His brain switched off thoughts of weddings and dresses and, well, everything, flew from his head.

Because Celeste appeared.

Good God, she was stunning.

Oh, she was always pretty—even when she was frowning at him—but this... Wow.

Her dress was the same beautiful light blue, but had a plunging neckline and a series of fluttery skirts that flowed around her as she moved. Her hair was done up in an almost whimsical style that framed her face. And...had he ever noticed how striking her gray eyes were? Surely he had. But in this light, they were almost silver.

He didn't realize that a silence had settled over the room until she broke it, saying in a snippy tone, "What are you staring at?"

"Ah..." Suddenly, there he was again, that gawky teenager who couldn't make a sentence around her. "You..." He sucked in a deep breath and composed himself. "You look magnificent."

Dear Reader,

I don't know how many times I've made assumptions about people in my life—based on what I saw, heard or experienced—and was *wrong*. I was very excited to tackle this sticky subject in Celeste's story. As a young woman, she formed a vision of Ben Sherrod in her mind, and it colored her perception of him for years. It wasn't until she was willing to look beyond the curtain (one she had created, by the way!) that she was able to open her heart and see him as he truly was.

What a gift that was. Not just for Ben, who craved that redemption, but for Celeste as well. And, in fact, for everyone involved, especially his daughter. Celeste's willingness to look again, to see him as he really was—rather than the way she had decided he was—changed everything.

I hope their story inspires you to be more generous with others, to try to look past the masks they wear to protect their wounded hearts, to accept them as they really are. I hope this story inspires you to give someone a second chance now and again.

Because doesn't everyone deserve love?

Happy reading.

Sabrina

A FATHER'S REDEMPTION

SABRINA YORK

HARLEQUIN

SPECIAL
EDITION

HARLEQUIN®
SPECIAL
EDITION™

Recycling programs
for this product may
not exist in your area.

ISBN-13: 978-1-335-59460-0

A Father's Redemption

Copyright © 2024 by Sabrina York

For questions and comments about the quality of this book, please contact us at CustomerService@Harlequin.com.

TM and ® are trademarks of Harlequin Enterprises ULC.

Harlequin Enterprises ULC
22 Adelaide St. West, 41st Floor
Toronto, Ontario M5H 4E3, Canada
www.Harlequin.com

Printed in Lithuania

MIX
Paper | Supporting
responsible forestry
FSC® C021394

Sabrina York is the *New York Times* and *USA TODAY* bestselling author of hot, humorous romance. She loves to explore contemporary, historical and paranormal genres, and her books range from sweet and sexy to scorching romance. Her awards include the 2018 HOLT Medallion and the National Excellence in Romantic Fiction Award, and she was also a 2017 RITA® Award nominee for Historical Romance. She lives in the Pacific Northwest with her husband of thirty-plus years and a very drooly rottweiler.

Visit her website at sabrinayork.com to check out her books, excerpts and contests.

Books by Sabrina York

Harlequin Special Edition

The Tuttle Sisters of Coho Cove

The Soldier's Refuge
The Airman's Homecoming
A Father's Redemption

The Stirling Ranch

Accidental Homecoming
Recipe for a Homecoming
The Marine's Reluctant Return

Visit the Author Profile page
at Harlequin.com for more titles.

This story is dedicated to Susie and Nicole
with sincere thanks for the adventure.

Chapter One

Celeste Tuttle awoke to a weight on her chest and the tap of a soft, fuzzy paw on her cheek. She forced open an eye and stared into the furry face gazing down at her, then glanced at her alarm clock and made a face. It was before six in the morning. "Really, Pepe?" she muttered.

In response, the cat batted her again, this time with a little more insistence. When that didn't rouse her, he settled down on her chest and nibbled on her chin. While his warmth and rhythmic purring was pleasant, she could do without the nibbling—it tickled.

"Okay. Okay," she said with a huff. "I'm up." She lifted him onto the bed beside her, sat up and stretched. Once she was fully awake—which she was now, thanks to the insistent Mr. Le Pew—she liked to just start her day. It was far more productive than snoozing.

After a quick shower, she dressed for work and then headed downstairs to feed the cat, even before she put the coffee on. She knew Pepe would start yowling if she didn't, and she didn't want him waking Momma up. Momma's room was on the main floor, right around the corner, and had been since her stroke six months ago. And while the stroke had made it harder for Momma to get around, it certainly hadn't affected her hearing. She seemed to hear every tiny noise, so Celeste tried to be quiet.

She put in her earphones and listened to the wake-up playlist on her phone—a compilation of her favorite classical music, for which she'd always had a passion—while making her breakfast. Then she sat at the dining room table, looking out on the garden as she ate and sipped her coffee. She loved a quiet moment at the beginning of the day to set her intentions and get off to a positive start.

"Good morning."

Celeste hit Pause on the music when Momma came around the corner in her robe. She was using her cane, which meant she felt a little less stable today—she refused to use it otherwise.

The stroke been a devastating blow when it had happened, when Celeste had walked into the living room to find Momma lying, unconscious, on the floor. She'd spent some time in the hospital and rehab, and then, when she'd come home, Celeste had taken a leave of absence from work so she could take care of her. It was so wonderful to see her getting better every day.

"Good morning, Momma." Celeste popped up and went to pour her mother a cup of coffee with a splash of milk and served it to her at the table. "How did you sleep?"

Momma cupped the mug in both hands and blew on the rich Colombian blend, so she could draw in the redolent scent. Momma loved her morning coffee. Good thing she hadn't noticed Celeste had switched it out to decaf three months ago. Caffeine interfered with some of her meds. "Mmm," Momma said as she took a sip. "I slept well, but I had a hard time falling asleep."

"Really? Why?"

And goodness, Momma's smile was bright. "I'm just so excited about the wedding."

Ah. Celeste didn't make a face, but it took some effort. Not that she wasn't happy that her sisters, Natalie and Amy, were getting married in a few days—she was. But heavens, she was tired of everyone talking about it. Mostly because it brought back painful memories of her own scuttled wedding plans.

There had been a time when she'd believed in true love and romance and all that, but the dream had died the day she'd walked in on the love of her life…with someone else. Oh, she'd been devastated. And while she knew that not all men were feckless—her father certainly had not been—it had shattered her illusions. Now that she'd healed her heart, at least a bit, she wasn't so bitter, but that didn't mean it was easy to be reminded of that pain, or the creeping worry that there might never be that classic "happy-ever-after" for her.

She attempted a sincere smile, as she always did, because no one else needed to know the weight she carried, and said, "It's going to be beautiful." And before Momma could take up that conversational baton, she added, "Can I make you some eggs?"

"Oh, you don't have to. Sally will be here soon."

"I don't mind." It only took a few minutes, and Celeste liked cooking. Besides, Sally, Momma's day nurse, had plenty to do without acting as a chef as well. Since Celeste had been Momma's full-time caregiver for several months, she knew how much work that entailed. What a blessing Celeste's boss, Sheida Stringfellow, had helped them apply for assistance from a foundation that provided social services such as day nurses like Sally. They would never have been able to afford it on their own.

With Sally coming in on the weekdays, Celeste had been able to go back to work at the Elder House, where she was a geriatric care nurse. Soon Momma would be strong enough that she wouldn't need a day nurse at all. Or, at least, they hoped so.

When Celeste set the plate in front of Momma, Pepe leaped up onto the chair beside her and meowed. "No, sir," Celeste said sternly, and gently deposited him on the ground.

Pepe, or Pepe Le Pew, a beautiful black-and-white tuxedo cat, had been Natalie's pet…until he'd decamped and adopted Momma. Or perhaps it had been the other way around. Nat had brought him with her when she'd come to help Celeste after Momma's stroke, and Momma and Pepe had bonded. So, when Nat had fallen in love with Jax and moved in with him, they'd decided that the cat would stay here.

Living with a cat was a new experience for Celeste. Growing up in a military family, moving constantly from pillar to post, she'd never had animals growing up, but Celeste found she liked it. The little fuzzball brought so much comfort and laughter into the home, the litter box chores, tufts of fur on the furniture and shredded paper towels were easy to overlook. Despite his terrible habit of waking her up before the alarm, Pepe was affectionate and funny and brightened her day.

When Sally arrived, she and Celeste chatted for a minute about Momma—a shift change conference, a habit formed from years of nursing—and then she headed off to work. It was a beautiful late summer day and Celeste enjoyed the drive over to the tribal lands south of town.

Coho Cove was a small town on the beautiful coast of Washington State, and it was charming on a bad day. But today it was glorious. The late summer sun shone brightly, but not too hot. There was a sweet breeze stirring the air as she drove through the maple shaded streets, past tidy and well-kept homes and businesses to the edge of town, and then over the bluff where the Elder House and its adjacent community center stood. As she crested the bluff, and the vast expanse of the sea revealed itself, sparkling with light and life, she caught her breath. It was so pretty that the view of the hideous resort hotel glittering in the sunlight over on the Point didn't even ruin her mood very much.

Once she got to work, Celeste checked in with the out-going night nurse and got started on her rounds. It was an easy morning. Most of the residents just needed their morning meds and a blood pressure check. There were only twenty-six full-time residents in the retirement home who needed medical check-ins, so rounds didn't take long, but Celeste had a lot of other responsibilities as well. She supported the recreation staff and did some administrative work, but her main function was to be available if there were any medical emergencies; the facility always had at least one nurse on-site at all times.

The problem was that while there was a doctor in town, he was a general practitioner more attuned to prevention and health maintenance; he didn't have the facilities to handle any real emergencies. Aside from that, he wasn't well tuned to the challenges of aging care. So if any of her residents needed help beyond what she and the other nurses could provide, it was a long way to the closest ur-gent care. Even farther to a hospital.

Celeste smiled at Jana Parker, one of the residents,

who sped by in her wheelchair—because the art class was starting soon—as she made her way to the nursing station to log her morning notes. Yeah, her job had its challenges, but it was rewarding too. She loved her patients, and her coworkers were the absolute best. Everyone here had a servant heart—they lived to help others, which made for a lovely work environment.

Of course, their boss had a lot to do with that. Bosses often set the tone, but Sheida Stringfellow did so with intentionality, which made a huge difference. Sheida was more than the manager of the Elder House. She was a force within the Coho Cove community and, in fact, had been instrumental in raising support and funding for the beautiful new Elder House. The old place, where Celeste had begun her career, had been practically falling apart at the seams, dark and cramped. The new facility was bright and clean and served the whole community in a way that integrated all generations and met multiple community needs. Sheida was, in Celeste's opinion, a miracle worker, and she respected her immensely.

After finishing her log, she headed from the resident wing to the community center side of the building to grab a bite and sneak a peek at the day care. She loved the layout of the new building, because it was more than just a residence for the elderly. It had been designed with the whole community in mind, serving all ages. She was of the firm belief that being in a bright and active environment like this kept her patients young at heart. Celeste had even brought Momma here for classes and activities, as well as physical therapy, when she'd been recovering.

As she passed the day care, she waved to Maisey Light-feather, who was trying to corral a group of youngsters into a circle in the brightly colored playroom. The kids, of course, had other ideas. It was hard to hold back a chuckle.

Celeste loved the day care. It always lifted her spirits to see the sweet babies, and the toddlers were always good for a laugh. Sometimes she wished she'd been able to finish her degree in early childhood development, which she'd started while she was working in a pediatric ward in Portland just after she got her nursing license. Gosh, she'd loved working with children.

But then her world had crashed in, as worlds sometimes do, and she'd been desperate to return home and lick her wounds. This job had come up just when and where she needed to be. She'd started taking online courses again, once she got herself settled here, but with taking care of Momma after her stroke, she just didn't have the time to pick it back up.

She made a face as she caught herself in a lie. That wasn't true, was it? She could find the time. She was certainly able to find time to engage in her passion of civic engagement—though she'd had to step down from some of her committee work when Momma got sick. The Coho Days Committee in particular. Heaven knew it took up more time than was precisely necessary. But then, committees often did.

Yeah. Time wasn't the issue and never had been. It was the passion. The passion was gone. Her life had shifted and things had changed, and somehow, somewhere, her desire to finish her degree had just slipped away. It sucked when that happened, but sometimes you just had to realize when a dream had died, and let it go. Some dreams, though, were easier to let go than others.

"Oh, Celeste!" Lauren called from the coffee bar of the

community center, just adjacent to the childcare wing. She raised a to-go coffee cup. Celeste changed direction and headed her way, in the hopes the cup was for her. Lauren volunteered on Tuesdays as a barista; on Tuesdays, the coffee was always good.

Celeste grinned when Lauren met her halfway and handed the cup over. "Is this for me?" she asked, even as she was taking it.

Lauren nodded. "A new recipe."

"Really?" Celeste took a sip and raised her brows. "Good. Is that a little chicory I taste?"

"Just a pinch. You like?"

"Very much. And just when I needed a pick-me-up. Thank you. You're an angel."

"My pleasure. Hey, only a few days till the wedding, right?" Lauren waggled her brows.

"Mmm…" Celeste nodded. She couldn't wait until it was over.

"I think it's awesome that your sisters are sharing a wedding."

Well, that was true. Better than having two weddings to hear about, she supposed. "They're going on their honeymoon together too," she said. "An Alaskan cruise."

Lauren's eyes went wide. "Really? It's a good thing Noah and Jax like each other, I guess." Yep. That was what happened when good friends married sisters.

They both chuckled and Celeste said, with a minxish smile, "Well, I'm pretty sure they're going to have separate cabins on the cruise ship."

Lauren laughed. "Well, have a wonderful time at the wedding." She turned back to the coffee shop and then stopped short and whirled around again. "Oh. Almost for-got. Sheida would like to see you in her office."

Celeste stilled. A hint of unease swelled. It wasn't un-usual for Sheida to call her to her office, but recently Ce-leste had heard rumors that there were some big changes coming at the Elder House, and she really disliked change. Hence the unease.

Because she believed in the maxim of doing things when you're thinking of them—and because she'd rather know than wonder—she went straight to Sheida's office and knocked on the open door.

"Hey," she said when Sheida glanced up from her com-puter with a bright smile. Sheida was in her late twenties, just like Celeste—in fact they'd gone to high school to-gether, just a year or so apart. She had long jet-black hair and deep brown eyes. She was also the smartest person Celeste had ever met, with three master's degrees, includ-ing an MBA. She could have rocked the business world anywhere she landed, but she, like Celeste, chose to serve the community they loved.

"Oh, Celeste." She broke into a grin. That was good. Wasn't it? "Come on in. Oh, and can you close the door?"

Close the door? Uh-oh. Sheida *never* closed her door. "Is this something bad?" she had to ask.

"Oh, it's good," Sheida said with an almost lurid de-light. "It's very good."

"Phew." Celeste felt herself relax and Sheida laughed.

"You worry too much, hon. Go on. Have a seat." Sheida was a great boss, and Celeste loved working for her. How weird was it that Celeste's sister Natalie was marrying Sheida's brother, Jax? So, in addition to being her boss,

Sheida would be her sister-in-law too. It happened like that, she supposed, in small towns.

"So, what's up?" Celeste took a fortifying sip of her very excellent coffee.

Sheida folded her fingers together and blew out a sigh before she began. "Basically, here's the deal… And this is all preliminary right now, just because there are lots of pieces in motion, so please don't share it yet. Okay?"

"Okay."

"Great." She leaned forward, telegraphing her excitement, which lit the same in Celeste. "So, you know how the Health and Human Services Committee has been working to get the funding for an emergency clinic in town?"

Celeste's pulse thrummed. "Yes?" Oh, gosh. That would be wonderful. Coho Cove was fifty miles from the closest hospital. When Momma had had her stroke, she'd had to be medevaced out and it had cost a fortune. With the town growing so fast—because of all the developers with their incessant developing—the need for a clinic with some advance care services was becoming even more urgent.

"Well…" Sheida's eyes shone. "I think we're close."

"Sheida, that's great."

Her boss crossed her fingers and held them up. "It looks good. But I was hoping I could tap into your grant writing expertise for the initial phases."

"Of course!" Celeste had had a lot of success writing grants for many programs at the Elder House in the years since she'd come to work here, as well as raising funds for the local social services coalition. She loved writing grants. It was like doing a jigsaw puzzle. She was a nerd like that. "Any way I can help. You know I am all in on the clinic."

"I was hoping you'd say that." But then Sheida made a face.

Uh-oh. Celeste knew her well enough to know her tells. That face was one of them. Somewhere in this proposal was a catch. Still, this was Sheida. She loved Sheida. She'd walk over broken glass for her. "Okay. Just spit it out," she said in a joking voice. "What horrible job do you plan to fob off on me?"

Sheida sucked in a deep breath and blew it out in a gust. "I need you to take over my seat on the Health and Human Services Committee. Now that I'm on the governor's commission, I'm going to be traveling to meetings in Olympia a lot and I just don't have the capacity for both."

But Celeste had tuned out. Her heart gave one big thump. She'd been lusting after that job since she'd come on board. It was the committee created by the city council to deal with all the humanitarian issues impacting the community. Other than at the city council itself, it was where *everything* happened in the Cove. Everything that mattered to her, at any rate. It was a dream come true. "Are…are you serious?"

"I know you're busy, with your mom and all, but I'm not asking you to do this on your own time. I feel confident that we'll be able to rearrange your schedule to fit it in. And on that note…you may have heard that we've been conducting interviews?" Celeste nodded. Rumor mills were incessant here, and infallible. "Well, we'll be bringing some new nursing staff on board."

"Okay." Thank God. They'd been understaffed for months.

"But with two extra nurses, you should be able to fold the committee time into your work schedule. Yes?"

"Ah…" Celeste took a moment to form her question. She didn't want to deter Sheida from adding staff, but… "Do we need *two* new nurses?"

Her boss's response was a grin. There was a glint in her eye. "We will. But for now, let's focus on getting the new staff up to speed. In the meantime, I'll have Tony add you to the committee email list, so you'll get a notice for the next meeting and…" She pulled out a very thick folder and dropped it on her desk in front of Celeste with a resonant thud. "Here's the project file."

It was all Celeste could do to not drool as she picked it up. This was the most exciting project she'd ever gotten her paws on. She couldn't wait to dig in. It wouldn't have been proper to start snooping now, right in front of Sheida, so she maintained her calm. But it cost her.

Sheida tipped her head to the side and sighed. "Thank you, Celeste. I love that I can always count on you."

"Absolutely."

"Have I told you today how much I appreciate you?"

"Yes." She had. She said it nearly every day. "Well, I'm excited."

"Me too." Her eye gave a twinkle. "I'm excited about the wedding too."

"Oh yes." Celeste didn't roll her eyes, but just barely. Everyone, it seemed, was excited about the wedding. But this was a small town. A double wedding was something of an occasion, she supposed. And Jax was her only brother. So Celeste schooled herself to sit patiently and chat about the coming festivities, even though what she really wanted to do was find somewhere private to dig into these project files.

When someone knocked on the door, and Sheida called,

"Come in," Celeste figured their meeting was about to end, so she grabbed the file and her coffee cup in preparation to make her exit.

She nearly dropped the precious file when the door swung open and Ben Sherrod stepped in and said, in that rumbly deep voice he had, "Hope I'm not interrup—" And yeah. He cut himself off the second he saw Celeste.

Ben Sherrod always did that. Stopped talking when he realized she was there. He'd stop talking and then kind of look at her. It wasn't a leer or a glare or an ogle. Just a look. As though he was trying to figure out what kind of creature had appeared before him from the nothingness.

He always had looked at her like that. Even back in high school. Since the first day she'd walked into Coho High. Back then she'd thought he was cute, with his mop of black hair and thickly lashed big brown eyes. But then she'd found out who he was.

They'd been at war ever since.

Oh, it was a nice, civil cold war. But they both knew. And they kept their distance from each other.

Well, she did.

He seemed to turn up here a lot. Though, to be honest— rumor mill, again—he was here to see Sheida, not to aggravate Celeste. Still, he managed to do both.

It was a well-known fact that Sheida and Ben were dating. They often had "meetings" over dinner at restaurants in town and even had occasional weekends together in Seattle and Olympia. Heck, they had been seen canoodling at Smokey's, the local barbecue joint, twice in the last week.

Gotta love the rumor mill.

It didn't bother Celeste that they were seeing each other. Why should it? Ben was a widower, and he had a daughter who needed a mother, and Sheida had been single for a while. Besides, he was nothing to her other than a too-attractive agent of chaos and overdevelopment. It had been his family's company that had destroyed this town, stripping it of its folksy charm. His company that had built that glittering eyesore of a resort on the Point, along with an enormous planned community to follow. And, of course, the swanky gated community of Coho Shores.

Yeah, she didn't care if those two were together, but she didn't want to have to watch them canoodling, so she quickly rose and said, in a rush, "Not a problem. I was just leaving—"

But at the same time, Sheida said, "Ben, I was just giving Celeste the news."

She froze and glanced at her boss. Something in her belly curled. It was that unease again. What did Ben have to do with her Health and Human Services assignment? He was a developer. It was his job to raze historic buildings and put up cheesy hotels, not make the community a *better* place.

They'd both been active for years on committees and commissions the city council had set up—Ben for business purposes and Celeste to enhance and maintain social services in a small town with few resources. They rarely, if ever, agreed on any issues. But apparently, he was interested in her Health and Human Services assignment.

His eyes widened and glanced from Celeste to Sheida to Celeste again. "And you're okay with it?" he asked.

"Uh, yes." His tone confused her. Why wouldn't she be happy with a plum assignment on the committee of her dreams? And why did his voice have to have that timbre? Why did he have to be so attractive too? With his dark hair, soulful eyes and that charming, boyish demeanor, one might be forgiven for assuming that he was a laid-back, easygoing fellow. One would be wrong.

He was a shark. A heartless businessman through and through.

"Good," Sheida said, snapping her laptop closed. "I know the two of you are going to do a fabulous job. You'll make an excellent team!"

Team? And she said it with such delight.

The unease flooded back into Celeste's gut as she stared up at Ben. His stupid beautiful eyes were filled with a vexing mix of sympathy and humor. He attempted a smile large enough for his dimple to kick up, and then he said the most horrible thing she'd ever heard. "Looks like we'll be seeing a lot of each other, Celeste."

And her blood froze in her veins.

Oh, Lord. What on earth had she agreed to?

She said yes.

Ben Sherrod wasn't sure how to feel about that. When Sheida had suggested Celeste Tuttle to fill in for her on the HHS Committee, he'd been shot through with twin strands of excitement...and trepidation.

The trepidation was easy to understand. She always filled him with trepidation, didn't she? She always had. Just her presence could tie his tongue up in knots.

The excitement was a little more complicated. He'd had a pretty big crush on Celeste Tuttle in high school, and even though she'd made it clear back then that she did not return the feelings—she had, in fact, intensely disliked him, his father and the family business—a remnant of that early attraction lingered somewhere in his soul and occasionally rose to the surface when he thought of her.

They'd both moved on, of course. They were both adults now and tacitly cordial, but the energy between them was always, somehow, at odds. He had the sense that, if she didn't hate him as a *person* now, she definitely still hated his line of work. And since his work was such a large part of his identity, the distinction felt like a moot point.

She blamed the Sherrod Group for all the changes the little town of Coho Cove had gone through in the past few decades, and she wasn't totally wrong. Under his father's hand, the company had cleared out the old-growth forest to the east and built a bunch of houses in its place. The company had snapped up every available piece of property on Steelhead Drive to create a retail district—including claiming the holdout properties through eminent domain, with the support of the old city council. Even though he'd been a kid, Ben had protested that decision because the use of eminent domain basically forced people to sell their homes and properties, which he thought was wrong. But his father hadn't listened. His father never had. His father had also been the primary developer of Coho Shores, a wealthy enclave on the south end of town, turning the area from a sleepy little hamlet into a swanky summer getaway spot for rich tourists.

But the company—at least since he'd taken over—had done a lot to develop town infrastructure and support much-needed social programs. The way he saw it, since he lived in his town, he wanted to make it the best place possible to raise his daughter, and his decisions reflected that.

Of course, Celeste wasn't aware of any of that. He doubted it would matter if she was. Their history ran too deep.

So, he was a little leery to be working with her on such an important project. But at the same time, there was a part, deep inside of him, that was hopeful for an opportunity to make some kind of peace with her so he wouldn't have to deal with this awkwardness every time he saw her.

"Well," she said in a particular tone, with which he was very familiar. She was getting ready to run. She did that when she could, when she was trapped with him. "I'd better get back to work." *Yup. Running again.* "Thank you, Sheida."

Sheida, who was oblivious to the currents of energy skittering in the room, chuckled. "Thank *you*, Celeste. I can't tell you what a relief it is to have that project off my list, and in the hands of someone I know is going to rock it."

"My pleasure." Celeste nodded to him—not making eye contact—and slipped past him from the room and was gone. What was it about her that utterly disarmed him? It happened every time he saw her, and afterwards, he was left feeling…out of sync.

He'd fallen in love with her at first sight—granted, he'd been sixteen, and sixteen-year-olds fell in love at first sight a lot. But then she'd ripped his teenage heart out in debate class during a discussion on civic responsibility and social development—where she'd made clear her disdain for him and his family's company to the point that all the kids in the classroom—including all his favorite bullies—had laughed at him. That had been rough, but it hadn't been the last time he and Celeste had been at loggerheads. They'd had many similar run-ins throughout the years because both of them had been active on various city council committees, usually on opposite sides of the table.

At any rate, they'd been at odds for years. Even having a simple conversation with Celeste was a challenge for him. He hoped that didn't impact the project. The town needed the best from both of them.

"Ben?"

He whirled around and fixed his attention on Sheida. Or tried to. Part of his brain was still working on Celeste. *Idiot.* "Yes?"

Sheida cocked her head and shot him a look. "Was there something you wanted to talk about? Or did you come all this way to see me just to say hello?"

He had to grin. Sheida had a dry sense of humor that he appreciated. She had a way of pointing out absurdities in people's behavior—including his. "I came to pick up Quinn from her playdate." It wasn't really a playdate so much as a therapy session working on integration skills for children with special needs, but they called it a playdate.

Quinn's speech therapist had recommended the program for his five-year-old daughter, as she was nearing school age. It was one thing raising a nonverbal preschooler, but if he wanted his daughter to thrive in life, and school, he knew he had to help her figure out how to navigate life within her own parameters.

He had no idea why Quinn didn't speak—no one did, not even the expensive specialists he'd paid an arm and a leg to consult. The best theory they'd all come up with was that her mutism resulted from the trauma of the car accident that had killed her mother three years ago. That was all fine and good, and made logical sense, but he needed something more. He needed to hear his daughter speak again.

It hadn't always been this way. She'd been very verbal as a baby. As a toddler, she'd even been precocious. But then, tragedy had struck. His wife Vi's car had been hit by a drunk driver and forced off the road…and Quinn had been in the car with her. The accident had taken her mother's life, and Quinn hadn't said a word since.

Ben had taken his daughter to every expert he could think of, who'd run every kind of test *they* could think of, but so far, they hadn't landed on anything definitive. No one had been able to figure out *why* she couldn't speak. Or wouldn't. It was frustrating as hell, not being able to help his daughter. She meant the world to him.

Funny, wasn't it, how such a tiny person had come to mean so much to him.

He'd never forget that day when they'd placed her into his arms, squalling and red-faced and perfect. He'd never seen such a beautiful sight. Never held something so precious, so fragile. It had humbled him.

Even with her challenges, and the stress and worries he carried for her future, frankly, she was the reason he woke up in the morning. She was the reason he did everything he did. She, in short, was his world.

"Oh!" Sheida's expression brightened. "Quinn's here?"

"It's Tuesday."

She made a face. "Is it? Sometimes I lose track."

"It is. And, since I'm here," he continued, "I thought I would pop in and say hello." Sure, he could have had Ellie, Quinn's nanny, come by and pick her up, or sent his driver, Greg, but Ben had wanted to get out of the office for a while. Besides, he loved when his daughter ran to him and threw herself into his arms, as she did when he came to get her. It was healing somehow.

"Well…" Sheida stood. "I could use a break. Let's go down there together, shall we?" As they headed out into the hall, toward the community center, she shot him a glance. "How is Quinn doing?"

He gave a shrug. "All things considered? Fine. I mean, everything seems fine." It was hard to know when you had a nonverbal child. Not that Quinn couldn't make herself understood. She could...most of the time. If she was hungry or thirsty or tired, he could see to her needs, but she was getting older. Her needs were changing. She'd be starting school soon and he knew her issues would require special resources that the local school district didn't have. One option was to move back to Seattle, where there were more specialized programs, but Ben loved it here in Coho Cove. And so did Quinn.

When his father had died five years ago, and Ben had taken over the company, he'd moved everything, lock, stock and barrel, to the Cove to consolidate assets and save the business his father had frittered away. Aside from that, he hadn't liked living in Seattle—that had been one of the main conflicts he and Vi had had—and now that the company was on solid footing with his development on the Point, he hated to rock the boat. He'd resolved himself to exhaust every possibility in helping Quinn before he made such a drastic change.

"Any results from the MRI?" Sheida asked.

Ben shook his head. He didn't ask which MRI she was talking about, because it didn't matter. They'd all had the same result. The MRIs, the CTs, the EEGs...all of the tests showed nothing. Nothing physical, at least. "The doctors are leaning more toward behavioral therapy now. Thanks for getting her into this group, by the way."

Sheida huffed a laugh. "For you? Anything. Besides, Maisey is excited to have her participating." Maisey, the facility's psychologist, had developed this program to teach communication skills to kids who had challenges. Ben wasn't sure if it was helping, but he knew Quinn enjoyed the sessions.

They came around the corner and his heart did a kerplop as he spotted his daughter in the playroom through the window. God, she was beautiful. She had long golden curls—like her mother—and a bright, pretty smile and stunning blue eyes. She was sitting in a circle with Maisey and the other kids and playing a drum and laughing. His chest tightened. She was so precious. So perfect. She was a happy, sweet, physically healthy five-year-old angel.

What he wouldn't give to hear her call him *Daddy* again.

Quinn saw him as soon as he stepped through the door. She leaped to her feet and did a little dance before heading over. It was so cute how she always did a funny little dance when she was happy. She ran to him and lifted her arms, which meant, in Quinn-speak, that she wanted him to pick her up.

But before he could, Maisey called to her in a cheery voice. "Hey, Quinn, can you help clean up the toys?" As his daughter nodded and skittered off to help the others put away the musical instruments in the toy chest, Maisey sidled up to him. "Hello, Ben," she said.

"Hi, Maisey. How was class today?"

"Oh, we had a good day." She smiled like the cat that caught the canary. She was young and energetic and lively. Her innate enthusiasm made him grin.

"Really? What happened?"

"It's soooo interesting." She turned to Sheida. "You know I've been teaching the kids some simple sign language." Like a Ping-Pong ball, she turned back to Ben. "A lot of nonverbal kids are able to use ASL for conceptual communication."

"Sure."

"Anyway, I was blown away at how quickly Quinn was able to pick it up. I think it's a strategy you might be able to use with her."

His heart lifted. "Really?"

"She's very clever." Yeah, he knew that. "But there's more..."

"More?"

"Have you been teaching Quinn to read?"

"I, ah, read her stories every night."

"Mmm-hmm. But actually teaching her letters and sounds?"

Ben shook his head. "She has a tablet she plays with. It has educational games on it." He was embarrassed that he didn't know for sure, but when he was with Quinn—in the evenings and weekends, when he wasn't working— she wasn't on her tablet. He liked to do things with her, like hiking and fishing or going to the zoo. He spent as much time as he could with her. As far as he could tell, she only played with the tablet when she was with Ellie.

"Well, Ben, your daughter can read." Her eyes widened and she nodded enthusiastically. "I know. I was surprised too. She's only five. See, we played a game today with word cards, and she was able to identify the word cards consistently...without the pictures."

"What does this mean?" Given Maisey's excitement, this was good—great—news, but Ben didn't really understand what it *meant*.

"It means, whatever her issues are, she isn't developmentally delayed. She can learn to communicate in written form, and through ASL. We may have found a path for her to start school in September."

"Oh." He should have said more. Could have. But emotion—something akin to relief and hope—had seized his brain.

"That's great," Sheida said.

He nodded. "Yes."

Quinn ran back over to him and held up her arms again, but Maisey prompted her by lifting her index finger to the sky while saying, "Up." Quinn watched with solemn eyes and then repeated the gesture, breaking into a huge grin when Ben lifted her into his arms.

"Good girl," Maisey said. "Up."

Ben caught and held his daughter's gaze and smiled at her. "Up," he said, and when Quinn made the gesture again, he laughed. "You're so smart," he said. "My smart girl."

Quinn made another gesture, crossing her fists over her chest.

"Aw," Maisey said. "Oh, how cute. She says she loves you."

Ben's throat closed up as adoration swamped him. "Aw, Quinney." He pulled her into another hug. "I love you too, honey. So much." It was kind of mind-boggling to realize, after so long, that he maybe could communicate with her after all. "Well," he said, "we should probably get going." After all, the day was wasting, and he had some sign language to learn.

But with his announcement, Quinn wiggled free from his hold and ran back to the toy chest, riffled around in it and then returned to him with a look of determination on her face. Then she thrust out her arm and handed him the flash card she had found. It was the cartoon of a fluffy orange cat, with the letters *CAT* on the backside along with a sketch of the ASL sign.

"Yes, Quinn. That's a cat," Ben said.

Maisey chuckled. "It's her favorite card."

Indeed, when Ben took the card and handed it back to Maisey—it was her card, after all—Quinn put out a lip. When he said, "This belongs to Maisey. We have to leave it here," her frown became even darker. She crossed her arms and stomped her foot in a gesture he needed no special language skills to decode.

When he chuckled, her expression became even darker, so he pulled her into his arms and gave her a loud wet exuberant kiss on her cheek until she giggled.

God, he loved her. She was the best thing that had ever happened to him. Above all, he wished he could be a better father for her, wished that he knew what to do or say to make life easier for her. He tried his best. He studied books on parenting and consulted with experts and talked with his friends who'd been through it. But it was hard, going it alone, always wondering if there was something, anything, he could have done or should have done differently.

That was the hardest thing about having kids. They didn't come with a user manual. And being a single parent made it even harder. How nice would it be to have a partner to help share the load? He was always second-guessing himself, wondering what he was missing, if he was failing her somehow.

But he didn't have all the answers. All he had to give her was love, and he could only hope that would be enough.

Chapter Two

After her shift, Celeste still had some time before she had to be home to relieve Momma's caregiver, so she stopped by her sister Amy's bakery.

She didn't visit the bakery often, because it was far too tempting—and lately, there was an awful lot of talk about weddings—but today she felt she needed a little moral support. Just that short interaction with Ben Sherrod had left her feeling prickly and irritated. She hated to think about what hours trapped in a meeting room with him would be like.

It was a beautiful afternoon, so a lot of people were out as she drove through town. She waved to her friend Marilee, the owner of the B and B, who was watering the flowerpots on her broad front porch, and then waved again when she saw Angus Crowley coming out of the liquor store. She even waved at Sherrill Scanlon when she saw her walking her little dog in the park. Even though she and Sherrill had never been friends, waving and smiling was just part of the culture here, and Celeste liked it. She liked that she knew everyone in town—or almost everyone. When she'd lived in Portland, for nursing school and then working at the hospital, it hadn't been like this.

It had been busy and impersonal and cold. Coho Cove was…intimate.

There was a parking spot right in front of Amy's store and Celeste snagged it with gusto. She smiled to herself as she pushed through the bakery doors. That was another thing she appreciated about a small town. Parking was definitely easier.

"Ugh," she said as she dropped into a chair next to her sister, who was sitting by the window at one of the cute parlor tables, taking advantage of the summer sunshine while doing her accounts. Celeste couldn't blame her. Amy's office, in the back of the bakery, was gloomy at best.

Amy looked up from her ledger and made a face. "Bad day?"

"The worst." Well, not the worst. The worst had been the day of Dad's fatal heart attack back when Celeste had been in high school. Or the day their brother, Nate, had died suddenly from anaphylactic shock just after they'd moved to Coho Cove. Or the day of Momma's stroke. Okay. There had been a lot worse days if she was being honest. Celeste gusted a sigh, perhaps in acknowledgment of her melodrama. "My boss gave me my dream assignment."

"Oh, yeah. I can see why you're upset." Amy was a master at sarcasm.

Celeste snorted. "Well, it comes with a catch."

"Dreams often do."

Oh, bother. "Don't get all philosophical on me," Celeste said snippily. "I just want to complain about my day." There was no one else for her to complain to, other than Momma, and Momma didn't have a lot of tolerance for whining. And maybe it was wrong, but sometimes a person just wanted to whine to someone who would pat their hand and say, *There, there*. Was that too much to ask? Really?

Amy, who'd carped her share to Celeste over the years, gusted a sigh. "Fine. Complain away. What's the problem with this dream assignment?"

"I have to work with Ben Sherrod."

"Ben Sherrod?" Amy's eyes widened and she snorted a laugh; though Amy and Ben were good friends, she was well aware of Celeste's feelings about him. "Well, that'll be fun." Another sarcastic note.

Celeste gave a frustrated groan. "It's such a great project too. Why does it have to be *him*?"

"What's the project?" Amy asked.

"Oh. Sorry. Sheida asked me not to share. Not yet at least. But it's important." Really important. Who knew if access to closer medical services could have saved their brother? Or lessened the impact of Momma's stroke? As a nurse, Celeste knew that accessibility to trained personnel and the right medicines and machines in a moment of crisis might have helped in both those cases. That was all she needed to be fully on board with the new clinic. Even if it meant working with Ben.

"Well, if it's important, you do it." Amy shrugged. "I mean, no matter what. Right?"

"Yes." She was right. *Suck it up, buttercup*.

"Besides, I like Ben. I always have."

Celeste sent her a glower. "Of course you do. You only see his glad-handing side."

"Glad-handing?"

"Oh, yes. He's always so friendly and nice—"

"He *is*."

Honestly, Amy was so naive sometimes. "You don't

have a clue what his company is doing to this town. You don't pay any attention to things that happen on the City Council Planning Commission, do you?"

"No." Amy made another face. She did that a lot. "Because it's boring. Honestly, Celeste, I don't understand why you like doing that kind of stuff."

"Like serving on committees and making real change for the people in this town?"

"Mmm-hmm." And then, in a singsong voice, Amy added, *"Boring."* She was probably kidding. Maybe. "Besides, wasn't it Ben who led the charge for redeveloping this retail district?" She waved toward the bustling street in front of her thriving business. "The bakery was practically dead in the water before all the other shops opened up here."

"Tourist shops," Celeste mumbled.

Amy leaned closer. "Tourists love pastries. And they have lots of lovely money and your nephews need new shoes." True. Some of the changes in town had helped her sister's business. And yes, the town coffers were in much better shape because of the increased tax revenue. But that was hardly the point. Developers were, in their hearts, rapacious and greedy. Why, look what Ben's father had done back in the day in the name of "redevelopment." Ripped out some lovely historic buildings to put in an ugly strip mall, and condemned a bunch of old homes on the shore to make way for the fancy marina. Her friend Huck Garner, from one of the town's founding families, had lost his ancestral home because of the ravaging development.

"Honestly," Amy said with a sniff, "I don't see why you think so poorly of him. You know the Point was going to be developed eventually. I'm just glad it's Ben who's doing it."

"You can't know that."

She huffed a laugh. "Development is everywhere. It's human nature. Aside from that, the town is growing. We need more housing options. Most developers would focus on the high-end customers, the mansions and stuff, but Ben makes it a point to fold affordable housing into every swath he develops."

Celeste made a face. Perhaps it was better to let the topic of Ben Sherrod, and his crimes, drop, especially with Amy. So she picked up on a lighter thread instead. "Did the boys wear out their shoes?" Although, to be honest, Amy's sons, John J. and Georgie, six and almost seven, were notorious for wearing things out.

Amy laughed. "They don't have to. They outgrow the shoes before that can happen."

"They're growing fast."

"Tell me about it. I just bought them new suits for the wedding—the cutest little things. I can only pray they still fit on Friday."

Celeste tried not to wince, even though she'd expected wedding talk when she'd made the decision to see Amy. She hated that she got that hard ball in her stomach every time it came up. Both her sisters had found the men of their dreams. They were in love. They were both over the moon. Of course Celeste was happy for them, but it kind of felt like she was losing them both—so she tried not to think about it.

Right now, however, it was about all Amy thought about, and the reminder spurred another question. "Oh.

Did you get your dress back from the seamstress?" her sister asked.

Celeste held back a cringe, but just barely. "I did." It was a fluttery bit of nonsense. She'd let her sisters choose it for her, but only because she was in the wedding party— maid of honor, how *fun*. It wasn't a dress she would ever have chosen for herself—she was far more sensible—but she'd read on the internet that the bride should be able to pick the dresses. The internet, Celeste decided, after seeing the dress, should probably keep its opinion to itself. But she'd wear the damn dress to the wedding and smile and pretend she didn't feel like a child at a costume party.

"Does it fit?" Amy was like a pit bull sometimes.

Did it? Probably. "I'll try it on tonight."

Amy made her eyes huge, the way she did when she wanted to pretend to be horrified. "You haven't tried it on? What if it needs more altering?"

"I'm sure it'll be fine—"

"The wedding is in *three days*, Celeste." Eek. Her tone was rising to a critical pitch.

But before Amy could build up any steam on her screed, the bell on the bakery door dinged and their sister, Natalie, came in with her fiancé, Jaxon Stringfellow.

"Hey. What's going on?" Jax asked with a grin. He probably didn't really want to know, but he made the mistake of asking Amy.

"Celeste hasn't tried on her dress yet," she blurted. "What if it doesn't fit?"

Ugh! "I said I'll try it on tonight!"

Nat set her hand on Celeste's shoulder, perhaps as a sign of support. They both knew how Amy was when she got wound up. "I'm sure it'll be perfect," she said in a calming voice. Both Jax and Nat were artists; they were good at manifesting calm. Thank God.

Jax nodded. "No need to borrow trouble, Amy," he said.

To which Amy snorted. Because Jax had said that exact same phrase multiple times since the two couples had decided to share a wedding. And on that note, maybe weddings were stressful enough without taking everything to committee. But whatever. It wasn't her wedding. All she had to do was show up. In a ridiculous dress.

"Oh, by the way," Amy said, switching topics. She did that a lot. "Celeste is going to be working with Ben Sherrod on a big project. She can't tell us what the project is because it's a huge secret."

Celeste sent her an aggravated look.

Jax just chuckled at the news, and when Celeste glared at him, he shrugged. "That should be interesting." Jax knew how she felt about Ben and his family's company. And because Ben was one of his best friends, going all the way back to the third grade, he probably knew Ben's side of things as well. His smirk was not appreciated.

"Oh, I love Ben," Natalie said. Of course she did. Natalie loved everyone.

"I love Ben too," Amy said, even though she'd already said it. Celeste suspected she was repeating herself to be obstreperous. "And John J. absolutely adores Quinn."

All right, at that Celeste had to smile. While she didn't care much for Ben, his daughter was adorable, and Quinn and Amy's son really did have a special relationship. Though she was nonverbal, and had been since the accident, somehow she seemed to be able to communicate with John J.

"Those two are so cute together," Natalie said on a laugh.

Amy nodded. "He told me they're probably going to get married."

"Aw." They all said it, in chorus.

"Speaking of Ben…" Amy said.

"We were speaking of Quinn," Celeste thought it only prudent to remind her.

"You *are* going to dance with him at the wedding, aren't you?"

Celeste nearly rolled her eyes out of her head. *Not this again.* Both Amy and Natalie had mentioned that they thought it would be a great idea for her to join the first dance. And because Ben was the best man and she was the maid of honor, they'd decided that *she* would be dancing with *him*. "I'm sure Ben has other plans."

"Not really," Jax said with a shrug, and Celeste gored him with a glower.

"Come on, Lesty," Natalie said in the voice she used when she cajoled. "It'll be fun."

"Will it?"

Amy frowned at her. "We don't want you to feel left out."

"I promise you. I won't feel left out."

Amy's frown deepened. "Just think about it, okay? It can be your gift to us."

"I already got you a toaster."

As usual, her sister ignored her joke. "And make sure that dress fits. I want you to look good in the pictures."

Okay. Enough of this. Celeste glanced at her watch and sighed. "Will you look at the time. I better get going," she said briskly. "Momma's helper leaves at four today."

"How is that going?" Nat asked.

"Great." She forced a smile. Her sisters both worried about Momma—of course they did—and they worried about Celeste too, bless them. After Momma's stroke, someone had had to stay with her full-time, and since Natalie had been living in California and Amy had a business and two small boys to raise, it had fallen to Celeste. Most things did, but she didn't mind. She'd long ago accepted that taking care of others was her calling in life, so she'd been happy to step up to the plate. Not that it hadn't been a challenge. It had. But things were better now. Having help with Momma was a huge relief. Huge.

Amy reached out and grabbed her hand. "We know you're the one carrying most of the weight with Momma," she said. "I just want you to know we're aware. And we appreciate it."

Nat nodded. "We do."

It was nice to hear. But the fact was, she liked living with Momma. She'd lived by herself for a little while in nursing school—before she'd met Randall—and she hadn't liked it at all. Living alone had been...far too quiet. She much preferred having someone else there to talk to, and to do things for.

"Well, if you need a break, you must let us know," Amy said in a stern voice.

"I will. I will," she said. But she knew she wouldn't. They probably did too.

First of all, she didn't need a break because taking care of Momma was normal life. It was what she'd always done—take care of others. Aside from that, there was nothing else going on in her life that she might be inclined to take a break for. Was there?

With that thought, a familiar prickle of dissatisfaction rose up in her soul, but, as she always did, she squelched it.

When Ben and Quinn returned to the hotel—where the two of them lived in an apartment on the seventeenth floor—he headed to his offices on the second floor to check in with his assistant, Char Taylor. He'd hired Char as his assistant years ago, when he'd started working for his father. When he'd taken over the company after his father's death, and moved the headquarters to Coho Cove, he'd brought Char with him—promoting her to his executive assistant, with her own assistant—because, frankly, she was phenomenal. She was the linchpin of all his ongoing projects and, somehow, managed to keep him on track. Of all his staff—and they were all phenomenal—Char was truly indispensable. Aside from that, Quinn adored her.

As he passed through the lobby toward the escalators, he scanned the space for any problems as he always did. Of course, there were none. He smiled a little when his gaze landed on the wood statue, rising above the pond in the center of the expanse, like an abstract Venus rising from the water. It always made him happy, that statue. His buddy Jax was the sculptor, and it was one of his best works.

They headed up the escalators and over to the wing where his company kept their offices. The second they entered the executive suite, Quinn spotted Char and rushed over to give her a hug.

"Ooh, what's this?" Char cooed as Quinn handed her something. Ben cringed when he realized what it was. "Is this a cat?" Char asked as she held up the flash card that his daughter had, apparently, stolen. Quinn nodded, and then took the card back.

Ben went down on his knees at his daughter's side. "Honey, is that Maisey's card?" he asked. When he tried to take it from her, she hid it behind her back and shook her head. He thought about taking it forcibly, but then decided against it. His father had been physically aggressive with him when he was a kid, and he'd hated it. Instead, he blew out a breath and said, "You know that doesn't belong to you, right, Quinn? It's wrong to take things that don't belong to you. Next time we go to see Maisey, you're going to have to give it back."

To which Quinn put out a lip.

He shook his head and sighed, and when he caught Char's eye, she gave a chuckle. "Think of it this way, Ben. The girl knows what she wants."

"She certainly does," he responded. "But she can't take things that don't belong to her." This he said more to Quinn than to Char. It was something his daughter needed to learn. Even though it was only a silly little card, learning to control impulses was an important lesson for a child to learn.

Parenting was hard, but it was even harder when your child had special needs that made typical two-way communication difficult. He was determined to be the best father he could be, and this was just another of those instances where not being able to just *talk* was a frustration. He was well aware that Quinn got away with more than she should because of it…he just wasn't sure what to do about it.

Quinn's nanny, Ellie, thought he was too easy on her, and recommended being more of a disciplinarian, but his father had been rigid and dictatorial, controlling Ben's every choice when he was young, and that had led to poor decision-making when he grew older—simply because he'd never had the chance to learn how to think for himself. Aside from that, he hadn't liked the way his father had treated him. He wanted better for Quinn.

He also didn't want her to be saddled with the kind of self-image issues he'd struggled with as a kid stemming from the constant criticism he'd received from his dad. It was, he supposed, a delicate balance.

"So—" He stood and shifted into work mode, maybe because it was easier for him than trying to figure out his daughter's mysteries. "Have we received the contracts from Raskin?" he asked. He'd been waiting for the draft agreement for a housing development his company was building near Olympia. It was the first new development they were launching outside of Coho Cove since Ben had taken over the company—and realized what a mess his dad had left him. It was exciting to be able to branch out again.

Char shook her head. "Not yet. But we did get the updated cost proposal from the construction team for the clinic project. I left it on your desk."

"Thanks." That review could wait until tomorrow.

"Oh, and I got a call from the city clerk. They've changed the next meeting for the clinic project to tomorrow at noon. You're available, but I wanted to check with you before I confirm it."

He swallowed that flash of dread at seeing Celeste again tomorrow. *So soon?* "Noon is fine. On that note, since today's meeting was canceled, I'm going to take the rest of the afternoon off."

"Good for you." She was always telling him he worked too much.

"Quinn's learning sign language in class, so I thought we could spend some time together practicing."

"How fun," she said to Quinn, who was far too entranced by the clacking ball toy on Char's desk to respond.

"But if we get the Raskin contracts, can you send them right up to my apartment?"

"Sure thing." That was one of the benefits of living so close to the office—easy access.

"Anything else going on?" he asked before he headed out for the day. Over the years he and Char had developed something of a shorthand. She knew what he meant. *Anything I need to know about?* There were thousands of details entailed in his hotel and construction activities. Char was very good at filtering through the dross to bring the right things to his attention.

"Well, there was an incident with a drunk guest who got injured on the pool deck last night," she said. "I notified legal, and got a copy of the security footage from Randy."

"Okay." Randy was the head of security.

"And a complaint about one of our subcontractors on the Seaview development…" She went on to highlight a few more issues and he listened attentively while watching Quinn play with the Newton's cradle on her desk, but he might not have been listening as attentively as he thought, because when she mentioned the Tuttle wedding, his attention snapped back to her. "Sorry. Can you repeat that?"

She glanced up from her notepad. "Yes. I said everything is going well for the Tuttle wedding on Friday." She grinned at him. She knew Jax—one of the grooms—was his best friend. Which was the reason the Tuttle wedding was on her list. "Caterers have ordered the supplies for the reception, florists have confirmed the order and I've reviewed the staffing schedules. As you requested, we booked extra childcare staff for the kids' club during the reception. There may be a problem with the best man, though."

What? Ben blinked. *He* was the best man. And then it hit him. "You're joking." He had to clarify sometimes. He'd never been very good at reading cues and Char had a deadpan wit.

"Totally joking." She flashed him a mischievous smile. "The best man will be there, don't worry."

"Good. Oh, by the way, your tux is back from the dry cleaners. I sent it up to your apartment."

"Oh, God." He hadn't even thought about what he would wear. "Thank you. Honestly, I'd be lost without you."

"Yeah," she said with a grin. "I know."

"Anything else?" he asked.

She glanced at her list. "Just…have a nice afternoon. You too, Quinney."

Ben reached out a hand to his daughter and she took it. But before he headed out, he said, "Oh. And don't forget. Raskin contracts." He knew she didn't need the reminder, but he did.

"As soon as they come in."

"Awesome." Damn. She was good. Also, she was willing to put up with all his foibles. That alone made her worth her weight in gold.

As he and Quinn walked down the hall to the elevator, he couldn't help but feel grateful for his staff. Not just

Char, even though she'd saved his sanity more than once. Everyone who worked at the hotel, as well as in the firm, was fantastic. There were occasional bad eggs—every company had them—but for the most part, he'd been really lucky.

When his father had died unexpectedly, and Ben had inherited the business and holdings, there had been a huge learning curve. Fortunately, when Ben finished his MBA and came to work for the company, he'd spent time training in each department, so he understood how the company worked on a granular level. But his father had been a larger-than-life character. He probably never expected God might dare take him as soon as He had, so he hadn't gotten around to including his son in any long-term planning or high-level management. In fact, other than a will, and a trust for Quinn, nothing had been done to prepare for succession.

And then, one day, out of the blue, his father was gone, and Ben had had to take charge of the whole shebang. He'd had to learn everything on the run. To make things worse, he discovered that his dad had overextended his property investments and the company was on the verge of bankruptcy. It had been a baptism by fire. Fortunately, because of a solid education, including a civil engineering degree and that MBA—as well as a team of excellent employees who knew their stuff—he'd been able to figure things out, determine the direction he wanted to take the business and implement the plan. As a result, the company was flourishing…and he no longer felt like an impostor.

Now his main worry was his daughter. If only he could figure out how he could help Quinn, everything would be perfect.

* * *

Even though Celeste had enjoyed spending some time with her sisters that afternoon—a treat usually reserved for Sunday suppers—it was nice to get home and relax. Although, technically, she didn't relax. First, she had a debrief with Momma's caregiver, made dinner, and then, after they ate, she helped Momma take a shower. Then, because Amy had called Momma, to make sure Celeste didn't forget, she had to try on the dress for the wedding and do a little fashion show for Momma. And yes, it was as frilly and impractical as it had seemed on the hanger, but it fit. Because of all that, she really didn't get a chance to relax until Momma went to bed that night.

Then she made herself a nice cup of tea and sat down with Sheida's big fat HHS file, slowly flipping through the notes and copies of filings. She'd scanned it a little at work, but this was a chance to really dig in and she couldn't wait. Most people didn't like paper files anymore, but Sheida had never been digitally inclined. It was a quirk Celeste could appreciate, because staring at documents on a screen made her eyes hurt. Also, there was something infinitely satisfying about flipping pages. It felt like she was actually doing something.

There were some really interesting notes and memos that helped her create a mental picture of the project so far, and get a grasp of who the players were and what they had decided. Above all, her favorite part was studying the sketches for the layout of the proposed clinic. She was a nerd like that. Blueprints had always fascinated her and the plans for the clinic were no exception.

These showed a well-planned-out facility. The front doors opened on a generous waiting room with an emergency bay to the left and a collection of treatment rooms on the right. The surgery and recovery rooms were in the back. It wasn't huge, but it had what a small-town emergency clinic should have to deal with everything from delivering babies to heart attacks. Though, if she had any say in it, she would recommend a change in the location of the supply cabinets. Any poor nurse working there would run her feet off trying to keep up.

She turned from the physical plans to the financial ones and scanned the budget—*hah! That was going to need to be amended*—and the funding recommendations. As she went through the notes, something caught her eye and she frowned.

According to this, the primary funding source for the construction wasn't the Coho Health and Human Services Committee fund, but the VSF, the same organization that paid for Momma's day nurse. She hadn't been familiar with the organization when Sheida had first told her about it, because she'd been so relieved to have the possibility of help, but seeing it again here made her curious. What was the VSF? The mystery spiked when, going through earlier projects the committee had tackled, she found the same entity had been a major donor when the new Elder House was built as well. And the city center redevelopment that had made Amy so happy. She had no idea what VSF was, but she fully intended to find out.

Celeste planned to ask her boss, but when she ran into her the next morning, Sheida's eyes went wide. "Celeste. Why are you still here? Didn't you get the email about the HHS meeting?"

Celeste grabbed her phone to check. "Uh, no."

Sheida made a face. "Ugh. Sorry. I asked them to add

you to the email list, but maybe they haven't yet. The meeting was changed to today at noon."

"At noon?" *Well, shoot.* It was nearly eleven now and she still had rounds. Thank goodness she'd reviewed the files last night. She hated project meetings when she didn't know what was going on.

Sheida must have seen the concern on her face because she said, "Don't worry. I called in Dee Dee to cover for you."

She should have known Sheida was on it. But her relief was short-lived, because almost immediately, she remembered who else would be at the meeting and her stomach tensed up again. "I should probably get going, then."

She was glad she left when she did, because she hit a lot of traffic on the way into town. It was aggravating, because she could remember a time when there had been no traffic in Coho Cove. It wasn't far from the Elder House to City Hall, but she had to drive past Coho Shores, the stupid, fancy, gated community that brought so many people to town for the summer.

Thanks, Ben Sherrod.

Thinking about the man, and the company that had brought all those visitors here, only aggravated her more. That, on top of being nervous about the first committee meeting, put her in a bad mood.

The current Coho Cove City Hall was a glamorous collection of double-wide trailers behind the grocery store, because the historic City Hall was in the middle of a much-needed refurbishment. It had been built at the height of the logging era, in the 1920s, back when the mill was in its prime and money was flowing. It was a beautiful, stately marble-faced structure with columns flanking its grand entrance, but as it was over a hundred years old, it had all kinds of structural problems. The trailers were hardly as beautiful, but they were a lot more functional. An added benefit was that she could park in the grocery store lot rather than hunt for a parking spot on the street.

The first person she saw when she walked into the conference room was Anthony Skinner. In addition to being the town's mayor, Tony was a Kiwanian, a Lion, a volunteer firefighter and a high school cohort of Celeste's. He was talking to Luke Larsen, her friend Lynne's brother, who was a local Realtor and the president of the chamber of commerce. She'd worked with both Tony and Luke on the Coho Days events for years. Just seeing them here calmed her immensely and made her feel right at home. It didn't hurt that they greeted her warmly.

The third person in the room was Susan Warren, one of the town's planning commissioners. She and Susan weren't pals, but Celeste knew and respected her work—even though they often disagreed on the direction the town should take. Susan was planning to run for city council next year.

And then there was Angus Crowley. Angus was one of the old guard. He and Celeste had stood together on a number of projects, fighting the inevitable erosion of the old Coho Cove. They'd both been against the massive development the Sherrod Group had proposed on the Point. Even though she didn't expect there would be any conflict over a project as vital as the clinic, it was nice to see an ally in the room.

Celeste greeted them all and took a seat opposite Angus. It didn't occur to her that the only empty seat was to her right until Ben walked into the room. The way he filled the doorway, blocking out the light, made her heart skip a beat. But then it switched to an annoying patter when he headed in her direction and sat at her side.

"Good afternoon." He said it to everyone, but the way he said it, in a low voice, made her feel as though he was speaking only to her. It sent a shiver up her spine, so she shot him a frown. She regretted her reaction immediately, of course, because it was rude, and she tried to make it a point to be polite to everyone. Aside from that, she could tell, by the way his expression tightened, that she'd hurt his feelings—if he even had feelings. That frown had been a petty, knee-jerk response to her discomfort, and she knew it, so she softened the blow with a mumbled "Afternoon."

Ugh. If it was going to be like this, working with him, it was going to be harder than she'd expected. It would probably be a good idea for her to at least pretend to be nice to him. But that was something for her to think about later, because Tony cleared his throat to signal that the meeting was starting.

"Welcome, all," he said from the head of the table. "Especially welcome to Celeste Tuttle. You all know Celeste, right?" Everyone nodded and waved. "Celeste will be filling in for Sheida and working with Ben to write the grants for some of the specialized medical equipment we need. They will also be handling the negotiations with the state lawmakers and coordinating with the federal funding sources. A quick review for you, Celeste, as you're new. Susan is our liaison with the planning commission, Luke with the chamber and Angus with the Coho Cove Historical Society. Ben's our liaison for construction and is overseeing the funding portion of the project. I, of course, will be running point with the city council." He went on to outline recent updates to the project, some of which Celeste had seen in Sheida's file, and some she hadn't. She listened intently and scribbled notes, but focusing on the topic was a challenge with Ben sitting next to her.

She'd never sat next to him before—other than that brief stint in their AP civics class, before she'd switched seats with her friend Lynne. At least in high school there'd been an aisle between them. At this conference table, they were smashed so tightly together she could feel the heat emanating from his thigh. It was irritating. Aside from that, every time he moved, it sent a trail of his aftershave in her direction.

A man like Ben should not be allowed to wear...whatever that aftershave was. It was far too distracting.

At one point he shifted and their legs touched, and she jerked away. She felt—*felt*—him look at her, but she refused to meet his gaze. Next meeting, she told herself, she'd take care not to sit next to him.

Anywhere but next to him.

Chapter Three

The first committee meeting with Celeste had been as draining as Ben had expected. Just sitting next to her had been a distraction.

For pity's sake. It had been nearly ten years since high school. He'd been married, had a child, built a business. He was a leader in the community and—generally—respected by everyone. He had accomplished all of his dreams. Or most of them, at least. Yet, somehow, she still made him feel like a stuttering teen with a creaky voice. He wasn't sure why she made him feel like that. She never said anything overtly mean—even when they disagreed. It was more of a general vibe he got when he was around her. As though there was some invisible wall between them. Maybe there was.

He had noticed that each time they'd touched beneath the table at the committee meeting—and the touching had been unavoidable; he knew, he'd tried—she'd jerked away as though he'd burned her. She didn't meet his eyes when she talked to him and—it wasn't lost on him—she didn't talk to him unless she absolutely had to.

It probably only bothered him because of the irritating remnants of his teenage crush on her.

At any rate, he knew he had to steel his spine, especially

as they would be working together on the clinic project. At least they both agreed on how important it was. That was something.

He was still a little off-center—because of her—when his driver pulled into his friend Jax's studio that afternoon to pick his buddy up for the bachelor party. Ben had decided to have Greg drive tonight because he was planning to drink at the party and he never got behind the wheel if he drank. Besides, what groom didn't want to step out of a chauffeured town car for his bachelor party?

Ben was thrilled that Jax had asked him to be the best man at his coming wedding, and even happier to offer Jax and Nat the garden at the hotel as a site for their wedding. Things had gotten a little more complicated when Nat's sister Amy—another good friend—had fallen in love with one of Jax's military buddies, Noah Crocker, and the four had decided on a double wedding. But Ben hadn't minded the change at all, since both Amy and Jax were so special to him. He and Amy had become close after Vi had died. Amy had lost her husband as well, and the two of them were both at sea, suddenly finding themselves alone in the world with children to raise. It was a true honor to be a part of their weddings. The fact that he could host the party made it even more of a joy.

It would be the first wedding at the hotel, which had only been open for a few years, so it was a good opportunity for him to scope out how events might be improved or marketed in the future. He had a great team to carry out the details—Char had been a wedding planner in a previous job and was very excited about taking the lead on the event. But beyond the potential business enhancement elements, Ben was looking forward to the ensuing festivities, most especially because it was for his friends.

Especially tonight—the bachelor party. It wasn't going to be some fancy thing, because Jax wasn't that kind of guy and neither was Noah. They were perfectly happy with a keg of beer surrounded by all their buddies at the volunteer firefighters' hall, which was pretty much Ben's speed as well, when it came to parties.

The door to Jax's studio was open, letting in the fresh sea breeze, but Ben still knocked before he stepped inside. "Hello," he called.

Jax popped out from behind an enormous log he was sanding. "Hey, Ben." He glanced at the clock. "Jeez. Is it five already?"

Ben chuckled. Jax often lost track of time in his art. But it made him happy. That was all that really mattered. "Yep."

Jax grinned. "Sorry. Sometimes I get carried away. Let me clean up." He was, indeed, covered with wood chips. Fortunately, his studio had a living space with a rudimentary shower.

"I'll grab beers." Ben headed to the fridge and snagged a couple brews, then shouldered off his suit jacket and tie and unbuttoned his shirt a bit. It was nice to shed a bit of the formality that went along with his job. With Jax, he could always be just-Ben.

It had been like this since they'd met in the third grade. Ben had been a shy outsider, coming into a small town where everyone knew one another, and to make matters worse, there had been a lot of opposition to his father's plans for redevelopment in the area, which had made Ben unpopular in school as well. His dad hadn't cared about any of that, of course. He'd just pushed along with what he wanted, never giving much concern to how his actions impacted his family. He never had. It shouldn't have been a surprise, Ben thought in retrospect, that a few years after moving here, his father had divorced his mother to marry his young secretary.

And yeah, that had been rough. Through it all, Jax had been a steadfast friend. Through that nasty, highly contested divorce, Ben's awkward middle and high school careers, and even when he'd lost his wife…Jax had always been there for him.

Ben was halfway through his beer when Jax emerged from the shower, raking back his jet-black hair. "Wow," he said with a grin. "That felt good. Sorry to keep you waiting."

"Hey, it's your party."

Jax laughed. "Well, then I might as well get started." He popped the top on his beer and took a slurp, finishing it with a gusted "Ahh. Nothing like a cold beer after work on a summer's day."

"Yep."

Jax plopped on the sofa, glanced at Ben, waggled his brows and said, "So…" But he didn't finish the sentence.

"What?" Ben had to nudge.

His buddy's grin widened. "I heard you and Celeste are working on a project together."

Ben tried not to grimace. "We had our first committee meeting today."

"And how did *that* go?"

"It was fine," he lied and Jax laughed, because he knew better. "Everyone on the committee is on board with the proposal—and that's a relief. You know how difficult some of the old guard can be."

"Who's on the committee?"

"Well, Tony and Luke…" Jax nodded. He knew them both from the good old VFF—they'd be seeing them tonight. "And Susan Warren from the planning commission."

"Yeah."

"And Angus Crowley."

Jax wrinkled his nose. "From the historical society?" Jax knew the Coho Cove Historical Society was notorious for opposing practically every new development. They often fought to preserve old buildings that were crumbling to pieces—mostly because they'd been poorly maintained—just because they were old. The nastiest fight had been over Huck Garner's fishing shack near the pier, which had been a rattrap filled with code violations. That fight between the historical society and the town's planning commission had even gone to court. The suit had only been settled when, after a particularly nasty winter storm, part of the building had collapsed, and it had had to be torn down and rebuilt with redevelopment funds. Fortunately, there were no buildings out on the Point to gum up the works for the clinic, now that the mill was gone. That had been a public nuisance as well, over a hundred years old and a ramshackle hazard.

"So…" Jax interrupted his musings with the worst question ever. "How did you and Celeste get along?"

"You mean, was there a fight?" Ben chuckled. "Sorry to disappoint you. No. We were both perfectly civil."

"Well, good. I know she was nervous about it."

She was? He would never have guessed it. But then,

he'd always had a hard time reading her. "Did she tell you that?"

Jax shook his head. "Nat did."

Oh. He didn't bank on hearsay—there was always something left out. "I'm sure there won't be any problems. I mean, it's an important project for the town."

"Yeah. I know Celeste feels that way too." Jax tipped back his head and finished his beer. "You 'bout ready to go?"

"Yeah." The party was scheduled for six, and they still had to pick up Noah at Amy's house.

They headed out to the yard and Jax's eyes widened as he spotted the car. "Ooh," he said. "Fancy."

Ben slapped him on the back. "Nothing but the best for you, my friend," he said.

After picking up Noah—and saying hello to Amy and the boys, because he could hardly stop by without visiting for a little while—they headed to the firefighters' hall. It was just as old as all the other buildings in Old Town, but it had a kind of ratty elegance that Ben liked. Also, it was filled with lots of memories for him. It was where he'd forged most of his friendships when he'd returned to town after his dad died.

Most of the guys were already there when they arrived. They hadn't waited to tap the keg and dig into the food Ben had sent over, but they did pause in stuffing their faces to greet them with a rousing cheer. Although it was probably for Jax and Noah.

Tony and Luke were there, as well as Baxter Vance, who ran one of Ben's favorite restaurants in town, and Vic Walton, who ran another. In fact, it looked very much like a chamber of commerce meeting, though there were a lot of other people there too, including some of the older VFF members who'd known Jax for years and respected him. A few of Jax's and Noah's military buddies, who had come to town from all over the country to attend the wedding, were there as well. Though Noah was relatively new to town, he fit in just like any of them.

There was a lot of laughter and teasing directed toward the grooms, because, after all, their bachelor careers were coming to an end. Most of the guys were already married, especially the older ones, and they got a kick out of sharing horror stories from their weddings. Some of them had tales of woe about failed marriages as well—which Ben thought was inappropriate, but he kept his mouth shut, even when Baxter Vance jested, "It's not too late to run, guys."

But yeah. It just didn't feel right to chime in on the topic. Maybe it was because he knew what it was like to be in love and have things go south. Or maybe it was because he was hopeful that Nat and Jax, and Amy and Noah, would be happy, that their marriages would last. They certainly seemed to be happy. But things had been wonderful with Vi in the beginning too. Didn't it always start out that way?

He'd met Violetta Gold when he was in college. His housemates had been throwing a party, but Ben had been up in his room studying, because his father expected him to finish his undergrad in three years, just as *he* had. Ben had been prepping for an important exam the next day and was deep in the books—trying to ignore the cacophony downstairs—when the door burst open and a vision walked through. Man, she'd been gorgeous, with blond hair, blue eyes and a slender build with curves in all the right places. He'd been poleaxed.

She'd been looking for the bathroom, but she'd found him instead. They'd talked for a while, longer than it took to point out the direction of the bathroom, certainly—and he was taken with her radiance, intelligence and sharp sense of humor.

They'd started dating and it wasn't long before they were living together, and happily so. They lived in that love as he finished his undergrad and his MBA, both in record time. His dad hadn't approved of the relationship because he'd considered her a distraction, but those had been wonderful years. Damn, he'd been in love. His only regret was that he'd been so wrapped up in Vi back then that he hadn't spent much time with his mother, who still lived back in the Cove. He should have done that, when he'd had the chance.

Shortly after Ben had married Vi, his mom had been diagnosed with cancer, a particularly virulent strain. She'd died when Quinn was a baby.

At least she got to hold her granddaughter. Ben could still remember the look in her eye when he settled that precious bundle in her arms. She'd looked like a Madonna.

God, he missed her.

After he got his master's, he started training under his father—ostensibly to take over the company one day—and the schedule was brutal. That was when the first cracks in his relationship with Vi started to appear. Ben was working long, hard hours and Vi started to feel ignored. He should have focused more on making her happy, rather than pleasing his father, but at the time, he just couldn't see any other option. Working for his father had seemed like his only path. It was only now, looking back, that he could understand how narrow his vision had been.

His vision had been narrow in a lot of places, though, hadn't it?

When Vi found out she was pregnant, they'd decided to get married. It had seemed like the right thing to do. And honestly, he suspected they both hoped that having a child would smooth out the rough spots between them.

His father had been furious when he found out about the baby. Called him sloppy. Yeah, his dad hadn't had an ounce of compassion. He hadn't even attended Ben's wedding, because he'd never approved of the relationship. Only his mother and her new husband, along with a few of his friends, like Jax, had been there.

So there had been tension in their marriage pretty much from the start. At the time, Ben had blamed it on his father for being so damn demanding and overbearing, but now he was mature enough to realize that he could have done better. Aside from that, things had only gotten worse when his father died, and Ben had moved his little family to Coho Cove and thrown himself into saving the company. Vi hadn't been happy here at all, partly because all her family and friends were in Seattle—she'd always been a city girl—and partly because, as Ben was restructuring the company, he was almost always working. It didn't help that money had been really tight; they'd had a lot of conflicts about that. By the time of her accident, they'd been heading for a divorce.

It made him sad to think about it. He'd loved her. He still did. But they'd never been a good match, despite the passion between them.

"Hey." Jax sat down next to him and handed him a frothing beer. "You okay?"

"Me?" Ben forced a grin, pushing away his miserable

past and his present loneliness. "I'm great. How about you? Are you enjoying the party?"

"I am."

"Sorry there are no strippers."

Noah, who'd just come up, huffed a laugh. "Amy would eviscerate me if there were."

Jax barked a laugh. "She'd eviscerate Ben first."

"I did bring a karaoke machine," Ben said helpfully. He'd thought it might be fun because he knew that Jax had a tendency to warble popular songs when he got drunk. And Ben had a tendency to tease him mercilessly after the fact. He'd even been known to shoot videos of the performance for said teasing.

His buddy barked a laugh and waggled a finger at him. "*That* is not happening again," he said adamantly.

But he was wrong.

And Ben got the videos to prove it.

The day of the wedding was a flurry of activity, especially for Celeste. She'd never been a maid of honor before, and because she wanted the day to go flawlessly for her sisters, she was a little nervous. Fortunately, there was plenty to keep her occupied.

"Are you ready for this?" she asked Momma over a nice breakfast of tea and toast.

Momma sniffed. "To be honest, I'm a little weepy. My two babies are getting married."

Celeste patted her hand. "I know. I feel the same." She didn't mention the odd disquiet in her heart, though. For some reason, as the oldest, she'd always thought she'd be married before her little sisters. But it hadn't happened, had it? Her one great love with Randall—along with her faith in romance and marriage and fidelity and all those fairy tales—had burned to the core and collapsed into ashes.

She'd met Randall Abbot when she'd been in nursing school in Portland. She'd been away from home for the first time, and had been painfully naive. At least, that was how she explained it to herself. When she finally realized what a terrible, toxic relationship it had been, she'd ended it…and vowed never to make that mistake again.

But this wasn't the time for that familiar lament. She forced herself to smile at Momma. "I'm happy for them."

"So happy. I love the boys." Though Jax and Noah were hardly boys. They were both grown men and military veterans to boot.

"Me too."

Momma sent her a side-eye. "Now all we need to do is find someone for you." It wasn't the first time the subject had come up between them, so Celeste let the comment slide away into oblivion rather than mention the salient fact that there weren't a lot of fantastic options around the Cove. Oh, there were some wonderful people—and some of them were men—but, ridiculously perhaps, Celeste had always wanted some great romantic love, a sizzling attraction, a real connection…and, other than that one brilliant and disastrous affair that had left her more than a little gun-shy, she'd never felt anything like that in her life.

Maybe there was just something wrong with her. Or maybe she and her soul mate had just never found each other. Not that she believed in soul mates. Why would she?

"I'm happy with the way things are, Momma," she said instead, because it was true. She loved her job, she loved the Cove, and her life was full and interesting. And because Momma looked as though she might launch into a list of all the eligible men in town, Celeste quickly said, "Well, I'd better get started. It's going to be a busy day."

She told Momma to sit and enjoy her tea while Celeste packed up the car. It was amazing how much stuff was needed to be in a wedding. There were dresses for both herself and Momma, makeup, gifts and more. The wedding itself was in the garden of the Sherrod Hotel in the late afternoon, and after that, there was dinner and a reception, but Nat and Amy had booked a suite for the family so they could enjoy the entire day at the resort. Though Celeste doubted she would relax all that much. It was her job to make sure her sisters enjoyed their day, after all.

Though she'd seen the fancy hotel on the Point from afar many times, Celeste had never been inside. On purpose. She'd opposed the project when the Sherrod Group had submitted the proposal to the planning commission, and she'd fought against it tooth and nail throughout the development…and lost. It still stuck in her craw. So she was totally prepared to hate the hotel, simply out of principle. How annoying was it then that, when she stepped inside the grand atrium, it stole her breath. For one thing, the ceiling soared over her head, probably ten floors or so. The color scheme was so natural that, combined with the artful design of the decor, the plants and the gorgeous sculptures hewn of beautiful woods, she felt as though she were outside. The enormous floor-to-ceiling glass panes amplified the effect. Even the chandeliers were stunning.

Goodness gracious. Seeing it made her understand why everyone in town always gushed over how gorgeous it was. How annoying.

She didn't mind gorgeous hotels in general. It was just this one that irritated her.

"Oh," Momma said. "This is lovely."

How irksome that she was right.

Before they had a moment to reflect, a pretty woman with long blond hair and a perky aura came up to them with a smile. "Wedding party?" she asked.

Celeste smiled back because she couldn't stop herself. Some people's energy was just contagious. "Mother of the brides and the maid of honor," she said.

"Oh. Pearl and Celeste?" Goodness. She didn't even need to check her iPad to know their names. "Welcome to the Sherrod. I'm Char. I'll be managing the wedding events, so if you have any problems or concerns, here's my number. Call me right away." She handed them both her business card. It was on thick paper with raised print. Fancy. "Now, let's get you settled. To the Grand Suite." She twirled her finger to the bellhop, who was following them with a gold-gilded cart laden with all their accoutrements. "Please, follow me."

Char led the way to a glass elevator on the eastern wall of the enormous lobby. Celeste had always hated elevators because they made her claustrophobic, but this one had a huge panoramic window on one side. As they rose up the first ten flights, Celeste realized that the elevator overlooked not only the stunning space, but the ocean to the west as well. She could only imagine how gorgeous this would be at sunset. And yes, it was difficult to not grind her teeth.

It was petty of her, and she knew it. Amy was right. Development would have come to Coho Cove eventually. It was just too beautiful a place to keep people away. She should be thankful that when it came, it was done well. Regardless of what she thought of the Sherrod Group, or developers, or change in general, this property was well done in every way.

When the elevator moved up past the atrium, and the dark shaft closed in, she turned around and tried to focus on the numbers lighting the header so she could keep her anxiety at bay. Fortunately, the elevator was swift, and before long, it opened.

Char led them out into a wide hall with thick carpeting to a set of double doors at the end of the hall. The Grand Suite was, in a word, gobsmacking. It opened to a living area that faced west and the vast expanse of the sea, but there were several bedrooms with en suites, a powder room and a small kitchen area as well. While Celeste was gaping at the vista, because she simply couldn't tear her eyes away, Char offered them both a glass of champagne, though they opted for sparkling water—Momma because of her medications and Celeste because she had *responsibilities* and it would be a long day. There was also a selection of canapés and chocolate-covered strawberries arrayed on the dining table.

"Isn't this lovely?" Momma said. She picked up the card next to the food and sighed. "Oh. Compliments of Ben Sherrod." She sighed again. "Isn't he a doll?"

Char smiled. "He's so thrilled to be hosting Jax's wedding, you know. He's just bursting at the buttons to have the festivities here."

After Char left them to relax and unwind, Celeste and Momma unpacked and organized all their things. After that, Celeste found a classical music station on the television, which both she and Momma enjoyed, and they relaxed by the windows and enjoyed the view.

All relaxation ended abruptly when the door opened and Amy, Noah and the boys poured in. It was an explosion of chaos, but a lovely chaos. John J., her youngest nephew, who had just turned six, ran to her and threw himself into her arms. "Auntie C!" he warbled. "Aren't you excited?"

"I am." She lifted him onto her lap. "How about you? Being a ring bearer? Such responsibility."

He wrinkled his adorable nose. "I have to wear a monkey suit."

She had to laugh. His expression of disgust was hilarious.

Georgie, the eldest, sauntered up. "That's what Noah calls it, but Mom says it's just a suit."

Celeste reached out to give him a hug, which he graciously allowed. It was always wonderful to see them, but they were growing so fast. She'd seen them both on Sunday, yet, somehow, they seemed older. It always surprised her when she noticed changes in them after so little time. "Are you getting taller?" she asked Georgie, to which he preened a little.

"I am almost seven," he reminded her.

"True."

In that moment of silence, the lovely Beethoven piano concerto playing from the speakers swelled into its crescendo and Amy made a face. "Ugh. Why can't you play anything normal?" she said. It wasn't the first time she'd complained about Celeste's taste in music, but it was *her* wedding day, so Celeste chuckled and turned off the TV.

"What's normal?" Momma said. "Besides, the reason

you girls are so smart is because I played classical music for you in your cribs. It's good for the brain."

"Is that true?" Noah asked.

Celeste shrugged. "There are some studies that suggest the patterns in the music help build neural pathways."

"Oh, look, Noah," Amy said. "There's champagne." She poured a glass for him and a sparkling water for herself.

Amy and Noah barely had a chance to sip their drinks before the door opened again and Ben Sherrod stepped through with his daughter, Quinn.

Quinn was a beautiful child, with long blond hair, startling blue eyes and an adorable smile. She was a shy thing, but the second she saw John J., she lit up. He lit up as well and squirmed from Celeste's lap to run to her and squire her over to the snacks. The two were so cute together, but to be honest, even as Celeste watched them, she was preternaturally aware of one looming presence.

Ben Sherrod.

Good glory.

Did he need to hover so?

Not that he was hovering. He was talking to Amy and Noah over by the door, but it *felt* like he was hovering. When he did make his way over to them, he greeted Momma first. "Good morning, Pearl," he said with a far-too-charming smile. "What do you think of the suite?"

Oh. Momma could go on. It was outstanding, she said. Sumptuous. Fabulous. The view was stupendous, the ambience divine… And on and on. Celeste was happy to sit and listen, because it meant *she* didn't have to talk to him. She was free to simply stare out at the sea and pretend he wasn't here at all—

"And how are you, Celeste?" She should have known he would ask.

"Very well, thank you, Ben." What else was there to say?

"Thank you so much for the refreshments." Oh, yes. That, probably. Good thing Momma remembered. "So thoughtful."

Ben's eyes twinkled. "My pleasure. Please call Char if you need anything today. You have her card?"

This last bit was directed at her, so Celeste nodded. And then, as an afterthought, because he had gone to considerable effort to ensure it would be a lovely day, "Thank you."

He seemed inordinately pleased at that, which made her feel small for not saying it sooner, but then he turned away and called to the kids. "Hey. Are you guys ready to go swimming?" And yes, he'd planned a full day for the boys at the resort's modest water park so the brides could focus on their special day.

The boys whooped, grabbed their day packs and galloped from the room. Before he left, Ben went to Amy and gave her a long hug with a heartfelt congratulations. "I'm so happy for you," he said, and he meant it. The hint of tears in his eyes as he smiled at Amy and Noah was kind of gutting. Celeste knew that Amy and Ben were close—they'd both lost spouses and were raising kids alone and all that—but she hadn't expected how his expression of emotion in that moment would hit her.

It was almost like he was a human or something.

"Oh," Amy gushed after Ben left. "Isn't this amazing?" She twirled around the room like a cartoon princess. "Can you believe this suite?"

"Didn't you book it?" Celeste had to ask.

Amy stopped short and gaped at her. "This suite?" She

snorted a laugh. "This suite is thousands. I booked a normal room. *Ben* upgraded us...to this."

Noah picked up a strawberry and snorted. "And then he refused to let us pay for it."

"For the room?"

"For the wedding."

"What?" Celeste stared at him.

Noah nodded. "He gave us some nonsense about using the wedding for marketing purposes and how we'd be doing him a favor and all..."

"We couldn't let him pay for the dinner, though," Amy said. "Not after the guest list got so large."

"Who knew we had so many friends," Noah muttered dryly.

"Amy is something of a celebrity now," Momma said. Indeed, Amy's bakery had recently been featured on television. Granted, it was a somewhat obscure travel show on Channel 11, but in Coho Cove, that counted as celebrity. And yes, the wedding guest list had expanded tremendously from when they'd first started planning.

Nat and Jax, along with his sister, Sheida, arrived shortly after, and the wedding party was complete. Well, other than Ben, who was the best man, but he had explained he would be popping in and out because he had a lot of other things going on. Unlike the rest of them, he hadn't taken the day off work.

And oh, it was such a nice day. After getting everything organized in the suite for Natalie and Amy, they all made their way down to the pool deck—where Ben had reserved cabanas for them—and they had a lovely lunch.

After lunch Celeste, her sisters and Momma went to the salon while the men went off to do whatever men do.

And heavens, it was wonderful. They each had manicures and Momma even got a pedicure, giggling all the way through it. After that came makeup and hair. And goodness, that was something.

Celeste wasn't one to wear makeup very often. She thought it was a waste of time and, frankly, didn't fit with her lifestyle very well. And her hair was, generally, wash and go. So she was fairly stunned when the stylist spun her around, once her work was finished, and she was faced with the creature in the mirror.

Heavens. It looked nothing like her.

Her sisters and her mother oohed and aahed so much she started to wonder what a drudge she was on normal days. But oh well, this was a special event, and her sisters had wanted photos, so she tolerated the praise and merely thanked them.

It wasn't so terrible being pampered, she decided.

"Oh," Nat said, pulling them all to the mirror to gaze at the picture they made in their finery. "Just look at us."

"My girls," Momma said with a sniff. "My beautiful baby girls are all grown up." Caught up in her emotion, and the emotion of the day, they all rushed to hug her, snuffling right along.

"Don't cry," Amy commanded. "It'll ruin your makeup." So, after that, no one dared.

But Natalie sighed. "I just wish Dad and Nate could be here with us."

Momma patted her on the hand. "They're here, honey. I know they are." Which made tears threaten again. "Family truly is what life's about, you know. People you love, coming together. Enjoying the journey…together. What a joy it has been to be your mother. To watch you grow into the beautiful, unique women you are. I am so proud of all of you. Your father would be too."

"Thank you, Momma," they each said.

She sighed heavily, but it wasn't a sad sigh, it was a hopeful one, and with a twinkle in her eye, she added, "But I wouldn't mind having another grandchild…or two."

Amy and Natalie exchanged a glance and their smiles widened. When they each set their hands on their bellies a prickle ran up Celeste's spine. "Shall we tell them?" Amy asked, and Natalie nodded.

"I think this is a good time."

"Tell us what?" Celeste asked, but her voice cracked, because somewhere, deep in her heart, she already knew.

"We're pregnant!" they said in an excited chorus.

And though Celeste joined in with Momma's delighted congratulations, a part of her had gone numb.

Both her sisters, *her baby sisters*, were expecting.

It was great news. Glorious news.

She had no idea why it made her chest hurt.

Chapter Four

As fate would have it, Ben had a very busy day. Aside from his best friend's wedding, there had been a huge hiccup on the Raskin project—a problem with a construction schedule that took him most of the day to work out. Because it was a time-sensitive project, he'd needed to deal with the snag right away. By the time he was done with work, the day had waned, and it was time for him to head to his apartment and get dressed for the wedding.

He wasn't a fan of weddings in general, but he'd kept his opinions from Jax and Amy while they were coordinating this one. Just because his marriage hadn't been as idyllic as he'd dreamed it would be—and his parents' had been worse—it didn't mean that every union was destined for tragedy. It was probably best to keep his cynicism to himself.

Oh, he thought about getting married again—in a general sense—but just because it bothered him, being a single father. He'd been raised by a single parent after his father had left his mother, and he knew how much Quinn was missing by not having a mother, but after his experience with Vi, at least after the romance had gone sour, he was leery about engaging in another romantic relationship. It was probably common for people who'd had a challenging marriage, he supposed, but the desire for something he both yearned for and dreaded had kept him from dating at all.

By the time he got to his apartment, Ellie had already helped Quinn get into her dress, and his daughter was flitting around the living room like a bright blue butterfly.

"Oh, sweetie," he said, going down on one knee. "You look beautiful."

He loved the way she smiled, the way her cheeks pinkened with delight.

It was so sweet, and warmed his heart, that Amy had asked Quinn to be her flower girl. Quinn loved dressing up on a regular day, but today especially so. She wore a gossamer blue dress that really brought out her eyes, and a pretty tiara of woven flowers in a blue-and-white motif. She even had matching patent leather shoes. "You are going to be the prettiest flower girl ever." He glanced up at Ellie. "I'm going to get changed, but after Quinn and I head down you can take the rest of the day off." He'd made arrangements for Quinn to join John J. and Georgie and the other guests' children in the kids' club after the wedding.

"That would be great," she said. "Thanks."

"Well, I'm going to go get ready, then," he said, but before he did, he pulled Quinn into his arms and gave her a very loud smooch on her cheek, mostly because it made her giggle when he did that.

Once he'd showered and shaved and wrestled his way into his tux, he and Quinn went over to the Grand Suite to check in with the rest of the wedding party, and honestly, it seemed a little like a circus when he stepped through the door. The boys, in tiny tuxes as well, were running rampant—probably because there were no adults present. No doubt they'd gotten the boys ready first before getting dressed themselves. When John J. spotted Quinn he stopped short, and his mouth dropped open.

"Gosh, Quinn," he said. "You look so pretty."

It was cute the way she blushed.

"Hi, guys," Ben said to the boys. "Are you ready for the wedding?"

Georgie, who was older and a little more jaded, shrugged. He tugged at his bow tie. "I suppose. It does seem like an awful lot of nonsense, doesn't it?"

Ben had to laugh. "I suppose it does. And where's your mom?" he asked.

"I'm here." Amy came out of one of the rooms, tying her sash. She gave a little twirl. "What do you think?"

Ben could hardly answer, he was so choked up. What was it about a wedding dress that was so magical? Maybe it was the fact that it symbolized a transformation in not just a woman's life, but her man's too. Maybe it was because he remembered the first time he'd seen Vi in hers. Something had caught in his throat then too.

Because he didn't answer quickly enough, Amy put her hands on her hips and glared at him. "Well?"

He had to laugh, mostly because she was so darn cute. "Amy, you look stunning. Noah is going to be blown away." The guys were getting ready in another room closer to the venue, because Amy and Natalie had been adamant that they not get a peek of them in their wedding finery before the ceremony.

"What about me?" Natalie asked as she followed Amy into the room. They had each chosen a different style of gown, but damn if they hadn't captured their personalities to a T. Natalie's was a sleek, formfitting nod to art deco, as befitted her artistic style, and Amy's was a Cinderella-like froth with a sparkly bodice, nipped waist and a full skirt.

"Gorgeous, Nat. Just gorgeous."

Pearl came out next and was exquisitely outfitted as the mother of the brides in a blue that echoed Quinn's dress. Sheida followed, looking gorgeous as well. What was interesting was that, though the color schemes were similar enough for continuity of theme, each woman wore a dress that fit them—in style and nature—which Ben thought was nice. Vi had chosen the bridesmaids' dresses for their wedding, and they'd all been the same cut, to varying effect. He'd never told her, but he'd overheard her friends and sisters complaining about that during their reception. Many had changed out of the "uniforms" right after the ceremony. But these dresses—

His brain switched off abruptly and all thoughts of weddings and dresses and, well, everything, flew from his head.

Because Celeste appeared.

Good God, she was stunning.

Oh, she was always pretty—even when she was frowning at him—but this... Wow.

Her dress was the same beautiful light blue, but had a plunging neckline and the skirt was a series of ruffled tiers that flowed around her as she moved. Her hair was done up in an elegant style that erupted in curls around her face. And...had he ever noticed how striking her gray eyes were? Surely he had. But in this light, they were almost silver.

He didn't realize that a silence had settled over the

room until she broke it, saying, in a snippy tone, "What are you staring at?"

"Ah…" Suddenly, there he was again, that gawky teenager who couldn't make a sentence around her. "You…" He sucked in a deep breath and composed himself. "You look magnificent." And then, because his awkwardness had consumed him again, he said, to everyone in general, "You all do. Just beautiful."

"Aw." Amy gave a little curtsy. "Thank you, sir. You look rather handsome yourself."

"Thanks."

"Oh, I don't know," Sheida said as she stepped closer. "Your tie is a little crooked." As she adjusted it for him, he couldn't help noticing Celeste's frown had melted into a glower. "There." Sheida patted him on the chest.

"Well, if everyone's ready, shall we go down to the venue?" he said, mostly because he couldn't think of anything else to say.

"Let's go." Amy hooked her arm in one of his, and Natalie took the other. Ben let the kids go first—just so they could all keep an eye on them—and Sheida and Celeste followed with Pearl.

Amy insisted they use one of the tower elevators—the ones without the panoramic view—just in case Noah or Jax could be in the lobby and might see them before they should, which made Ben chuckle. Vi had not allowed him to see her before the wedding either. So they took the roundabout way to the antechamber just off the garden, where the bouquets and Quinn's flowers were awaiting them. It was all Ben could do to keep his eyes off Celeste, but he tried.

Once the ladies were settled, Ben headed to the room

where his buddies were waiting. It was amusing to compare the energy levels of the two groups. Where the women had been excited and aflutter, the men were lounging. They both looked fantastic in their matching tuxes as they came to their feet at the sight of him.

"Wow," Jax said. "You clean up nice."

"Stuff it," Ben grumbled, but he was only playing. "Well, your brides are about ready." He glanced from one to the other. Surprisingly, neither one of them ran away.

"Well." Jax tugged down his vest and glanced at Noah. "I guess we do this, then?"

Noah shrugged. "I guess so."

Even though their tones were blasé, Ben knew better. He remembered his nerves on his wedding day, and he could tell his friends were feeling similar bouts of fear and elation. "Don't worry," he said, clapping them both on the shoulders. "It'll be over soon."

"Thank God," Noah said, raking back his hair.

"Before you know it, you'll be on that cruise ship headed for Alaska." He shot them a wink. "I'm jealous."

Char poked her head in and grinned. "Everything is ready," she said in a gentle voice. Apparently, she knew which tone to use with grooms. "Shall we?"

Jax looked at Noah and Noah looked back. They both swallowed heavily. "Let's do this," Jax said.

"Hooah," Noah responded with the Air Force battle cry. And they were off.

Celeste became oddly calm when it was time for the bridal procession to begin. Quinn, with her basket of petals, was the first to step onto the cream carpet that formed the aisle between the two rows of chairs, followed by

Georgie and John J., each carrying a velvet pillow with a set of rings. Char had cleverly pinned the rings to the pillows so they didn't go flying off on the short journey to the altar. Boys, after all, would be boys.

Sheida, the bridesmaid, arm in arm with her and Jax's father, Alexander, followed close behind.

When it was her turn, and Celeste stepped out, she got her first full look at the garden, all decked out in wedding finery, and her heart thumped. Heavens, it was gorgeous. The decorations, certainly, but the natural background of the sea and the afternoon sun were breathtaking as well. The arbors were festooned with white and blue flowers, and goodness, there was quite a crowd. And they were all looking at her.

Jax and Noah were already standing at the altar, both staring attentively, anticipating a glimpse of their bride. They both held one wrist in their other hand, as though they'd practiced, and while they looked suave and sophisticated, Celeste could see the nervousness in their faces. Her heart blossomed with love for them both. Her brothers.

She sensed a presence approach her side. She didn't need to look to know it was Ben. His aftershave preceded him. Aside from that, Natalie and Amy had designed the march to the altar in a very particular fashion. They'd been adamant that she and Ben, as maid of honor and best man respectively, come down the aisle right before them. The brides would follow, with Momma between them, as she would be giving them away. Usually the mother of the bride was the first to walk down the aisle, but this pleased everyone better. Especially Momma.

"Are you ready?" Ben asked softly, totally disrupting

her thoughts. The warmth of his whisper danced over her bare shoulder, sending a shiver through her.

She glanced at him. She shouldn't have. He was far too close. She could see every whorl in his eyes, every thick, dark lash, every twitch of his lips. "Yes—" she tried to say, but it wouldn't come out. She had to clear her throat and try again.

He put out his arm and she took it, trying to ignore how warm he was, how imposing, how absolutely resplendent he looked in that tux. Instead, she tried to focus on the dance of the gulls in the distance, the play of the sun on the water. It was hopeless, of course. He filled her senses.

It was nearly a relief when they came to the end of the aisle and separated, he going over to Jax and Noah, and she joining Sheida to face the assembly.

When the bridal march began, and her sisters, flanking Momma, stepped out, Celeste's emotions swelled and tears pricked her eyes. But to be honest, that had been happening all day, hadn't it? Today was a big day for the whole family. It was probably normal to be emotional. Even seeing Amy's sons, dressed in their tiny little suits with their hair slicked back, made her weepy. It was funny how much they looked like Nate.

She forced a smile, though, as the couples were declared husbands and wives, and it even became real for a second there when John J. hollered, "Woo-hoo!" but when the two couples kissed, she got all choked up again.

As her sisters swept down the aisle with their new husbands in tow, Celeste ushered the boys and Quinn in behind them and then helped Momma out of her seat to follow along as Sheida and Alexander made their retreat. Momma had refused to bring a walker or cane, of course, and without the support, she was a little unsteady, so it was nice that Ben waited there as the rest of the wedding party passed, and offered her an arm.

He glanced at Celeste over Momma's head as they made their way with the rest of the wedding party through the patio of the hotel toward the sumptuous banquet room, where the reception would be held. A shiver walked through Celeste when their gazes met.

She always hated when that happened—when their gazes met. It always made something in her tummy slosh. But because he was being so kind, she knew she had to at least make an effort to be civil.

"Thank you," she said to him in an undertone.

"Of course," he responded, and the shiver returned, even though she was no longer looking at him.

When Celeste stepped inside the banquet hall, her breath caught. It was certainly grand.

"I think we're over here," Ben said to Momma as he led them through the maze of circular tables to the front of the room, where a long trestle had been set up for the wedding party. Celeste scanned the nameplates and then winced when she realized one of her sisters—maybe both—had decided to sit her right next to Ben. They should have known better. When she sent him an irritated glower, he responded with an apologetic look. They both knew it was a bad idea.

She settled Momma next to Jax's dad, Alexander—which had been an excellent seating choice because they began happily chatting right away. Momma and Alexander had become friends during Nat and Jax's courtship and they both had an interest in rockhounding, of all things, so they had plenty to talk about. Once she was settled, Celeste headed off to the bar to get Momma a wine spritzer. Momma had to watch her alcohol intake because of her medications, but she liked an occasional wine spritzer. Celeste didn't realize Ben had followed her until he said—in that annoying voice of his—from right behind her, "We can do this, you know."

She stopped short. Too short, in fact, and he barreled into her. She didn't mind being bumped. It was the warmth of his hands on her waist as he steadied her that irritated her. She whirled on him. "Do what?" She tried not to snap; it was a wedding, after all. She'd had lots of conversations with herself about how she would handle any interaction with Ben Sherrod prior to today and she'd decided she would be civil. She would be polite. She would be distant. All that went out of her mind whenever he was close.

And he was close.

For some reason, he smiled. It was one of those sad smiles she hated. "We can be nice. At least, tonight."

The little hairs on her nape prickled. Was he lecturing her about being nice? She was the nicest person she knew. So she said, in a very nice voice, "Well, *I* can be nice." And to prove it, she effected a credible smile.

His response was a chuckle and a murmured "Well, okay then," which, thankfully, required no response. She picked up Momma's drink, gave him a nod and headed back to the table, leaving him to wait for his.

After handing Momma her drink, she rounded up John J. and Georgie and followed Char, who had charge of Quinn, to the kids' club, where they would have a fabulous evening of pizza, movies and video games. The kids' club was brightly colored and filled with games and toys and soft sofas and beanbag chairs. It was such a comfy space she hated to leave, but she knew she had to, because there was one last torture on the menu for tonight—that dance with Ben.

Naturally, once she got back to the banquet room, she headed to the bar and grabbed a glass of wine for herself. If she had to spend the evening sitting next to Ben, it was probably a good idea to lubricate at least a little. She checked in on Momma—who was having a wonderful time with Alexander—then she meandered around the room and mingled. She was emotionally exhausted and physically tired from running around making sure everything was in order for the two brides, but the thought of sitting down—next to Ben—kept her on her feet. There would be plenty of time to ignore him once dinner was served. Fortunately, there were a lot of people to talk to as they all enjoyed their drinks and waited for the newlyweds to arrive to the party.

Everyone was at the wedding. Even Tony and Luke— the mayor and the president of the chamber of commerce— had shown up. Many more of Celeste's friends were here too, so it was fun to catch up with them—although it did remind her how sad her social life had become. Sheida was there too, of course, so talking about work was a great way to kill some time.

The arrival of the newlyweds was announced with fanfare and applause, and shortly after that, everyone found their seats for dinner.

Maybe it was the wine, but it was a lovely dinner. It seemed more like restaurant service than a catered event. Everything was fresh and delicious. Momma was next to Alexander and throughout the meal they had their heads together, chatting and laughing, which left no one for her to talk to...except Ben.

It probably wouldn't have been so difficult, having a simple conversation with him, but the only thing she could think about was the coming dance.

It came shortly after dinner was finished. Natalie and Jax came out on the dance floor, followed by Amy and Noah. And even though it was charming to watch them embark on their first dance together, all Celeste could think about was the fact that she would soon be joining them. With Ben. Her stomach tightened when Momma and Alexander—the mother of the brides and father of one of the grooms—headed for the dance floor as well.

"Shall we?" Ben asked in a rumble, far too close to her ear.

She glanced at him, at his outstretched hand, at his hopeful yet oddly anxious expression. While she was tempted to say no—she'd lost sleep over this, after all—she knew she couldn't. And not just because it would disappoint her sisters. Honestly, it was because she knew it would wound him, and after he'd been so generous and kind, that would be a terrible thing to do.

So she sucked it up, straightened her spine and took his hand.

She ignored the shiver that wracked her. Another one? She might be coming down with something. Surely that was the reason she was overset whenever they were close. Probably.

He led her onto the dance floor and she turned into his arms.

Steeled spines were all good and well, but they did little to protect one against a tsunami of sensation should it occur, and this was definitely that.

Oh heavens. She'd noticed his enticing aftershave earlier, but it had been easy to step away or focus on something else, but there, in his arms, held close, dancing slowly to a very romantic song, with nowhere to look but at him... it was devastating. She stumbled once or twice—probably due to lack of oxygen because she was trying desperately to hold her breath—but he was the perfect gentleman, steadying her easily.

It seemed to last forever. Probably the longest rendition of "The First Time Ever I Saw Your Face" in existence.

When the song ended, and they came apart in the darkened room lit only with the sparkles of a spinning disco ball, their eyes met. It was only for a second or two, but it felt like an eternity. And then his lips quirked in a smile, and he said softly, "Thank you for the dance, Celeste," and then he walked away. She had no idea why she felt so cold in his absence.

After the dance Celeste didn't go back to the table. She danced with a few friends, chatted here and there, and even had another drink. But after a while, she found a quiet place on the sidelines where she could be alone with her thoughts.

Her heart was so full...but at the same time, somehow, so empty.

For some reason, watching her sisters say their vows had awakened the realization that life, apparently, had passed her by. She didn't know how it had happened, but she was turning twenty-eight soon, and was still single.

So, mixed with the tears of joy at seeing them beam with happiness, there might have been a tear or two of despair.

They irritated her, those tears, because she wasn't the kind of person who thought a woman had to be a wife and a mother to have value, or to have a full life. Quite the opposite. And she was happy with the life she had created, wasn't she?

Her life was full. She was certainly busy. Aside from her job and working with the city council and the chamber of commerce on community events and social services committees, she was also Momma's caretaker. But watching her sisters get married had been a stark reminder that, somehow, she'd left out the most important part. Love.

But since that disaster with Randall, she found it really hard to trust men. She didn't trust herself much either.

What kind of intelligent woman let herself be lured into an emotionally abusive relationship?

She'd seen a therapist for quite a while after it ended; working through it had been a long slog. She'd come to the conclusion that if she ever found someone who could rouse her passion, a man who had the qualities she was looking for in a life partner, she'd make damn sure she knew him very well before giving him any power over her.

She'd been happy with the decision. Happy being single.

She *was* happy. She was.

All she needed to do was ignore that dream floating around in the back of her head, the dream most little girls had, to one day marry a man she loved, to have a happy marriage—like Momma'd had—with a house full of children and laughter.

But now, as she felt that wisp of a dream fading away

forever, her chest ached and her lungs locked. She could barely breathe.

Suddenly, it was all too much. The crowd. The chatter. The overwhelming joy.

With a sigh, Celeste headed from the banquet hall in search of a quiet spot where she wouldn't have to pretend to smile anymore. At least for a little while.

He couldn't deny it. Ben was shook.

The evening had been wonderful, a real triumph for his staff on all notes, but something else had knocked him completely awry. Celeste Tuttle.

He was used to her giving him the cold shoulder. He was used to it by now. It was water off a duck's back by now, wasn't it? But he hadn't been prepared for the impact of seeing her in her flowing dress with her hair and makeup done. Smiling. Oh, yeah, that had thrown him for a loop. But it was nothing compared to that dance.

That dance with Celeste had hit him hard. He hadn't expected that. Hadn't expected his body to *react* like that, holding her close, inhaling her fragrance every time she brushed against him. He had no idea how he made it through the charade. After the dance ended, he quickly found Sheida and they engaged in a lively and amusing conversation, a convenient distraction to bury his emotions and ignore those very inconvenient reactions to Celeste Tuttle.

He couldn't ignore Celeste herself, though. His brain had some bizarre kind of tracker; he always seemed to know where she was. He watched her dance with one guy after another. She talked to them, he noticed. She laughed with them. She had drinks with them. It was silly to be jealous, petty even, but it was hard to ignore those feelings. They had a life of their own.

He figured it was probably cowardly of him to avoid going back to the table, where he'd have to sit next to her and try to make conversation until the cutting of the cake, but he avoided it anyway.

Since everything was going smoothly in the banquet hall, he slipped out to head upstairs to check on his daughter in the kids' club. But as he came off the escalator and rounded the corner, he stopped short. Celeste Tuttle stood there, at the window, watching the little ones entertaining each other with their games and sharing desserts. He was about to move away quietly when she turned and caught sight of him. Her beautiful face tightened up immediately. His gut clenched when he saw that expression. It always did. It always made him want to run. But something else caught his attention, something that wiped the trepidation from his heart and replaced it with empathy.

Her cheeks were stained with tears.

Well, damn. So much for avoiding her.

Celeste gusted a sigh as Ben stepped up to the window next to her. She'd been having a perfectly wonderful time watching the children enjoy their innocence—and weeping heartily. Trust Ben Sherrod to come along and ruin that too.

"Are you okay?" he asked. She could feel his attention on her face—she always could. It was irritating that there was sympathy in his expression. She ignored it.

She sighed and turned from the bright colors and the sight of children laughing, and stared out across the atrium of the hotel. Why had he followed her? Why couldn't he just let her be miserable in peace? "I'm fine."

"Why did you leave the party?"

"I have a low tolerance for crowds." To prove it, she walked to a bench farther down along the hall. Naturally, because he was annoying, he followed.

"Are you sure that's all it is? You're crying." It was so nice of him to notice. She gave him a glare.

"It's a wedding. People cry."

"Not like that." And then, when she didn't respond, he added, "Celeste, I just want to help." Why did it only make things worse that he was being nice?

"You can't help me." The words came out in a bubble of a sob.

"Try me."

She blew out a breath and gave him a telling glance. Why would she open up to *him*? They'd never gotten along. They'd never agreed on a thing. She didn't like him and he didn't like her, and that was all there was to—

"Look," he said, interrupting her inner diatribe. "We're going to have to figure out a way to talk to each other. Now that we're going to be working together and all." Her gut churned at the thought, but damn it, he was right. "What's wrong, Celeste?"

She shot him a frown. "Isn't it obvious?"

He just stared at her, so maybe it wasn't. To a man, at least. They were, after all, somewhat oblivious creatures. "My sisters are married." She tried to contain the slightly maniacal rise in her voice, and failed.

"That's good, though. Isn't it?"

Oh, bother. She hated when he was right. "Of course it's good. I'm so h-h-h-happy for them." This, she said on another lamenting sob. "But there's more. I suppose I can tell you. Both Nat and Amy are e-e-expecting."

Ben nodded. "Yeah. I know." She frowned at him. Because how irritating was it that *he* knew a family secret? And, since she'd just found out today, he'd probably known it before she had. "Jax told me." *Of course he had.* She gritted her teeth. "But that's great news. Why are you upset about that?"

Ooh, he aggravated her. Fine. He wanted to know? She'd lay it out for him. "I'm not upset about that."

He sent her a look. "You're crying."

She glared at him. "My point is," she said forcefully, as though her ire could dry up the tears. It often did. "My baby sisters are both married now. They're moving on with their lives. I can't help feeling…left behind."

He huffed a laugh and it made her hackles rise. When she glared at him, he said—in the kind of tone that made you want to punch a guy for being too nice—"Celeste, you're not left behind."

Men. They understood nothing. "I'm pushing *thirty*. I don't even have a *boyfriend*." Even as the word came out, the inanity of it hit her. She didn't want a boyfriend. What she wanted was a companion. A partner. Someone to share her life with. *Boyfriend* was a flimsy word for all that.

She didn't know why she was telling him this. She usually evicted thoughts like this when they arose. She most certainly never shared them. Certainly not out loud. It was probably the wine. Another good reason not to drink.

He gaped at her. "Do you *want* a boyfriend?" Why did he seem so surprised?

She snorted a laugh and shrugged. "I don't know. I guess sometimes I'm just lonely."

His smile was sad. "Yeah. Sometimes I'm lonely too." She stifled an urge to mention Sheida, but didn't. You never knew the truth of other people's relationships anyway. But before she could think of a different response, he said, "Well, if you want to date, all you have to do is say the word," and her heart lurched. She stared at him in shock. What was he saying? Was he suggesting— But before the thought completed, he added, "I mean, guys were lined up to dance with you tonight." *He'd noticed?* She didn't know why that made her face hot. "I know a few of them would ask you out in a New York minute if they thought you were interested."

Sure. Yeah. There were a few guys in town who had asked her out over the years. She was the one who'd suggested they just remain friends, simply because there had been no spark there. To be honest, she knew that if she really wanted *someone*, just anyone, she could have that. The truth was, she wanted more. Something…soulful. Barring that, her own company was preferable. So yeah, being single was her choice.

Ben shot her a sideways glance and teasing grin. "Baxter Vance is single again."

She rolled her eyes. "I hear the third divorce is the charm," she said wryly and when he laughed she had to join in.

"There you go," he said. His smile was warm and sincere. "Do you feel better?"

Oddly, she did. She felt much better. She shot him a smile. "Why, yes, I do. Thank you."

"My pleasure." They sat in silence for a minute, just enjoying the sounds of the party in the distance, and then he turned to her. "I meant what I said earlier," he said.

She blinked at him. He'd said a lot of things.

He noticed her confusion, so he elaborated. "What do you think? Can we make peace?"

"Peace?"

"I mean, now that we'll be working together on this project, we'll be spending a lot of time together. It will be so much easier if we're not...at odds. Can we just at least try, Celeste? What do you say? Truce?" He held out his hand.

For a second, she thought about not taking it, but considering how much progress they'd made in this one little conversation, she decided not to be small.

She wished she had been small a second later when her hand touched his, because the warmth of it shocked her. It lured her a little bit too. She released him and immediately regretted it.

She didn't want to see him in this light. She didn't want to have comforting conversations with him. She certainly didn't want to know he was *warm*. But it was too late. It had happened. She could feel her resistance melting away.

It disturbed her because her feelings for Ben Sherrod had been solid for years. She didn't like him. She never had. But now that was changing. And it kind of felt like the earth beneath her feet was shifting, putting her in peril.

And all because she'd taken his hand.

Chapter Five

Celeste didn't have much time to think about Ben—or anything else—because she had plenty of other things to deal with after the wedding. The newlyweds were heading out on a two-week honeymoon to Alaska, and Celeste and Momma would be taking care of the boys while they were gone. During the weekdays, things would go on as normal—with Celeste taking the boys to the sitter on her way to work and picking them up at the end of the day—but on the weekends, she'd have them all day.

She and Momma weren't strangers to watching the boys. They'd done so often in the early days, when Amy's business was just starting out and she couldn't afford a sitter, but they'd been little then, hadn't they? Now they were getting older. They were more energetic, heinously curious and seemed to be everywhere all at once.

The first day with them, the Saturday after the wedding, was exhausting. Celeste learned very quickly to check the pockets of their jeans before tossing them into the wash—John J.'s were, for some reason, full of worms. And though they'd never been a family that crowded around the TV, she learned to appreciate the value of a nice long animated feature.

Honestly, by the afternoon, she was pooped...and she

still had supper to make. Fortunately, Momma noticed how tired she was and said, as Celeste was perusing the contents of the freezer, "Why don't we order in?"

Celeste gaped at her. Momma never wanted to order in. She considered it a waste of money.

"Do you have anything in mind?" she asked Momma, but the boys, who'd been skulking around looking for a snack, answered for her.

"Pizza!" This from Georgie. And "Barbecue!" from John J. They ended up getting both, and along with a couple of nice salads from Bootleggers for her and Momma, she cobbled together a smorgasbord. It was a lovely meal, a fine meal, but still, in the middle of dinner, Momma sighed.

"What's the matter?" Celeste had to ask. She knew if she didn't, Momma would continue sighing until someone did.

"Oh, nothing. It's just… There's only four of us."

"Momma, it's usually just the two of us."

"Oh, I'm not thinking about today. I'm thinking about tomorrow. It doesn't seem right, does it, just having the four of us at Sunday dinner. I can't remember when we've had only four."

It was true. They typically had a crowd—usually a mix of friends and family. The four of them, staring at each other around the table, did seem terribly odd. And quiet.

"We can invite some friends over," John J. said.

"Yes." Celeste smiled at him. "Let's. Who would you like to invite?"

She shouldn't have asked. She should have known. "Quinn."

"That's a lovely idea," Momma said. "A small way

to thank Ben as well for all he did to make the wedding special."

Though her first response was something along the lines of *Ugh*, Celeste bit her tongue. For one thing, the boys were here, and it was important to be a positive role model and not say unkind things in their presence. For another, Momma was right. Ben had been exceedingly generous. And she had, after all, agreed to a truce. Sadly, it was one thing to agree to make peace with Ben. It was another thing entirely to remember. She was so used to feeling annoyed with him and grumbling about his business, it was almost a habit. And a bad habit to boot. For one thing, it always made her feel…small.

He'd never been mean to her, like so many of the kids had been when she'd first arrived at Coho High. In fact, he'd been kind then, friendly even—until she'd ripped him to shreds in their debate class. After that, he'd just withdrawn.

And then, after graduation, she'd gone away to nursing school and he'd gone off to college. They hadn't really encountered each other again until they'd both moved back to town and she'd been appointed to the planning commission…and they'd clashed over his downtown redevelopment project. And his development of the Point. And of course, his hotel project. Perhaps the fact that she'd lost out on all three skirmishes had fed her resentment toward him.

"Maybe we can invite Alexander too," she said. And not just because having Alexander here might help diffuse the tension between Celeste and Ben.

"Oh yes. We should. After all, he's family now." It was cute the way Momma's eyes lit up at the suggestion.

* * *

Celeste was a little nervous about Sunday dinner, though she had no idea why. She'd been making Sunday dinner with Momma for years. But then, Ben was coming, wasn't he? It had been nerve-wracking enough, calling him up to invite him for Momma. Thank heavens he hadn't been there. She'd left a message with his service, and when he'd called back to accept, it had been on her voice mail.

Given the fact that they'd agreed to be on friendly terms, it was good that he was coming, so she could get in some practice, but she was still on pins and needles as she prepared the meal.

She got the boys involved—it seemed to keep them out of trouble, she'd found. They helped her make the lasagna, ice the bread with a thick swath of garlic butter, toss an enormous salad and bake a cake. What a mess that was! The boys wanted to decorate the cake too, so that was an adventure as well. It was hardly the kind of elevated dessert they were used to, but Amy—the baker in the family—was off on her honeymoon. At any rate, it would be delicious.

Making the meal with the boys was fun and filled with laughter, and served to distract her from obsessing on the fact that she'd be having an evening with Ben. Alexander arrived first and he sat with Momma in the living room as Celeste and the boys continued making the preparations. Momma had wanted to invite Sheida too, but she hadn't been available.

Celeste had nearly forgotten to be stressed about Ben's arrival when, as she and John J. were setting the table, the bell rang. Her stomach tightened immediately.

Fortunately, Georgie was there to open the door and welcome them in.

"Wow," Ben said from the foyer. "Something smells wonderful."

"We made lasagna," Georgie said proudly as he ushered them in.

John J. abandoned the table, of course, running over to greet Quinn and give her a hug, then they both did their little happy dance. Honestly, those two were beyond adorable. But all thoughts of cute kids were whisked from her mind as Ben stepped into the living room. Celeste's heart gave a little thud at the sight of him.

The last time she'd seen him, he'd been wearing his tux and he'd been devastatingly handsome. Today, it was jeans and a T-shirt, and somehow, he was just as gorgeous. He smiled when he saw her, a little hopefully perhaps, so she had to smile back. "Welcome," she called. "Can I get you something to drink?"

"Quinn likes orange soda," John J. announced, and indeed, Quinn grinned and did another little happy dance.

"A beer is fine for me, if you have one," Ben said and then he turned to greet Momma and Alexander—which was the perfect opportunity for an escape into the kitchen. After a quick check on the lasagna, which was bubbling away happily, she grabbed their drinks and headed back out, taking a moment to steel herself at the door.

She'd always thought that Ben was good-looking, but today something was different. They'd both agreed to a truce, which somehow had changed everything. She wasn't sure how or why it put her nerves on edge, but it did.

She set both the drinks down on coasters on the coffee table because Ben had taken a seat on the sofa. "Oh, thank you," he said with another smile. Gosh, he was even more stunning up close. It was clear he'd freshly showered and shaved, as his hair was a little damp and his cheeks glowed.

"Where are the kids?" she asked. They were nowhere to be seen, and by now, she knew that could mean trouble.

"They're trying to find Pepe," Momma said.

Alexander chuckled. "They got a glimpse of him, but he shot up the stairs."

"Smart cat," Ben murmured.

Momma nodded. "The hunt should keep them busy for a while." Her smile was sly. Then she frowned. She did that sometimes—flipping from a smile to a frown like someone flipped a light switch. "Don't tower over everyone. Sit down, Celeste."

There was only one place to sit—right next to Ben on the sofa. She sucked in a breath and took a seat anyway. "Dinner is coming along fine," she said, just to have something to say. "I'll put the bread in about fifteen minutes before we eat."

Everyone nodded, but no one spoke. To fill the space probably, Ben said, "It smells amazing."

"Celeste made lasagna," Momma said. "I love her lasagna."

"Really?" Ben's brows rose.

"She loves to cook," Momma said, before Celeste could respond.

"Well, the boys helped with the assembly," she had to say. "Lasagna is all about the layering. They seemed to enjoy it."

"I can't wait." Ben put his hand on his stomach. "I haven't had a home-cooked meal in…well, I can't remember."

It was probably rude to gape at him like that. "Really?" Nearly every meal she had was home-cooked. Granted, that was mostly because it was what Momma preferred.

"That's what happens when you live in a hotel, I guess," Alexander said.

"Right." Ben took a sip of his beer. "I miss it, though. My mom was a great cook."

The conversation was interrupted by a squeal somewhere upstairs, followed by the thundering of footsteps across the hall and then down the stairs. Something black-and-white and furry sped past Celeste's legs and entrenched itself safely under the couch before the kids came roaring around the lintel and into the living room.

John J. surveyed the room and put out a lip. "Where'd he go?" he muttered.

"I think he's hiding," Celeste had to say. The poor cat probably needed a moment alone and she wasn't going to be the one to reveal his refuge.

"But Quinn wanted to pet him!" Oh, so much melodrama in that wail.

"Perhaps we can coax him out a little later," Celeste said to Quinn, who looked very sad indeed. "He's shy, you know."

Ben chimed in to help. "Look, Quinn. Celeste brought you an orange soda."

Her eyes lit up at that and she took a delicate sip. And then she caught Celeste's gaze and nodded, her way of saying thank you.

"Come into the den, Quinn," John J. commanded. "We can play a video game until dinner's ready." Fortunately for Pepe, all three of them tromped away.

The conversation then turned to Coho Days, the annual

celebration of the end of summer, which was coming up. Celeste had been on the committee up until Momma got sick, so she was able to fill the others in on all the plans. It was pleasant, chatting about one of her favorite projects, just the four of them, despite sitting so close to Ben, being preternaturally aware of him as she was—his warmth, his presence, his scent. She'd never met a man who distracted her quite as much as he did. In the past, she'd been able to mask her fascination with that convenient irritation, but now that she was making an honest effort to be friendly, all that had been stripped away.

Her inclination was to revert to her familiar defenses, but when she was able to discipline herself not to do so, she found she enjoyed his company very much. He was clever, funny and well-informed. When the timer sounded from the kitchen, she was actually disappointed to have to excuse herself from the conversation.

Dinner was the same. It was a very casual, family-style affair, with great conversation—much of it about Alexander's most recent rockhounding adventures—delicious food and much laughter. It wasn't the same as having everyone there, but it was still very pleasant.

It was clear Ben was having a nice time as well. Celeste had known that Jax and Ben were besties, but she hadn't realized that he was close with Jax's dad too, but the conversation, and his respectful manner to the older man, made clear that the two men had spent a lot of time together. Of course, that made sense, didn't it, if he was dating Sheida? The thought put a pall on her mood.

After Ben cleared his plate, he leaned back, patted his belly and groaned. "I'm stuffed," he said.

"Not too stuffed, I hope," she said. "There's cake."

"Oh no." He made a face at Quinn, who giggled. "Where will I put it?"

Well, he found a place. He had two slices and a cup of decaf.

After they ate, they all retired to the living room. No one was in the mood for the evening to end. Momma opened a jigsaw puzzle onto the coffee table and they all sat around to work it.

At one point, Celeste noticed Quinn had moved away from the group and was down on the floor staring under Momma's easy chair. It didn't take a rocket scientist to work out what had caught her attention. Celeste went over and sat beside her, then peeked beneath the chair as well. Two glowing eyes looked back. "What did you find, Quinn?" she said softly. "Is that Pepe?"

In response, Quinn pouted.

"He's hiding, isn't he?"

A nod.

"Well," she said with a gust. "I know a secret about cats. Would you like to hear it?" Quinn's eyes went wide and she nodded. "They like to play hard to get. Most people don't realize this, but it's true. Let's both pretend we're not in the least interested in the cat, shall we? And here." She reached into Momma's knitting basket and pulled out two lengths of yarn. Not that she'd spent countless evenings teasing the cat, but she had. She knew what he liked. She handed one of the lengths to Quinn. "You and I are just here playing with our yarn, yes? No interest in cats at all." She dangled her yarn and made it dance, just where Pepe could see it, and Quinn quickly joined in, adding a second thread to the dance.

It wasn't long until a furry black paw popped out and

batted at the tempting array. The delight on Quinn's face was glorious. They played with the phantom paw for a bit and then Celeste drew her yarn a little farther away, and Quinn copied her action. They diddled it there until the paw emerged again and, soon after, a whiskered face. Before long, Pepe was fully engaged, running and leaping for Quinn's yarn at full tilt, causing laughter from them both. Celeste had stopped playing once Pepe emerged, so Quinn could have him all to herself. And oh, she loved it. But what little girl didn't love a kitty?

After a bit, Celeste went to get a couple cat treats so Quinn could coax Pepe into her lap, and before long, she was sitting on the floor with Pepe in her arms and petting him gently.

She looked up at Celeste and smiled. It was a smile of such joy, such unbridled delight—and it hit Celeste hard. A wave of emotion rushed through her, warming her. What a precious child. It broke her heart that she'd been through such hard times. So much trauma for such a young soul. All she wanted to do was take Quinn into her arms and hug her tight, to make everything right.

If only she could.

Ben swallowed hard as he watched Celeste interacting with Quinn. It was a beautiful scene, the two of them there on the floor together, petting the cat. Celeste had been so patient as, together, they'd coaxed the furball out from under the chair and finally into Quinn's arms. And Quinn—she was so happy. Had he ever seen her this happy? He couldn't remember.

He couldn't remember an evening he'd enjoyed this much either. He hadn't realized how much his work had crept into every corner of his life. That was what happened, he supposed, when you lived where you worked. What a treat it was to get out and spend time in a real home. Maybe it was time to move.

After his father's death he'd poured everything into his job—he'd had to, to save the company his father had frittered away—but he'd always made time for Quinn. But lately he'd been feeling as though he should be, could be, giving her more of him. Aside from that, she deserved a proper home, didn't she? Hotel life was fine for a single man—even one with a baby—but she wasn't a baby anymore. It just didn't feel right calling for room service for every meal, having her watched by sitters, not having a yard. All the things he'd loved as a kid were missing for her.

She deserved better.

"Aha!" John J. crowed triumphantly as he placed the final piece into the puzzle and everyone cheered.

"Great job." Alexander patted the boy on the shoulder.

Ben gusted a sigh and stood. "Well, this sure was fun. But we'd better be going." He didn't want to leave, not at all, but he didn't want to overstay his welcome either.

Pearl stood as well and smiled at him. "It was lovely having you. You'll come again, won't you?"

"I'd love that, I really would." He glanced over to where Quinn was back to teasing the cat with the yarn. "And so would Quinn."

"She is precious," Pearl said with a sigh. "Oh, how I would like a granddaughter. Just think. All the little dresses and frills. Boys are fine, mind you, but not nearly as much fun to shop for."

Celeste huffed a laugh. "Well, Momma," she said. "You

may not have long to wait now that Natalie and Amy are married."

Pearl sniffed. "Amy seems only capable of having boys. My odds would be better at getting a girl if you would get married too," Pearl said. Ben didn't miss Celeste's grimace. It seemed as though this wasn't the first time she'd heard that exhortation.

"Well," he said, to divert the tide of that conversation. "You're welcome to borrow Quinn anytime you like."

Pearl's eyes sparkled. "I shall. When can you come back again?"

"Next week?" John J. suggested hopefully.

Ben had to chuckle. "Anytime you'll have us, John J. And we'd love to have you over too. You can come and swim anytime you like."

John J.'s eyes went big. He turned to Celeste. "Ooh. Can we do that? Can we?" He whipped back to Ben. "I'm not afraid of the big slide anymore."

"I'm glad to hear it." He'd taken a spill on it the last time he'd been at the water park. "How about Saturday?" He glanced at Celeste, just to check her reaction. "Would that work?"

To his surprise, she smiled, and it was a real smile, tinged with gratitude. "That would be wonderful." Then she added, with a little laugh, "To be honest, I'm still learning how to keep them busy. I have no idea how Amy keeps up."

Pearl made a face. "I had four. I managed."

"Yes, Momma," Celeste said, "but you are a superwoman."

"That is true," Pearl said, and everyone laughed.

"Come along, Quinn," Ben said, holding out a hand. He

had the suspicion the only reason she responded was because when all the adults stood up, the cat sprinted from the room. "Again, we've had a great time. Thank you so much for inviting us."

"Oh, it's been our pleasure," Pearl said, giving him an unexpected hug.

He didn't expect a hug from Celeste either, which was prudent of him, because he didn't get one. But she did give him a small wave and say, "See you at the meeting on Tuesday," with a bright, sincere smile. That was plenty fine for him.

"Sure. And, if you like, I can stop by and pick you up at the Elder House a little early, and take you out to see the proposed site before the meeting." He'd been thinking it would be a good thing for her to check out the location.

Her eyes went wide. "I'd like that. Thank you."

All in all, it had been a lovely evening—mostly because he and Celeste hadn't been at odds. He'd been nervous about how the evening would go, but it had turned out much better than he'd expected.

With work and Momma and the boys, it was Tuesday before Celeste knew it and Ben picked her up from work right on time. The drive over to the Point didn't take long, which was a shame because Ben's car was comfortable. The seats were much more luxurious than her ten-year-old basic-model Honda. But then, of course his car would be luxurious. As they passed the hotel and rounded onto the vast expanse of the Point, she was surprised at how different it looked. The last time she'd been out this far, years ago, it had all been scrub. Now, down close to the water, what looked like a small village had sprung up, with shops and restaurants fronting the beach, followed by a neat grid of stylishly designed houses—large and small—all with similar beachy vibes. It wasn't all homes and shops, though. A swath of green ran through the development, spotted with trees and sand traps. Ah, yes. The infamous golf course she'd heard so much about. But what surprised her the most was that only a tiny area had, as yet, been developed. She could tell that there were plans for much greater development by the terraces and roads that had been carved out of the hill.

Ben pulled into one of the empty lots about midway up the vacant hill and stopped the car. "Well," he said. "Here it is."

"This?"

He grinned. "Yeah. Come on. I'll walk you through it."

She got out of the car and followed him as he headed… somewhere in the vast field. It seemed he knew exactly where he was going, so it only made sense. From here, she had a great view of the development down by the water, as well as the resort to the north, but the town proper was around the bend and out of sight. It struck her then, just how massive the Point project was. She'd seen the plans when she'd been on the planning commission, but it was very different to see it for real.

"Okay," he said, once he'd gotten to wherever he was going. "See that flag over there?" He pointed to the west.

"Mmm-hmm."

"And that one over there?" To the east.

She squinted her eyes. "Yeah."

"Well, those mark the lot size."

She gaped at him. "It's huge."

"Don't forget, we have to add parking too. But yeah,

it'll be a good size." Even though she'd reviewed the blue-prints, she hadn't really understood until now just how large the clinic would be. "And the lot goes back to those flags there." He pointed out two more on the other side, fronted by the main road from town.

"Wow."

He grinned. "We're standing right in the middle of the waiting room. The treatment rooms will be here." He waved to his left. "And the surgeries back there."

She struggled to visualize it all, and failed. But she did know one thing. "This is going to be awesome."

"I hope so. I know it seems large, but we want to plan for the future."

Judging by how enormous the overall development was—it would more than double the size of town when it was done—she appreciated his point. Still, it was a little overwhelming.

"And on this plot over here, we're planning a commu-nity center with a park, and on the next plot, we're putting in a fire station. The facilities in downtown are limited as it is, so we're going to need a place out here with all the equipment as well."

She nodded dumbly. She knew he was a member of the volunteer firefighting crew, so it made sense that he'd in-cluded this in the plans, but she was still a little stunned. The city council hadn't required him to do any of this. She knew. She'd read the minutes from every meeting like a hawk. "This seems very…generous of you."

He cocked his head to the side. "What do you mean?"

"It's a lot of land. I mean, these three lots, well, you could put in quite a few homes right here."

She was surprised that he chuckled, but he did. "Yeah,

I suppose," he said. "But putting in as many houses as possible isn't the goal. I want to build something that's... livable."

"But the views from here..." They were stunning.

He laughed again. "Yes. But remember, when all the houses are built, those views will be obstructed. So yeah. We did take that into consideration when we chose these plots. But they're also the closest to the road to town so it makes them most accessible." He gave her a minute to process everything and then said, "So, what do you think?"

"I think it's perfect." Sure, she didn't have a developer's eye and she struggled to imagine exactly what it would all be like when it was finished, but she didn't have to, did she? He was the visionary. He'd already done it.

"Once we get the final approval on the plans from the council, we'll come in and block everything out and you'll be able to get a better idea of how it will look. We can come back then. But this gives you a good sense of how everything will flow."

"Okay." She couldn't deny that his plans excited her. There was just so much space for everything they needed in an emergency clinic, and with him adding a fire station and community center as well, this would become a hub for social services—not just for the new residents, but for everyone in Coho Cove.

Somehow, suddenly, seeing all this, his plans coming to fruition, seeing the kind of community he had in mind, seeing it actually...becoming, made her rethink everything.

Yes, she hated the changes his company had made when she'd been in high school. They'd been predatory and ugly. People had been turned out of their homes and businesses had closed because the developers had taken over the town—the city council to be exact—and forced their ideas on the community.

But Ben had been in high school then, hadn't he? A kid. He hadn't had any part of his father's business, had he? And somehow she'd blamed him for all of it. Heat suffused her at the thought that she might have been wrong about him all this time.

To give herself a moment, she turned to review the whole of the Point again, scanning from the empty terraces on the hill waiting for structures, down the already paved roads to the understated elegance of the finished homes close to shore. On the southern side of the property she noticed a long wooden fence running along the crest of the hill, beyond which the natural flora had not been disturbed. "What is that?" she asked. She knew he owned the entire property. Wouldn't it make sense to develop there too? And yet he hadn't.

"Why don't we go look?" Together they headed for the car—it was pretty far to walk—and he drove toward the southern edge of the property. When they got close, he put on his blinker, even though there were no other cars on the deserted road—which made her smile—and headed to a naked cul-de-sac in the undeveloped section.

He parked and they walked over to the fence. Once she got closer she realized it had been designed to have a rustic look, but was hardly rustic at all. It was clearly a quality build, designed to last.

"You're not planning to develop this area?" she asked. You would think, with the stunning views down to the estuary, that the area he'd cordoned off would be prime real estate.

"No. This whole area has been designated as a bird sanctuary." He pointed her to a sign to the left that notified visitors that this was a restricted area and natural preserve.

"Doesn't that cut into your profit?" She wished immediately that she hadn't said it—they were both working hard to maintain a nonconfrontational conversation—but the words were out.

The look he sent her was only a little wounded. "You could think of it that way. Or you could consider that nature is one of the draws to a place like this. People aren't coming here just to party on the beach, but to feel closer to the sea, and the animals that live here."

"I suppose." Yes. He was right. "It is very peaceful." The estuary was beautiful and wild and she could see the appeal for bird watchers, painters and people who just liked to stare at creation.

"When we were doing the environmental assessment for the project, the naturalist we hired found a couple rare species nested down there. There's also a couple of eagles that nest nearby. We wanted to make sure whatever we did here on the Point didn't impact their habitat."

"That's nice." She shot him a glance. "Are you a bird person?"

He snorted a laugh. "I wouldn't say so, but I do think it's important for a developer to exercise balance. And to make quality of life a primary consideration. When I was planning this place out, I was thinking of Quinn, and what she would want her legacy to be. You know, would she be proud of what I did?"

"Were you proud of what your dad did?" She hadn't intended the question. It just slipped out.

He snorted again but, this time, with no humor. "All he

cared about was money. And look how that turned out." She frowned, because she had no idea what he meant. When he saw her expression, he shook his head and looked away. "He overextended himself, and the company. By the time he died, we were nearly bankrupt because he wasn't paying attention to anything but profit."

"Oh. I...didn't know."

"When I inherited the business, I inherited a mess. I had to do a complete restructure."

She had no idea what a *restructure* might entail, but judging from his dark expression when he said it, it hadn't been easy. "A lot of work?" she asked.

He huffed a breath. "A. Lot. Long hours. Rough negotiations. Sometimes I was away from Vi and Quinn for weeks putting together deals or cleaning up problems."

"Well, you're doing well now." There was really no doubt about that.

He leaned on the fence and blew out a sigh. "Yeah. But really..." He threw out his arms to encompass the view. "With a resource like this, with a really great team that is environmentally and socially conscious, and with a clear, solid plan moving forward—and a tight grip on waste— well, it seems logical that the company would prosper. Don't get me wrong, my dad had good instincts, but he made some flawed decisions, mostly driven by his desire to be some great and famous developer. When his own ego overpowered good business sense and logic, well, everything lost traction. I narrowed our focus. We still have some properties in Seattle and Portland and Olympia, but the majority of our development focus is here in Coho Cove." He gave a chuckle. "Granted, that's because this is where I want to live, but still...it makes logical business sense given the local economy and the demand for retirement housing and the market for holiday homes. And we're close enough to metro centers like Seattle and Portland to attract a variety of customers who are looking for both."

"So you chose to move the company headquarters here?"

He quirked a brow. "Wouldn't you? If you could live anywhere in the world, wouldn't it be here?"

It was a beautiful vista with the bluer than blue sea reaching to the distance, the puffy white clouds dotting the azure sky and the hint of a sea breeze ruffling her hair. In the distance she could see a couple of crab boats bobbing along and, over to the left, a gorgeous sailing yacht. She sighed. He was right.

Chapter Six

Ẅhen they arrived at the City Hall trailers, they were a little early for the meeting, so Celeste stopped at the reception desk to say hello to Darlene, the town's receptionist and her friend from the Coho Days Committee. Ben headed straight back to the council chambers, where the meeting would be held. After catching up with Darlene, Celeste stopped by the kitchen to grab a cup of coffee and was surprised to see Huck Garner, another of her friends, there, doctoring up his own cup.

Huck was one of the town's old guard. He'd been on the city council several decades ago—and had served on the planning commission with her as well. He was also the founder of the Old Town Coalition, a group of people who wanted to keep Coho Cove the way it had always been. Most of the members were older residents, but Celeste had joined the coalition when she'd come back to town and heard about the plans to tear down the old mill and build a hotel on the Point. She'd been horrified and determined to stop all the coming development.

She wasn't an active member anymore, mostly because after the hotel went in, it seemed pointless to sit around and complain about it. And frankly, with all of her other commitments, she hadn't had time. But she and Huck had been friends for years, and it was a nice surprise to see him.

"Hi, Huck," she said with a smile. "What are you doing here?"

"Celeste!" He set down his coffee and gave her a bear hug. His long, scraggly beard scraped her cheek. "I'm just here filing a public information request." She nodded. He did that a lot. Practically everything the town did was public record and a lot of it was even available online, if you knew where to look, but occasionally some information had to be requested. Because of open information laws, the city clerk would provide any information a citizen requested, if it was available. However, Celeste knew that Huck often used public information requests as a strategy. To, as he put it, *let them know someone is watching.* "Why are you here?" he asked. His bushy eyebrows rumpled. "Are you on the HHS Committee now?"

She nodded. "Sheida is giving me a shot at it."

"Hmm." He leaned closer. "Working on the clinic project, eh?"

It surprised her that he knew about the project, because it was still in the planning stages, but when she thought about it, it really shouldn't have. Huck knew everything that was going on in town. He made it a point to. But before she could answer, he added, "I'm so glad you're on the committee. You'll make sure things are done right."

"I certainly hope so." She grabbed a cup and filled it from the coffeepot. City Hall coffee wasn't always the best, but it was hot and caffeinated, and with the boys running her ragged, she needed a hit to get through the meeting without falling asleep.

Huck leaned against the counter, as though settling in

for a long chat. "I mean, I couldn't believe it when I saw that they're planning to put the clinic way over on the Point. It should be in town, don't you think?"

Celeste bit back her response, but only because she didn't want to have an argument with Huck—who was, in general, argumentative—and frankly she didn't agree, not now that she'd read through the project files and seen the site. The location out on the Point made sense for the future, because as the development continued, soon there would be just as many people living out there as there were in town, and the clinic location was midway, easily accessible and, frankly, less expensive because Ben was donating the land and a large chunk of the construction costs. Finding a convenient location in town would have been a lot more complicated, more expensive and a whole lot less convenient. Out on the Point, for example, the facility could be as large as they wanted it to be, and would be designed to fit their needs.

But Huck was staring at her, waiting for a response, so Celeste forced a smile and said, "You know that everyone on the committee has the community's best interests at heart."

His brows furrowed again as though he hadn't liked her response at all. "But *we* should have the clinic. Here. In town. Why is it going to all those rich people on the Point?"

They weren't all rich. There were swaths of affordable housing in the plans, but that was hardly the point Huck was making and Celeste knew it. He had always opposed the new development and fought against any changes to Coho Cove. For pity's sake, so had she. But Huck was a hard-core Old Town advocate. Old Town was all he really cared about. Celeste, on the other hand, despite her dislike of all the new development, cared about community services being available to everyone who needed them. That fed the true soul of the town.

Knowing Huck, recognizing his expression, Celeste knew where this conversation was going, and she didn't want to engage. So she was happy when Ben poked his head around the doorjamb and said, "Oh, hi, Huck. Hey, Celeste, we're about ready to start the meeting."

Thank heavens. She shot Huck a smile and patted him on the arm. "It was good to see you, Huck," she said, and then, before he could respond—and drag her back into a conversation she really didn't want to have—she took her coffee and left.

Ben didn't say anything to Celeste as they made their way to the council chambers, but he'd overheard part of her conversation with Huck and it made him a little leery. He knew the Old Town Coalition had been grumbling about the proposed location on the Point, and he'd hoped that the issue wouldn't crop up as a conflict with Celeste, but now he wasn't so sure. She and Huck had been close friends for years, aligned on many past issues. The fact that Huck was lobbying her to push for a location change bothered him. But what bothered him more was that a conflict like that might spoil their tentative friendship and that would be a terrible shame.

He really liked where they were now, the ease of their relationship and that tentative peace. It would stink if all that collapsed in on itself over something as important as the location of the clinic.

But he didn't say anything, because frankly, he didn't

want to bring it up. And also, she was entitled to her opinion, whether he agreed with her or not.

The council chambers were a lot larger than the cramped meeting room they'd used last time, so they weren't all crammed together around one table, which was nice. The other committee members were already there. Tony, Angus and Susan sat on one side of the long dais, while he, Celeste and Luke sat on the other. There was plenty of room for them to spread out the plans, and the room had a whiteboard as well, should they need it.

Also, this time, Tony had brought doughnuts. He flipped open the box as a way of calling the meeting to order. "Dig in, everyone."

"Are these from Amy's bakery?" Luke asked. "Yum." Everyone grabbed a doughnut except Susan, and Angus took two.

"Thank you, Tony," Celeste said before biting into a chocolate cruller. "You have no idea how much I needed this."

"Busy day?" Luke asked.

"Well, no more than usual," she said with a smile to everyone. "But Momma and I are watching the boys while Amy's on her honeymoon." Ben couldn't help noticing how Luke's expression fell at the mention of Amy's honeymoon; Luke always had a thing for Amy but had made the mistake of never actually telling her he was interested. Then, when Noah Crocker roared into town on his Harley and swept her off her feet, Luke had no one to blame but himself.

Tony chuckled. "You don't realize how much energy goes into raising kids until you have them." Tony and his wife had two of their own. They chatted a bit about this and that and then Tony blew out a breath. "So, shall we begin?" And, at everyone's nods, he said, "The big news is that the grant paperwork has come in." He held up a thick envelope that he then passed over to Ben. Ben passed it to Celeste, since she was the one who would be doing most of the grant writing. While Ben's company could support the construction costs, there were many other expenses in setting up a medical facility. They would be reaching out to a number of organizations, foundations and block grant agencies to find the funding for everything from furnishings to equipment to medical imaging machines… which weren't cheap. Celeste opened the file and began flipping through the sheaves as Tony continued. "You're going to want to set up a meeting with the grant coordinator in Olympia. His contact info is on the card in the file."

Celeste found it and smiled. "Oh. Maxwell Carver. I've worked with him before. He's great."

"Given the scope of the project, I think it would be a good idea to make the trip out there to meet with him as soon as possible," Tony said.

Ben nodded. "Celeste and I can drive out there this week."

Her eyes widened. "It's a long way," she said. "I'm sure I can handle it myself."

He nodded. "I know you can, but I'd like to go as well, just so I'm up-to-date on all the requirements." Ben shot her a glance. "If that's okay."

She nodded. "Sure. I'll give him a call and see when he's available."

"Excellent."

After setting the goals for the grant applications and discussing several other issues quickly, they came to the end of the agenda in record time. That was one of the things Ben really liked about Tony's leadership style. His meetings were congenial and quick, and he was a master at keeping everyone on topic.

Trouble was, at the end of the agenda, at the end of nearly every city government meeting agenda, there was this tiny little item called *New Business*, which was, undoubtedly, an opening for a time suck. And indeed, when Tony said, "Okay, guys. Any new business?" Angus's hand shot up.

"It's not new business," he said, "but I'd like to discuss something that wasn't on today's agenda."

Oh. Great. Ben forced himself to relax. He'd been in enough meetings with Angus to know he probably wasn't going anywhere soon. Ben thought about grabbing another doughnut to fortify himself, but when he looked, the box was empty. Darn.

"Okay, Angus," Tony said. "What is it?"

Angus took a deep breath and shot Ben a sharp glower before gusting, "I think we should address the clinic location again."

Tony glanced at Ben—a look that said, *Here we go*—and then nodded to Angus. "Okay. What are you thinking?"

Angus snorted. "Well, it should be obvious. The current site is way out on the Point. The clinic should be in town." He went on to explain, at length, why this was so. By the end of his, well, tirade, his voice was getting pretty loud.

Tony was a patient man. He listened to everything Angus had to say, and then responded with a gentle calmness Ben found almost saintly. "Well, we talked about a lot of those issues in our earlier meetings, Angus," he reminded him. "And the committee agreed that the location on the Point was superior for a number of reasons. I believe we have those meeting minutes available if you'd like to review them."

Angus nearly growled, "I don't need to review them. I want to open the item up for discussion. The committee has changed." He waved toward Celeste. "We should have another vote."

Ben nearly rolled his eyes. That wasn't how project meetings worked. If you had a revote anytime committee members changed, nothing would ever get done. Besides, if Ben recalled correctly, the vote on the location had been everyone else to one. Even if Celeste voted with Angus, the majority would still hold.

But again, Tony was the mayor for a reason. He was good at this kind of stuff. He folded his hands together before him and said, "Okay, Angus. Let's discuss it."

Angus swung his attention to Celeste. "I want to know what you think, Celeste."

Ben steeled himself for her response, dreading it, because he knew what she was going to say. She and Huck and Angus had been aligned on many issues in the past. It was pretty clear that Angus thought he had gained an ally in her as well.

But again, she was entitled to her opinion.

"Well," she said, toying with her pen. "Ben and I went to visit the site earlier, so I've had a chance to see it, and I have to say, I like the location. There's plenty of space and it is close to town. It'll be much closer when the new road goes in along the bluff."

It was all he could do not to stare at her, but the fact that she'd seen what he'd been trying to show her, and she agreed with him, made his heart do a little dance.

Angus, on the other hand, was not pleased. "Aw," he muttered. "You don't know what you're talking about." He glared at her. *Glared.* Ben wanted to step in and shield her from the animosity in his expression, but she was more than capable of defending herself against grumpy old men.

"I beg your pardon," she said in a crisp tone. "You know me, Angus. I've studied all the project notes, I've toured the site and analyzed the options. But if I've missed something, please enlighten me. What other sites have you proposed?"

Angus didn't have a response for that, because there were no other good sites—certainly not with the same accessibility, parking and functionality. Aside from that, an existing site would need to be purchased by the city and refurbished to a new use. In many cases, given how old some of the existing structures were, and how many permits would have to be pulled, that would take longer and cost more than a new construction. Still, Angus burbled and muttered a bit before he realized he wouldn't be making any headway with her and let the issue go. But not before saying in a belligerent tone, "I want this conversation reflected in the minutes."

Oh, good glory. It took an effort for Celeste not to roll her eyes. She should have known something like this might happen. Having Huck and Angus at City Hall at the same time should alone have warned her that the Old Town Coalition was upset about something, never mind the fact that it coincided with a committee meeting for the clinic. But it didn't matter. She was used to Angus huffing and puffing at someone, it had just never been *her* before. As it was, she was more amused than shaken.

After Tony ended the meeting and Angus noisily gathered his things and stormed out, Ben turned to her. "Are you okay?" he asked softly.

She appreciated him asking, maybe more than she would admit. "Yes, thank you." She shot him a smile to reassure him, because his expression was very concerned. "I should have expected Angus to bring the site up, because Huck mentioned it to me in the kitchen too."

Ben nodded. "Well, the point of having a committee is so everyone has their say, I suppose."

Yes. Yes it was. She was surprised he took that magnanimous stance, but she wasn't sure why. "And it will be recorded in the minutes," she said with a little laugh. It felt good that Ben grinned back. That he got the joke. Because, honestly, in projects like this, *everything* was recorded in the minutes. That was the purpose of having minutes. No one could remember everything that happened.

As they were cleaning up all the papers—and doughnut crumbs—Susan came over to Ben and leaned against the table. "It's almost five. Are you interested in grabbing dinner?" she asked. "It's been a while. I'd love to catch up."

Celeste couldn't help noting the hopeful expression in her eyes, or how it dimmed when Ben said, "Oh, I'd love to, but I have another meeting this evening, and I need to get Celeste back to the Elder House. We came straight from our tour of the site."

"A meeting this evening?" Susan shook her head. "Don't you ever get any time off?"

Ben chuckled. "I get plenty, I promise. But this week I have two projects coming to a head. Maybe some other time?"

"Of course," she said, but her smile was tight. With a wave to everyone, she left.

"You about ready?" Ben asked.

Celeste collected the heavy pile of grant applications and her empty coffee cup, and nodded. They waved good-bye to Luke and Tony, who were chatting about an up-coming golf tournament they were both in, and headed out to Ben's car. "Thanks for taking me back," she said. "I didn't realize how busy you'd be after the meeting or I would have driven myself."

He glanced at her and grinned. "No problem. Quinn's at the community center's day care anyway."

"Is she? I thought you have a nanny."

"I do, but recently Quinn has been having therapy sessions with Maisey on Tuesdays."

Celeste's eyes widened. "My Maisey?"

He chuckled. "*Our* Maisey…I guess. She's amazing."

"She really is." How nice was it that he opened the passenger door for her? "How have things been going with Quinn?" she asked once he had taken his seat and started the engine.

He blew out a breath. "Up and down. Since the accident, I've taken her to a bunch of specialists—psychologists, neurologists, linguists—every kind I can think of. The consensus is that the reason she doesn't speak is because of the trauma of the accident. She's been seeing a child psychologist regularly, but frankly, we're not making much progress there. We did, however, have a breakthrough with Maisey the other day."

"Really?" Celeste's heart thumped. She turned a bit in her seat, so she could face him. Quinn was such a sweet child. She really adored her and hated that she was struggling. "That's wonderful."

"Yeah." Ben's grin was brilliant. "Maisey realized that Quinn is pretty good at sign language, so we've both been learning that."

"That's wonderful." She herself had learned some ASL to communicate better with her patients who were deaf. She even taught a class at the Elder House every now and again for hard-of-hearing residents and their families.

"At least it helps with communication," he said. "Sometimes I feel so…"

"Powerless?"

"Yes. She's my daughter. I love her so much. I…" He paused. Swallowed, hard. "I just want to be able to talk to her."

How heartbreaking. "That must be difficult for you."

"Yeah."

"And for her."

"It kills me to see her struggle. I'd give anything to make it all better. A dad should be able to do that for his daughter, shouldn't he?"

She hated how rough his voice was, how hard it was for him to get the words out. She'd never seen him—big bad Ben Sherrod—vulnerable like this. It was a side of him he kept locked up tight.

But then, she did that too, didn't she? She put so much of her energy into her *persona*, what she wanted people to think of her, how she wanted them to see her. Most people, even those she was closest to, didn't really *know* her.

He probably felt the same way. He'd told her before that he was lonely, that he struggled being a single parent.

Her heart went out to him. "Well, I think you're a wonderful dad."

Thank goodness they were at a stoplight, because he turned to stare at her. So long that the car behind them honked when the light changed. "You do?"

Why did he seem surprised? "I do. And honestly, Ben, despite everything, she is very well-adjusted. She's obviously healthy and happy and she loves you so much."

He pulled into the lot at the Elder House before he responded. He met her gaze and swallowed, and then said, "Thank you, Celeste. That means a lot. Really. It does."

Something, some heat, rose within her and she looked away, because she knew she was blushing, though she didn't know why. "Well, it's true. And listen, I'd be happy to help you both with your ASL if you like."

His expression brightened in a way that made her sorry she didn't offer sooner. "Would you?"

The hope, the excitement, in his tone made her chest hurt. She didn't know why it made her feel suddenly discomfited. It was such a simple offer, but it had meant so much to him. She shot him a quick smile and fired off a breezy "Sure" as she opened the door and hopped out, but only to escape that suddenly-too-intimate moment.

They headed inside together. Neither talked, but it was a comfortable silence. She snuck a glance at him and was warmed even further at the smile on his face. When he caught her looking at him, it widened even more.

"Well, look who's here!"

Celeste was yanked out of a moment she hadn't been aware was cocooning them as Sheida called to them from down the hall. Her stomach dropped. She wasn't sure why she was disappointed when her boss captured Ben's attention, but she was.

And yeah, his grin went even wider. "Sheida."

Had she really forgotten, even for a minute, that Ben and Sheida were dating?

"How was the tour?" This question was directed at Celeste, so she quickly nodded and said, "Great. And we got the grant paperwork at the committee meeting." She waggled the folder.

"Excellent. Wow." Sheida eyed the package. "That's a lot."

Ben nodded. "It's going to be a lot of work."

Sheida's brows went together. She frowned at Celeste. "I'll need to find you somewhere to work."

"Well," Ben said. "We have office space available at the Sherrod for remote workers. It might make sense to have you work there." He shot her a glance. "If you don't mind."

"No, of course not." In fact, the idea of seeing him every day excited her. How…unexpected.

"Well, that sounds perfect," Sheida said.

"That is settled, then," Ben said. "Come over tomorrow, Celeste, and I'll have Char set you up."

"Great."

"Oh, and, Sheida, Celeste and I need to connect with the grant manager in Olympia. Tony thinks, with a project like this, it should probably be a face-to-face and I agree."

Sheida nodded. "Yes. We don't want any hiccups. You know how grants are." She rolled her eyes, but it was a well-founded gesture. Grants had gone south more than once for something as simple as a misplaced comma or a late submittal.

"I'll contact Maxwell Carver and see when we can

get a meeting." Celeste turned to Ben. "Do you have any preferences on a day?" It'd probably be a full day and he was busy.

But he shook his head and said, "I'll make it work," with such conviction, she had to believe him.

"Well, I don't know about you two," Sheida said, "but I'm getting really excited about this project."

Ben nodded. "Me too."

Celeste gave a little laugh. "Me three."

The next morning, Ben gave Char an update on the plans, and asked her to get Celeste set up in one of the empty offices down the hall. He was excited about the prospect of seeing Celeste every day, but that wasn't the only reason he'd suggested she have her base at the hotel. All of his division heads had offices here and were in and out on a regular basis. It made more sense having her work from here, rather than asking her to chase them down if she had a question or needed specific information.

He had a meeting that morning, but when he got back to the office and saw her through the glass windows, working away, his heart thudded. Damn, it was nice to see her there. Since the door was open, he gave her a courtesy knock before stepping in. She glanced up from the computer screen and smiled. "Good morning." Her voice was chipper.

"Morning. I see you're all set up."

"Yes, thanks. Char is amazing."

He chuckled. "I know."

"I thought she was the wedding planner."

He chuckled. "She used to do that, before she came to work for me, so she offered to help with the wedding. But she did such a good job, she just might find herself promoted to events manager." He was joking, but not really. She had done a great job. But then, that was what she did. "Not sure how I got so lucky, but she basically keeps this place running. So, how are things going?"

"Good. I'm just going through the paperwork and getting started."

"Great. Well, I'll let you get back to it, but if you need anything, just let us know."

"I will. Oh, by the way, I have a call in to Maxwell about setting up a meeting with him."

"Perfect. Let me know when you hear back and I'll put the meeting on my calendar."

Her brow furrowed. "You don't need to go with me," she said. "You're awfully busy."

He had to grin. Yeah. He was busy. He was always busy. And yes, she could handle the meeting by herself. But schedules could always be rearranged and he was oddly eager to spend more time with her now that they were getting along. Besides, he wanted to learn more about the grant process for future projects. "Don't tell anyone," he said, "but I like to escape every once in a while." To which she laughed.

He would have stayed and chatted longer, but he didn't want to dominate her time. Aside from that, they both had a lot of work to do. So he waved goodbye and headed to his office with a warmth in his chest. It was surprising how good it felt, knowing that she was in the office just down the hall.

Sadly, he only saw her one more time that day, but she came with good news. It was cute the way she peeked in through his opened door. "Ben?" Such a tentative tone.

He gave her a big smile, just to encourage her, just so she'd know she was always welcome to interrupt. "Hey, Celeste. What's up?"

"I just heard back from Max." Ben's mood dipped. She'd called him Max. "He's doing grant process reviews on Friday and says he can fit us in at one p.m. Will that work for you?"

"Perfect." It was an hour-and-a-half drive to Olympia—depending on traffic—so it would take up most of the afternoon, but he'd anticipated as much.

Also perfect, because he'd be spending all that time with her. The thought surprised him because a week ago, it would have been unthinkable.

On Friday, Ben picked Celeste up at the Elder House for the trip to Olympia. As they headed up the cliff road heading out of town, Celeste blew out a breath.

"What is it?" he asked.

She gave a chuckle. "I'm just trying to remember the last time I left town, and I can't."

"Really?"

"I think it was to visit Natalie when she lived in California." She sent him a pained look. "I don't get out much."

"Well, you've had a lot on your plate since your mom's stroke." He knew all about the weight it had been on her, but only because Sheida had told him.

"I suppose, but to be honest, I love the Cove. I don't see any reason to leave."

Funny. Vi had hated living in Coho Cove. She'd called it the boonies. Couldn't wait to get back to the city. "I feel the same. I mean, it wasn't always like that. When our family first moved here when I was a kid, the Cove was a lot smaller, and the community was supertight. It was hard to make friends at first."

Celeste nodded. "It was still that way when we moved here. Small towns can be closed up like that. I know Natalie had a really hard time fitting in."

"But you didn't." Man, she'd just kind of clicked into place.

She made a face. "I'm a joiner. That's always been the way I've dealt with feeling like an outsider—and as a military brat, moving every year or so, you feel like an outsider a lot. So when we moved here, I joined as many clubs as I could to meet people and get involved in things." He remembered that about her. She'd been on nearly every page of the yearbook, in one club or another. "Of course, we were all reeling from Dad's death. Oh, and learning how to live with our grandparents." She blew out a breath. "That was an adventure."

"I'll bet."

"I can't imagine what it was like for Momma. Losing her husband and her way of life in one fell swoop."

"Your mother is a really strong woman, though. She weathered it well."

"Yes. She did. But to be honest, Momma was the one who raised us. Dad was on temporary duty a lot, or at this school or that. Momma was alone a lot. She had to be strong. All military wives do."

Ben nodded. "I don't remember my dad being around much when I was a kid either. He was always working. He had this company and all those dreams. It seemed like he was always away somewhere. He traveled a lot."

"Wow. I didn't know that."

"I didn't realize it at the time, but when Dad moved us here, their marriage was already on the rocks."

"I'm so sorry."

He shrugged. "It was rough, but things were actually better after the divorce. Mom was happier, at least."

"But you still went to work for your dad after college?"

He nodded. "Honestly, I never felt like I had a choice. Even though he was never happy with anything I did, he still instilled me with all these expectations about the dynasty I would be inheriting."

"Did he really call it a dynasty?"

"He did." Ben huffed a bleak laugh. "The joke was, when he passed, I discovered it wasn't much of a dynasty at all. My dad had severely overextended his investments and mismanaged some large projects. We were at risk of losing everything. So when I took over, I had to make some pretty big decisions. Fortunately, I was able to sell off a lot of the real estate at a profit, and pay off the creditors. I downsized the corporate structure—I'd always thought it was overblown. Dad had hired a bunch of his friends who did basically nothing at exorbitant wages, and a bunch more who were totally incompetent."

"Wow."

"Yeah. It was bad. But to be honest, the financial crisis was actually a blessing, because it allowed me to start from scratch basically, building the company up the way I wanted. The way I saw it. But I gotta tell you, there were some lean years there."

"Well, I had no idea. I don't think anyone noticed."

He grinned. "Good. But now things are going well. We downsized and settled here and have a more focused perspective."

"And why did you pick Coho Cove to be your home base?"

"I always liked it here. I mean, from third grade to high school graduation, this was my home. Mom even stayed here, until she got sick. Aside from that, the company owned the land on the Point free and clear and all our projections pointed to the growing market for seaside living here in the Northwest. I wouldn't have been able to create that community somewhere closer to Seattle or Portland because of the elevated property values. But I think, mostly, it's because this is where I've always felt…"

"At home?"

He glanced at her. "Yes. Exactly." She knew. She understood.

"I felt the same way when we moved here. Oh, it had been a terrible time. Dad was gone and we'd all been uprooted from our way of life, and plopped down here. I know Momma chose this place because it's where her parents lived—and at a time like that, you need your family—but I can't believe how lucky we were to end up here."

"It's a beautiful place."

"It's heaven. From the day I stepped out of the car I knew this was where I wanted to be." She looked away then, then looked back. "That's why…"

When her pause grew, he smiled to encourage her. "Why, what?"

"Well." She gushed a breath. "That's why I was so upset about the development in town your dad was doing. I know I've never been shy about that."

He nearly chuckled. No. She had not. "I understand."

"No. You don't. I mean… Not really. I… It felt like

such a perfect place, and then all these bulldozers rolled in and started knocking down buildings…"

"Yeah." He nodded. "I know. I didn't like that either. Or the way my dad and his friends on the city council got around the building codes to do what they wanted."

She gaped at him. "You didn't like that?"

"Hated it. My dad and I fought about it all the time."

"I had no idea. Oh my goodness." Her cheeks went red. "I blamed you. Why did I blame you?"

He lifted a shoulder. "Everyone in town did. I understood. It was my dad's business after all. But I'll be honest, he undertook some business practices that I didn't agree with and, frankly, will not allow in my company today."

She tipped her head to the side and stared at him and said, "I am so sorry I was so mean."

"You weren't mean." She never had been. Not really. Not like some of the others. Granted, he'd hated the fact that he knew she didn't like him, but she was never mean.

"Well, I should have been more open-minded. I could have been."

He didn't know what to say, so he simply said, "Thank you."

She was silent for a moment, watching the fields and gas stations flick by on the long straight highway into Olympia. "Did your wife love it here as much as you do?" she asked, and his heart clenched.

"Ah, Vi. She made do, I suppose. It was rough on her to begin with, learning that the business was in trouble, that we had to really cut back spending. When we first got married, we were living the high life. In fact, most of my life I never had to worry about what things might cost, because there was always money. Or there seemed to be. After Dad died, I got a real wake-up call. Everything changed." Celeste nodded. She knew. She'd been through something very similar. "And after we moved here, I was spending a lot of time working, trying to save the company so we could have a decent life. Vi had Quinn, who was just a little thing then, but other than being a mother, there wasn't a lot for her to do here, and she missed her family and friends in Seattle." He shrugged. "She probably would have loved it if it was a vacation, but she really didn't like living here."

"That must have been hard for her."

"Yeah. I feel bad about it, but I don't know what else I could have done. If the company had gone under, we would have had nothing."

"Thank goodness that didn't happen. You've done so much good in town. We really are lucky to have you here."

Her eyes shone when she said it, and he could feel her sincerity coming through. His chest swelled because it was about the nicest thing anyone had ever said to him in his life.

And the fact that it came from her?

Priceless.

Chapter Seven

Celeste was surprised when they hit the outskirts of Olympia, because the ride had flown by. There might have been a hint of regret too, that it was over so soon. She hadn't expected to enjoy it that much. She'd never enjoyed the long haul to Olympia when she'd had meetings there in the past. But Ben's car was beautiful—so comfortable with wide cushy seats. And, goodness, that conversation.

She hadn't been open to getting to know him before. And now that she was, she realized how stubborn and closed-minded she'd been toward him in the past. It made her feel a little ashamed, that she'd made such reaching assumptions about him, and that she'd been so wrong. She was also surprised how easy it was to shift her perspective, considering how she'd felt about him in the past. But knowing he hadn't been like his father, that he hadn't even liked what his father had done, changed things. Amy was right. He had really helped make things better.

The capital hove into view and her heart fluttered a bit because it was so pretty. They passed it on by and headed down Capitol Way, toward the much more boring administration buildings nearby. Olympia was crowded with administration buildings, which housed employees for a huge array of services.

They'd made such great time, Ben pulled into the parking lot about twenty minutes before their meeting. Celeste shot him a smile. "We're a little early, but there's a coffee shop with sandwiches on the first floor if you want to get something to eat."

It was cute the way his face lit up. "I could eat."

"Excellent."

The building was unusually busy—there was even a line for drinks and food—but Ben and Celeste were able to find a table in the corner, which she liked because there was a window. It made it easier for her to forget how many people were milling about.

"Are you okay?" he asked when she didn't say anything for a minute.

She forced a smile. "I don't do well in crowds."

He nodded. "I don't like them much either. Maybe that's why I live in Coho Cove." Which made her laugh, and somehow, she relaxed.

They were both hungry, so they ate their lunch as she answered his questions about the grant procedure. Then, in a comfortable silence, they enjoyed sipping their coffees and staring out at the birds in the courtyard.

Max's office was on the third floor, so when the time for their appointment approached, they collected their trash and tossed it, then headed for the elevators. There were two elevators, but one was out of order. Celeste had been aware of how crowded the lobby was from the moment they walked in, but when they stepped onto the elevator, and about seven other people swarmed in after them, her heart began to thud. She glanced up at Ben.

"Are you okay?" he asked.

"Mmm-hmm." There might have been a thread of panic

in her voice. She was only a little claustrophobic, but when she was in a tight space with a lot of people, it tended to flare up. *Three floors. It was only three floors.* But then, just as the doors were starting to close, three more people ran up. As they filed in, everyone adjusted to make room and Celeste found herself pancaked between Ben, who was at the back of the car, and the large man in front of her. *Oh dear.* Her pulse kicked into gear, pounding painfully in her chest.

Three floors.

She drew in a—somewhat stale—gulp of air and tried to relax, attempting to calm herself as the doors slid closed. When the elevator started to move, it did so with a jerk, causing her to fall back against Ben. His hand came up to her waist to steady her.

It was warm.

He was warm.

She decided to focus on that, on him, and it calmed her. She knew she was safe. She was in an elevator, for pity's sake. She knew her reaction wasn't logical. But somehow, he soothed her. It helped even more to lean back into him.

She couldn't help but notice his reaction—stiffening ever so slightly—but after a second, he relaxed. And then said, into her ear, "It's okay." A hint of a whisper, and that was all it took to soothe her.

Well, it didn't soothe her, per se. Yes, she did stop obsessing about the other people in the elevator and how jammed in they were, and how they incessantly breathed in and out, sucking up all the oxygen…but with Ben's whisper, the warmth of his breath skating over her neck, something else, something deep within her, awoke.

Something like hunger.

She barely noticed that the elevator jerked again as it

stopped on the second floor—except that some of the in-habitants of their car gave a little squeal when it happened—and she hardly cared when two more people squeezed on, because she was then pressed, even more firmly, into Ben.

And speaking of firmness… When the elevator jerked again, she felt…*something* there against her buttocks. At first, she thought it must be her imagination, but when she realized it wasn't—when she realized that his body was reacting to her presence—a tumult of heat washed through her. It was a rush of emotion she hadn't felt in a long, long while.

The realization that Ben was…*aroused* by her presence knocked her for a loop.

Or had it just been a natural reaction to the proximity of their bodies in a crowded elevator, something he had no control over and, in fact, was embarrassed by? She didn't like that thought very much. What a shame she couldn't ask. Well, wouldn't. How embarrassing would it be to bring it up anyway? How mortifying if he denied it?

He was, after all, dating Sheida, wasn't he?

Oh dear. That reminder just made it even more awkward all the way around.

So, as the jerky little elevator finally opened onto the third floor, and they wormed their way out, she didn't mention it at all. She did flash a glance at him, though, and noticed that his ears were a little pink. Furthermore, she noticed that he didn't look at her at all when he said, "Okay, which office are we looking for?"

"Three-fifteen." Was it wrong that she had to bite back a smile when he finally peeped at her, looked away quickly and then blushed? Was it wrong that somewhere, deep in her soul, she was a little delighted about the whole thing?

* * *

Ben's mind was in a whirl as they headed for Maxwell's office. *Had she noticed?* God, he hoped not. It was his own fault. He should have been focusing on the grant and the questions he had, rather than thinking about how wonderful she smelled, or how nice it felt to have her lean against him.

He hadn't realized she got that nervous in crowds—they were so rare at the Cove—but he'd recognized the signs in her demeanor, in the puffs of her breath and her slight groan as more people filled up the space in the small car. Hell, he'd even been a little claustrophobic...until he'd been distracted. By her.

It didn't help that he'd thought about her a lot lately, or had been enjoying her company as much as he had. It didn't help that his thoughts had begun to wander about her.

Surely she hadn't noticed. She would have said something if she'd noticed, wouldn't she?

It took some effort, but he set those tantalizing thoughts about Celeste—and her body and how warm and comfortable she'd been—aside and tried to focus on the business at hand as they stepped into suite 315.

A tall, slender, good-looking man was talking with the receptionist when they walked through the door, and when he saw them, his eyes lit up.

"Celeste!" He came over and wrapped her in a hug. Like, a really long hug. Ben didn't know why something growled deep in his soul. The guy—finally—pulled back and stared down at her like a hungry wolf. Okay, maybe not that bad, but it felt like it at the moment. "How have you been?" he gushed.

She smiled. Her eyes sparkled a little. "Good. And you?"

He shrugged. "Same old, same old."

Ben nearly jumped when Celeste took his arm to draw him forward. Electricity at her touch sizzled through him. Even through his suit jacket sleeve, he felt it. "Max," she said in a chirpy voice, "this is Ben Sherrod, from the Sherrod Group. We're working on the grant together. Ben, this is Maxwell Carver."

"The Sherrod Group?" Maxwell's expression made it clear he'd heard of them, but then he would have done. Ben's company had done a few block grant projects in the past. Maxwell thrust out his hand. "Great to meet you," he said.

"Thank you," Ben said. "We're all pretty excited about this opportunity, so thanks for your time."

"No problem. Come on in. I have the presentation set up in the conference room."

But once they were seated, Maxwell didn't start the presentation right away. He and Celeste chatted about mutual friends for a moment. Ben couldn't help noticing how he looked at her. Maxwell Carver was a very handsome man, Ben noticed with a hint of a bitter taste in his mouth. And it was clear he and Celeste were very old friends.

Celeste was the one to steer the conversation back to the grant application. With a hint of reluctance, Maxwell turned on the projector. The presentation was a standard slide show, with each screen showing the different requirements for the grant application. Not the grant itself…the *application*. It went on for a while.

Ben had never worked at this level on grant funding, and he was blown away by how complicated it was. This was compounded when Maxwell completed the presentation, answered all their questions and then sat back with a sigh. "Just so you know," he said, "we just got word that the funding on this grant has been cut for the next quarter. So, for your best chance at getting the funding for the medical equipment, I recommend you submit your application on this round."

Celeste paled a little, which made Ben realize this might be a problem. "When is the deadline for this round?" she asked.

"September first."

Celeste gaped at Maxwell. "So soon?"

Ben glanced at her. "Is that enough time?" They'd only just gotten the paperwork, for pity's sake.

She swallowed. "We can try. It'll be a push."

"We can do it." He shot her a smile in an attempt to wipe that bleak expression from her face. By God, he'd make sure of it.

They hit heavy traffic all the way back, but Celeste hardly noticed. Her mind was in a whirl. It was like dueling banjos in there, swinging wildly from the memory of Ben's body against hers in the elevator to the fact that their deadline had been accelerated. Could she gather all the information, research all the medical equipment they needed, compile the proposal…and then write the grant in that time?

But yeah. Ben had been warm and hard and…what was that scent he wore?

"Are you okay?" he asked, his voice cutting through the silence of the car like a warm knife.

"Huh? Oh. Yes. Thanks." She huffed a nervous laugh. "I'm, ah, just thinking about everything." Well, that was true.

"The grant?" Was he asking her to clarify? Did he want

her to bring up the thing in the elevator? She shot him a glance, trying to decipher his expression, but he didn't give away anything. He never did. She decided to latch on to the topic he had provided. She was a coward like that.

"That's a short clock, Ben."

"We can get help if we need it. Which part is most challenging for you?"

She thought about it for a bit. "I think the medical equipment estimates will take the most research. I know a lot about general equipment costs, and supplies, but the X-ray and the MRI… I don't even know specs on those."

"Don't worry about it." Why did his eyes have to crinkle when he smiled? "I'll have Char find a contractor for that."

She blinked. "They have contractors for research work?"

His grin widened. "They have contractors for everything."

"Well, that would help." Heck, anything would help.

As they hit the curve in the bluff with the overlook of town and she caught a glimpse of his hotel glittering in the waning light of the early evening sun, a sudden thought hit her. Her stomach dropped.

"Oh, Ben."

He frowned at her. "What is it?"

"I just realized…we're going to have to cancel tomorrow." They had planned to take the kids to the pool, but there was no way she could do that now. "I need to get started right away. The boys will be so disappointed." So, in fact, was she.

"Why?"

She gaped at him. *Why?* She tapped her wrist. "Ticking clock? I'm going to have to work straight through. I can't afford to take a day off."

"I mean, why do we have to cancel the day for the kids? We can work in one of the cabanas by the pool."

Seriously? She huffed a laugh. "I don't think it's considered working if you're in a cabana by the pool."

He laughed. "I do it all the time. But if you're not comfortable—"

"Did I say I wasn't willing to give it a try?"

Warmth swelled in her as he laughed again. "We'll give it a try. If it ends up being too distracting, I can stay with the kids and you can work in the offices."

Well, that didn't sound like very much fun at all, did it?

When they pulled up to her car in the Elder House parking lot, he said, ever so smoothly, "I really enjoyed this." There was warmth in his eyes.

"Me too," she said. "It was a very nice day."

"But a long one."

"Still nice." She smiled at him.

When he smiled back, it warmed her. She thought about it all the way home. But all thoughts of Ben and his smile were wiped from her mind when she walked through the door, and heard Momma scream.

She was nearly into the living room before she realized it was a scream of laughter, not terror. Celeste skidded to a halt and stared.

Momma and Alexander were sitting on the sofa, each with a half-empty glass of wine, and between them, a cribbage board. "Oh, really," Momma huffed as she tossed down her cards. "I can't believe you did that." She looked up and saw Celeste. "Oh, hello, dear."

"Hey, Momma."

"Can you believe it? I just taught Alexander how to play and he won the game."

"That's not very sporting of you, Alexander," Celeste said with a grin.

Alexander chuckled. "She shouldn't have told me that I can steal her points."

Momma rolled her eyes. "Silly me. Well, Celeste, how was your meeting?"

"It was great, Momma. I'm sorry I'm so late." She was still reeling a little bit at coming home to find Momma and Alexander playing cribbage, like they were on a date or something. "Um, how are the boys?"

"They're fine. I put on a Disney movie in the den. We had a really nice dinner. Alexander brought ribs."

"The boys love ribs."

"They made a fine mess," Momma said with a tsk. "We had to put them out in the yard and turn the hose on them."

What? Really? Celeste blinked, then glanced at Alexander for confirmation.

He nodded and laughed again. "They had a blast."

"There's some leftovers in the kitchen if you're hungry." Momma waved in that direction, but then turned her attention back to Alexander.

Celeste chuckled to herself and headed to the kitchen, where she ate in the company of a very friendly cat, so Momma could enjoy a little more private time with Alexander, just because it looked like it pleased her so much.

It had been a good day, she'd said. She'd enjoyed it, she'd said. Ben couldn't help smiling to himself when he thought about it. It *had* been a good day. He'd liked spending it with her.

Better yet, he'd be seeing her tomorrow too.

But as good as today had been, the best part was still

to come. It was the part of his day he looked forward to the most. As he walked through the door to his apartment and called, "I'm home," Quinn came running out of her playroom and threw herself into his arms. He spun her around until she laughed and then he hugged her again. "Hey, baby. Did you have a good day?"

She nodded, then wiggled to get down. "Come," she signed, and in case he hadn't understood, she took his hand and dragged him into the playroom, where she showed him a Lego princess castle.

He waved to Ellie before he went down on his knees to check out her creation. "Wow," he said. "Did you make this?"

Pride shone on her pretty face as she nodded.

"Great job, Quinn. This is beautiful."

She nodded again and then ran to her worktable and grabbed a painting she'd done. Stick figures, a man—wearing a stick figure tie, he assumed—and a little girl with long yellow hair.

"Is this us?" he asked, though he knew.

She nodded and pointed to the picture, to a scribbled wad of black next to the little girl.

"What's that?" he asked. It obviously meant something to her, but he had no idea. He glanced at Ellie, but she shrugged. "Is that a ball?" It looked like a ball.

Quinn's face scrunched up. Okay. Not a ball.

"A cookie?"

She rolled her eyes...which was pretty darn cute.

"Sorry, Quinn. I don't know what that is." It was one of the frustrations of having a nonverbal child and it was aggravating.

She made a sign—pinching her thumb and forefinger

together next to her cheek and drawing it out. Dang. He'd seen that sign before, but he couldn't remember what it was. That was another frustration, learning sign when he didn't know it well enough to remember. And then it hit him. The sign mimicked cat whiskers. He should remember that. "Is it a cat?" he asked and Quinn's smile exploded. Yes. A cat. Of course it was. "A black-and-white cat…" It suddenly hit him. Pearl's cat had been black-and-white. "Is that Pepe?"

Her smile lit up her face and she nodded wildly.

"What a great painting, Quinn. Good job! Hey, are you ready to have dinner?"

Her nod was adamant.

"Good. I'm starving." He sent Ellie home and then sat down with Quinn to look at the menu. Even though it was a vast selection, tonight everything looked a little boring. He'd studied this same menu every night for years.

In the end, they ordered pizza and salad, and he even got Quinn to eat some veggies, which was always good. After dinner, she splashed around in the bathtub for a bit, and he got her in jammies and read her a story, all cozy in her bed, with a little Brahms playing in the background because he'd read online that his music helped children sleep. She'd fallen asleep to Brahms, with him reading her a story, more times than he could remember. Heck, he'd fallen asleep a couple times himself.

Aside from that, he'd always loved classical music. He found it soothing, and unlike most music with lyrics, it didn't intrude on his thoughts.

Quinn chose the book *The Tale of Tom Kitten* by Beatrix Potter, which didn't surprise him much, because she picked that book a lot, but tonight she kept signing,

"Again, again," once he'd finished. He read it three times, and then had to stop because reading the same children's book over and over again was teasing his sanity. So, when she signed, "Again," for the fourth time, he decided to try some classic parental misdirection.

"Hey, Quinn, tomorrow is Saturday. Do you know what we're doing?" She shot him a petulant look, probably because she was too smart for the old distraction ploy. "John J.'s coming over and we're going to play in the pool."

Yeah, that worked. Her face lit up. "JJ," she signed. It was her way of shortening his name and also, probably, because making the letter *J* was kind of fun.

"Yep. Georgie and Celeste are coming too. Won't that be fun?"

"Fun," she signed. And then, "Water fun."

"Yep. Playing in water is fun."

"JJ water fun."

"Yep. It is more fun playing with your friends, isn't it?"

She nodded. Her eyes were bright and her smile wide. He didn't think she'd ever been as beautiful as she was in this moment. But then, he thought that a lot.

"So, don't you think we should get some sleep, so we have lots of energy to play tomorrow?"

Her brow furrowed and she crossed her arms. No? She pointed to the book and signed, "Again."

He had to laugh. "Okay, okay. One more time, but then we definitely need to go to sleep. Okay?" Thankfully she was happy with that negotiation. He read the book—again—and then tucked her in, kissed her on her forehead as he always did and whispered, "Nighty night, Quinney." Before he left, she asked for one more hug, which he was happy to provide before shutting off the main lights—save her night-light—and leaving her room. He then headed to his study to catch up on the emails he'd missed during the day and review a couple of project updates that had come in while he'd been out. Of course, he got wrapped up—he usually did—and so he didn't even get to bed himself until after eleven.

He regretted it in the morning, because Quinn woke up so early. She was bouncing on his bed, trying to rouse him, before six. Naturally, he groaned and rolled over, but she was persistent, and in the end, he hauled ass out of bed and went into the kitchen to make her a bowl of cereal, which she ate watching *Sesame Street* while he brewed a pod of coffee for himself. Some days they ordered from the restaurant in the hotel, but most of the time, breakfast was easy, like this. Added bonus, they didn't have to wait as long for food. Sadly, anything more complicated than a bowl of cereal or a fried egg was beyond him. But hey, everyone had their skills, and cooking wasn't on his list.

Celeste and the boys weren't due to arrive until nine, so Ben and Quinn sat down to "play" with a workbook Maisey had recommended. Technically, it was an educational resource, but he loved that Quinn saw it as play. The older she got, the more he realized how curious and enthusiastic she was about learning new things. This one was a coloring book that showed how to make signs, and it was cool to do it together so they could both practice. Then they went on YouTube and watched some signing videos.

Quinn soaked this stuff in, but Ben's brain was a little more fossilized, so he had to repeat signs again and again to remember them, and even then, he sometimes forgot them. Still, it was a really nice way to spend a lazy Saturday morning.

When reception called to let him know Celeste and the boys had arrived, he was surprised that it was nearly nine. He'd gotten dressed in his swimsuit and a T-shirt when he first woke up, but Quinn was still in her jammies, so he hurriedly got her dressed and they headed down to the lobby.

The second Quinn saw John J., she sprinted over to him, and they both did the silly little dance they did whenever they saw each other. Ben followed at a more leisurely pace. When Celeste saw them coming, she broke into a smile that just about made his day. There'd been a time back in high school when he would have loved to see her smile at him like that. That it was happening often now was really nice. She looked very cute in a pair of shorts, a T-shirt and sandals; her toes were painted a cheerful pink. All of a sudden, it occurred to him that he'd never seen her toes before. He didn't know why *that* thought popped in—probably because the sight of her had discombobulated his usually logical mind—but it did. It bore noting, however, that they were very pretty toes.

Usually when he saw her, she was wearing her work clothes, so it was nice to see a different side of her. She did, however, have a fat sheaf of file folders poking out of the beach bag on her shoulder, reminding him that they would be working, despite their attire. Only the kids were really having a day off, though he hoped he'd get at least a dip or two in the pool if it got warm. "Good morning, all," he said. And then, to the boys, "Are you excited to get in the pool?"

"Yeah!" they both hollered.

"Well, let's go, then." He took Quinn's hand—John J. took the other—and led the way to the pool deck. It was summer, so the pool was busy. A lot of his customers came down from Seattle or up from Portland just for the weekend in the summer, so a busy Saturday at the pool was par for the course…which was why he'd had Char reserve a cabana for them right next to the kids' water play area. If they wanted to go into the kids' pool, Ben and Celeste could still keep an eye on them from here. But if they wanted to float the lazy river, they'd need to have an adult with them. It was safe—Ben had lifeguards everywhere—but as a dad, he just wasn't comfortable having Quinn out of his sight for that long, even though she was a strong swimmer.

After the kids stripped down to their swimsuits, and he and Celeste had slathered everyone with sunscreen, Ben let them know the parameters—and had them repeat them back, because frankly, he knew how boys liked to push the envelope. Then they set them loose. The kids yelled, "Hurrah!" and barreled off to the water.

Celeste shook her head as she watched them tear off. "I can't remember having that kind of energy," she said with a laugh.

"Right? Me either," he said. Must be nice. "Okay, ready for a tour of today's office?" he asked.

"Sure thing."

The staff had left a pile of towels, as well as drinks and snacks, in their cabana, and had even set up a table if they needed to spread the paperwork out. "Will this work?" he asked Celeste as she surveyed the setup.

She grinned at him. "Um, yeah." He loved the humor in her tone.

"Okay. But if there's anything else you need, just let me know and I'll get it to you."

"What else could I need?"

He took her question at face value. "Well, I didn't ask for a computer because we're still just figuring things out, but if you think you need one, I can have someone bring a laptop down."

She blew out a sigh and shook her head. "You think of everything, don't you?"

He couldn't hold back a grin. "That's my job." He really liked the way she smiled back.

Despite the setting, and the occasional interruption—when someone appeared, dripping and demanding a snack—they got a lot done before lunch. Basically, they went through the sheaf of applications together, giving each a priority, and making notes on the kinds of information they would need to pull together to complete each one. They realized quickly that if they put the time into writing a thorough proposal, they could use it as a base for each of the different funding applications the project required. Since they'd have to do that for the grant that was due on the first anyway, they decided to start with that. Then he and Celeste went through the specific requirements for that grant, splitting the list in two—the parts she could complete by herself, and the parts she'd need additional data on. And while she was working on filling in the blanks where she could, he and his staff would be collecting all the information she didn't have close at hand.

It was a fantastic plan, and, as fantastic plans always did, it gave him a very satisfying feeling of time well spent. But it was more than that, wasn't it?

Because he got to spend that time with her.

As a bonus, she was as logical as he was, scarily organized and so easy to work with.

The thought astounded him. Two weeks ago, if anyone had come to him and told him that Celeste Tuttle was easy to work with, he would have laughed in their face. He'd known it was probably true—based on her reputation in the community as a go-to resource and a very efficient project manager—but it hadn't been his experience… until now.

But then, now they were aligned. They'd never been aligned before, they'd always been at odds.

He liked this much better.

They got so much done that he didn't even feel guilty about taking the kids on the lazy river before lunch, and apparently, neither did she.

He was surprised that she'd even worn a suit under her outfit because that was an act of extreme optimism considering the task that lay before them, but he was really glad that she had. They had so much fun on the lazy river that they did it twice. He loved the way she looked, laughing as she engaged in a splash war with the boys. The way the sun glanced off her skin, the way her wet hair spiked up straight when she raked it back…and the way she laughed when she realized it.

And when, after they returned to the cabana and sat around, wrapped in towels, Quinn crawled up into Celeste's lap…he loved watching them. They looked so natural together. He loved seeing Quinn respond to her so warmly. Mostly, he loved seeing them laughing together.

Chapter Eight

Celeste took a sip of her soda and stared out at the pool, nearly blinded by the flash of the sun on the water. Gorgeous. It was nice to take a break from work, but even nicer when she reviewed how much they had accomplished just by organizing the project and breaking it into manageable pieces. It was hard to believe they'd completed so much…poolside. She would never have imagined it.

And aside from that, how fun was it to take a breather for lunch and just watch the kids at play? Georgie was older and a little more staid, but watching John J. and Quinn frolic in the water, gallivanting around the colorful structures and fountains, was so entertaining. She nearly spewed out a bite of her salad when she watched Quinn stalk John J. in the spray pool, and hit him with a blast from the water cannon. Ben laughed too, but fortunately, none of his food came out.

"Those two," he said, as John J. got Quinn back.

"Peas in a pod."

"Yeah," he said. "They are. I don't believe in soul mates, but those two make me wonder."

Celeste nodded. "It does seem they have a special connection." How interesting that he didn't believe in soul mates. She didn't either—only because she hadn't found hers—but that didn't keep her from liking the idea. It made her want to ask him about Sheida—she'd been thinking about the two of them a lot since that encounter in the elevator—but for some reason she held her tongue. Some part of her didn't want to talk about his relationship with Sheida. Some part of her didn't want to know.

They watched the kids for a while longer, laughing at their antics. When Quinn went to stand under the little waterfall—and mug being in a shower—they both chuckled. "She is so adorable," Celeste had to say.

Ben shot her a proud grin. "Thanks. She takes after her mother."

It was an opening Celeste welcomed, because she'd been wondering about his wife. They'd met a few times after Vi and Ben moved to the Cove, at one city function or another, but she didn't know very much about her. "So, how did you and Vi meet?" she asked.

Ben paused to chew and swallow his bite of burger. He took a drink of his soda and said, "We met at the U." She knew he'd gone to the University of Washington in Seattle, so she didn't have to ask him to clarify. "She came to a party my housemate threw. We hit it off right away. We were living together within a year."

"A match made in heaven, then." She meant it to be a flippant comment, but was surprised when his expression flickered.

He looked away and shrugged. "We had some good times. It got a little rough when we realized we both wanted different things. You know how it is when you're in love. You overlook a lot. And unfortunately, we were both young, and we didn't have the kinds of conversations we should have had."

She nodded. Yeah. She'd had the same problem with Randall. "I suppose it's common. Being too young and too in love to want to face big issues head-on in fear of screwing everything up. But it's important to be on the same page."

"And Vi and I weren't. Even early on, before Quinn."

"What was the problem?"

"She loved the city—nightclubs and restaurants and shows—and she wanted to go out every night after I got back from work." He gave a laugh, but it wasn't one, not really. "Back then, working with my dad… It was tough because he had such high expectations. And also, because he and I didn't agree on a lot of things, we were often at odds."

"I'm sorry." She hated confrontation. It did drain the soul.

He nodded at her acknowledgment. "So, by the time I got home at night, I'd be wiped. All I wanted was a quiet night to recharge. But Vi'd been bored all day and she wanted to go out."

"Yeah, I can see how that would be a problem."

"Mmm-hmm. For a while there I tried to accommodate her, going out one or two nights a week—the rest of the time, she went out with her friends—but man, it was exhausting. Aside from that, clubbing and parties aren't things I particularly enjoy, not even when I was younger."

"What do you enjoy? For fun?"

His face was transformed by a smile. "Spending time with Quinn, of course. She's such an angel. But I also like fishing with my friends."

"Hmm. Yeah. Probably not something Violetta would have enjoyed."

He snorted a laugh. "Not in the least. I took her out once when we moved here, but only once."

She leaned in and whispered, "I don't blame her. I hate fishing too."

He gaped at her with wide-eyed mock offense. "No."

"It's very unsporting. The poor fish just wants a snack." They both laughed, and then she added, "But I do love being out on a boat. I love the water."

"Hmm. You're probably not seasick."

"Oh no. Was Violetta seasick?"

"Barfed everywhere."

"Poor thing."

He nodded. "That wasn't the only thing she hated here, though. But to be fair, not everyone can live in a small town like this."

"Especially not if you're used to the city."

"And we had Quinn by the time we moved here. That was another huge adjustment for her."

She had to nod. "Yeah, being a mom does impact your freedom, I imagine." At least, that was the way it had been for Amy. Every decision had needed to take what was best for Georgie and John J. into account.

"At any rate, she wasn't very happy living here. But since what was left of the company was here, well, we had to stay here while the company got back on its feet."

"That must have been rough on her."

"Yeah." He shoved a french fry into his mouth and mused for a moment while he chewed. "We went to counseling, which was helpful. Our therapist coached us on finding compromises that would make both of us happy." He huffed a grunt. "You know how that works out."

She did. "What did you guys decide?"

"Ah." He took a quick slurp of his drink. "Our compromise was that I would stay here and work and she and Quinn would go and stay with her family one week out of the month."

"Did that work?"

"For a while. Yeah. She was a little happier. But that was when the reality of being a mom really hit her, I think. Because even though she was in the city, she still didn't have the freedom to do what she wanted all the time. She had a kid to take care of. Before long, she'd hired Ellie." He shot her a look. "Ellie had worked for her sister as a nanny, but her kids had started school, so Iris passed her on to Vi."

"Well, at least she came well recommended."

"Yeah, but imagine my surprise when my wife came home from a visit to Seattle with a nanny."

"Oh. You didn't discuss it first?"

"No. But that was Vi. She was used to having money—her family was well-off—so it never even occurred to her that it might be a problem. That was one of the other issues we had after I took over the company and realized how bad things really were. It's hard to be on a budget when you're used to having everything you want when you want it."

"I can imagine."

"To make things worse, at that time, I had nearly all our assets invested into the hotel construction. It was tight. But hey, those trips to Seattle did help, and Vi seemed happier. And honestly, Ellie is great with Quinn. Not to mention the fact that I was completely lost when Vi died. Thank God that Ellie was there to take care of my child while I pulled myself together."

A shiver walked through her. Another opening to something she'd been wondering about. "Do you mind telling me how Vi died?" She knew the basics—everyone did—but there was probably more to it than the grapevine offered. There usually was.

When he glanced at her, his eyes were shadowed and his expression tight, but he said, "No. I don't mind talking about it. Basically, she and Quinn were coming back from one of their trips to Seattle. Ellie was on vacation, so she wasn't with them. Anyway, it was raining, dark… Some idiot who'd had too much to drink veered into her lane and hit her car. The state patrol said she lost control and went over the verge and rolled the car." He paused and swallowed heavily. "They say she died instantly."

"Oh, Ben. I'm so sorry." She had to reach out and set her hand on his. He stared at it for a second and then swallowed again.

"Thanks. It was…pretty rough getting that call."

"I can't imagine."

"Quinn was in her car seat, thank God, but apparently she was all alone for nearly a half hour before the emergency crews got there to cut her out. And then…" Another gulp. "Well, she had to be airlifted out to Harborview."

"Oh no." Harborview was the large trauma hospital in Seattle. Harborview always meant something terrible. "How long was she there?"

He swallowed, hard. "A week. She had a concussion and some internal injuries. She was all banged up."

"Oh. Poor baby."

"It was hell to see her with all those tubes and wires. Her face all scratched up. They thought she was going to lose her eye for a while."

"Oh, Ben." She just couldn't imagine the horror. His wife dead, and his sweet daughter in the ICU...

"I just had to cling to the hope that she'd make it. Thank God she did. After a week, they said she was stable and transferred her to a children's hospital in Bellevue."

"Goodness."

"I got an apartment there so I could be close. Fortunately, she's a tough cookie. I mean, look at her now."

Celeste followed his gaze to the perfectly healthy, adorable child frolicking as though she hadn't a care in the world. "I'm so glad." No wonder she'd been so traumatized. She must have been horrified after the accident, being all alone in a wrecked car, in the dark...with her mother. Her heart ached for them. "Well, thank you for telling me."

He sent her a smile, though it was a crooked one. "Sure."

"I know it must be difficult to talk about."

"Yes, but we've worked hard to move past it, and I think we're doing pretty well."

"Of course you are. You're a great dad, you know."

She liked that his eyes shone at that. "Thanks. Sometimes I wonder."

She chuckled. "I think every parent has those feelings. Even Amy has the same worries."

"Surely not Amy!" It was funny the way he clapped his hand to his chest and said it so melodramatically. Amy liked to believe she was practically perfect in every way.

"Don't you ever tell her I told you that," she joked back. "I will deny it to my last breath." They both laughed then, but when silence fell, Celeste sighed. "I suppose we should get back to work."

"Yeah," he said, but he said it with a smile.

They worked for a bit longer in a comfortable silence whenever they didn't need to consult on a question. Celeste kept an eye on the kids, mindful of how long they'd been in the sun, and she noticed that Ben was checking on them too every now and again. She liked that.

At one point, Char came by with a folder. "How's it going?" she asked.

"Good." Ben shot her a grin. "Thanks for the setup. So much nicer than working in the office."

Char grinned back. "Might as well enjoy the sunshine while you can." Yeah. In the Pacific Northwest, sunny days were outside days—or should be. Char opened the folder. "Well, in addition to checking in, Ben, I have that VSF check for you to sign." She pulled out the paper and handed it over.

"Oh good." He reviewed the numbers and then took the pen Char had extended, signed the check and handed it all back.

The exchange piqued Celeste's curiosity because it reminded her that she'd been meaning to ask Sheida about the VSF. She was even more curious why Ben would be signing a check from the foundation. She waited until Char left before she asked, "What is the VSF? I've seen it mentioned all over the HHS files, but I'm not familiar."

How curious that his ears went pink. "Ah." He took a sip of his drink. "The VSF is the Violetta Sherrod Foundation. It's a vehicle I set up to fund and support social services in the Cove." He gave a little shrug. "I set it up in her memory."

It took Celeste's brain a minute to integrate that information with everything else she knew about the fund, but then it hit her with a resounding clang.

Ben *was* the VSF.

He was Sheida's angel investor. He'd funded the majority of the new Elder House construction, furnishings and features. And *he* had paid for Momma's day nurse.

It was a stunning revelation, but the most stunning thing of all for Celeste was the fact that he did all this *good* in the community—life-changing stuff for other people he probably didn't even know—and he did it humbly, quietly. Even she, with all her community connections, hadn't known he was the source of all those gifts. Lots of people would crow about their giving, crying, *Look at me!* But not Ben Sherrod. He just quietly did what needed to be done. It was an astounding discovery. And humbling.

Celeste was utterly stunned. All she could manage was a breathless, "Ben that's so...generous of you."

He sent her a crooked grin. "Is it? I think it's a little selfish."

She stared at him. "How could it ever be so?"

"Because," he said with a simplicity that warmed her heart, "I want my daughter to grow up in a world where people are generous and kind, and as I see it, healing the community we live in is the best way to make sure that happens. Besides, we teach our children by our example, don't we?"

And what could she say to that?

After that day by the pool, when Ben and Celeste got all their ducks in a row, the grant writing process really took off. Partly because Celeste worked on it every day, though she did take part of Sunday off to enjoy the weekly family supper. She'd invited Ben and Quinn to join them, and it had been one of the best Sundays in a long, long while.

One of the most enjoyable parts was teaching them some ASL; even the boys joined in on that game.

Of course, as soon as Monday hit, they were right back at it, full tilt. They worked on the initial document for several hours in his office, though when he was called away to handle a problem at the hotel or take a call, Celeste kept going, marking the spots where she needed his input with a little flag.

Just before their lunch was delivered, Quinn came in to say hello to her daddy. It was truly heartwarming the way the little girl's face lit up when she saw him, but even more, watching his response as she ran for him. He broke into a smile, dropped down to swoop her up in his arms and swung her around. Then he kissed her, all over her face, with loud smooches that made her giggle.

Once he set her down, she came over to Celeste—a little more tentatively—and crawled into her lap and gave her a hug. Gosh, it was so precious to get a cuddle from her. The boys were getting to the age where they didn't like to cuddle much and Celeste missed it.

Little girls, she was realizing, were very different from little boys.

She was sorry to see Quinn leave with Ellie, and not only because it signaled that it was time to get back to work. As she had all the information she needed from Ben for this portion of the proposal, it was time to go back to her office to start writing it up. She was a little torn about that because she really liked working with him, but he was just plain distracting.

Since that moment in the elevator, it felt as though something within her had awakened, and now she couldn't stop thinking about him…like *that*. He'd lean forward and she'd get a whiff of his aftershave, and all of a sudden, her heart would start pattering and her imagination would begin to play out scenarios that, well, frankly, she didn't have time to entertain. It didn't help that she enjoyed spending time with him, like the conversation they'd had at the pool, where she'd learned so much more about his life and his marriage, or the game of chess they'd played on Sunday evening while the kids and Momma watched a movie. Beyond that, he seemed to enjoy spending time with her too.

She often caught herself wondering if something beyond a working relationship might be possible for them—which in itself blew her mind, especially given their rocky past. Whenever the thought occurred to her, she had to push it away, because she couldn't think about any of this. Not really. Not now. This project had to be her top priority.

Aside from that, there was his relationship with Sheida. If they were romantically involved—and the signs that they had a very close relationship were undeniable—she could never allow herself to act on her attraction to him. She'd been cheated on before and wanted no part of something like that. She liked Sheida. Respected her so much. Celeste could never do that to her.

So yeah. It just wasn't in the cards, even if they were both interested in something more.

So stop thinking about it, doofus!

She was just about finished with her first draft of the base proposal they planned to use for all the funding when Ben poked his head into her office later that day. "Still at it?" he asked.

"Almost there." She sighed and stretched. "I wanted to

get it done today so you can review it tonight." She shot him a glance. "I mean, if you have time."

His response was a wide grin. "Wow. You're already done?"

"Almost."

"Why don't you finish that up, print out a copy and we can go over it together."

She glanced at the clock and frowned. "I have to pick up the boys from the sitter. And make dinner for them and Momma, but I could come back after that."

"Well," he said, with a glint in his eye. "If the sitter can take the boys home, I can send over dinner for all of them from the restaurant. Then you can stay until we knock through the review and start fresh on phase two tomorrow. Would that work?"

Oh, gosh. That sounded great. Then she could just dive into phase two. She shot him a grin. "Let me make a few calls."

Fortunately, Kim, the boys' sitter, was more than happy to take them home, and Momma was pretty excited about having a fancy dinner delivered…especially because she didn't need to pay for it. So once Celeste finished up the bits and pieces, and printed out two copies, she and Ben headed up to his apartment to start their review, and have their own dinner with Quinn.

It was a novel experience for Celeste, sitting at a table with a man and his daughter. It was fun to watch them interact. It was so cute the way he used sign with her, especially when he used the wrong sign and Quinn laughed. She was so pretty when she laughed.

It was also fun because Celeste knew enough ASL to converse with them, though because Ben's and Quinn's vocabulary was fairly basic at this point, the conversations were pretty simple. She was able to teach them a couple words here and there, which was nice.

After dinner, Ben set Quinn up with a coloring book and crayons as the two of them worked side by side in the living room, going over her draft proposal. It was such a pleasant evening, she didn't even mind working late, and the feeling of excitement as they neared the end of the review left her elated. She'd been so worried about the deadline looming over their heads, but now that this huge chunk was nearly ready, she knew it would be comparatively easy to make adjustments for the various portions of the funding package.

They were a great team.

Just as they were finishing, Ben received a call. When he checked the screen of his cell phone he made a face, so she knew it would be something bad. "Celeste, I'm going to need to go downstairs and handle an issue. Do you mind watching Quinn while I'm gone?"

"Not at all," she said, placing a mark where they'd left off on the paperwork so they could find it again.

"Thanks. I'm so sorry."

"Not a problem." She loved spending time with Quinn.

He was gone longer than either of them expected, and as it got later and later, and Quinn started yawning, Celeste decided to start getting her ready for bed. Quinn, she realized, was a lot easier to get ready for bed than John J. and Georgie. There wasn't any whining or complaining when she suggested it was time for jammies. Quinn just took her hand and led her to her bedroom. It was a beautiful little girl room with fairy lights on the ceiling and a princess bed.

Once Quinn had brushed her teeth and was in her pajamas, they collected some books and Celeste sat in the big comfy chair by the bed. It was sweet that Quinn curled up in her lap. She had to bite back a smile when she realized all the books Quinn had chosen featured a bunny or a princess or a cat. Her nephews preferred books about dinosaurs or tractors or trains.

When Celeste had finished all the books Quinn had chosen, she set them aside and told Quinn a story she made up herself. It involved a little princess who had a cat and lived in a beautiful hotel by the sea. Quinn seemed to enjoy it very much, even though it didn't have much of a plot. And then Celeste sang Quinn to sleep, as Momma had always done for Celeste and her sisters.

Quinn's weight got heavier and her breath slowed as she fell asleep in her arms. How precious was that? There, in the pretty princess room, with Quinn's warm weight beside her…she couldn't think of a nicer way to finish a day.

Damn it. The problem with the irate customer at the front desk had taken a lot longer than Ben had expected. His staff didn't usually call him about things like this, but the situation had escalated out of control. They'd ended up having to call the sheriff, because the guy was obviously high on something and had gone totally berserk. Things like this didn't happen often at his hotel, thank God, but when they did, it was a royal pain.

He felt awful about leaving Celeste with Quinn. She was probably as tired as he was after such a long day and just wanted to go home. So he hurried back to his apartment once the sheriff had taken the troublemaker into custody and the incident report had been finalized.

When he pushed through the door, the living room was empty, but he heard something coming from the bedrooms. He stopped in his tracks as the sound of singing hit him, along with a wave of nostalgia.

His mom had sung that song to him at bedtime, he realized. "Good night, my someone, good night, my love." It had been from an old movie or something, but she'd sung it to him every night. He hadn't heard it since he was a kid. Hadn't thought about it since then either. But all of a sudden, he remembered, and man, it hit him right in the solar plexus.

How many nights had Mom lulled him to sleep with that song? Wiped away the stress and fears of the day, all the heartache he'd suffered as a small boy with an abusive father? All the harsh rejection. The stress of his parents' fights? His mom had taken all that away, with just that little song. And love, of course. She'd been such a wonderful mom. Despite everything she'd been through, she'd always shielded him when she could, and soothed him when she couldn't.

He didn't know why it hit him so hard, that sudden grief, but grief did that sometimes.

He wiped away the tears that clogged his eyes and headed for Quinn's bedroom, called as though by a siren. And there they were. Quinn and Celeste, together in the easy chair by his daughter's bed. They both had their eyes closed and Quinn was curled up in Celeste's arms.

His heart thudded. Hard.

"Hey," Ben said in a whisper, just as she was thinking about him.

Celeste opened her eyes and smiled at him. "Hey."

"Everything okay?"

"Yes." She looked down at Quinn. "She's asleep."

"Here. Let me take her." Ben leaned in to take Quinn from her and Celeste's heart nearly stopped when his hand brushed against her breast. A bolt of raw sexual awareness shot through her. She must have jerked away because he flinched. "Sorry," he murmured. His voice was soft, his breath warm. Damn. He was attractive like this.

No, he was attractive always. She just hadn't let herself see it before.

"It's okay," she said, even though her entire world had been turned upside down. Good glory. How had that simple touch set her on fire the way it had? She hated when he lifted Quinn away, but even more, she hated losing his warmth when he turned away to tuck his daughter into bed. She watched as Quinn snuggled in, murmuring slightly without opening her eyes, and he bent over her and pressed a kiss on her forehead. "Good night, princess," he said softly.

And yeah, her heart melted. Tears pricked at her eyes. She was thrown back, deep into her own childhood, when her father used to do the same. It had made her feel so safe and loved. And content.

Funny, that was how she felt at this moment, just watching from afar. *Contentment.* She glanced at Ben as he stood staring down at his daughter, a tall, strong, handsome man. How had she never noticed it before? She had no idea.

He turned just then and caught her looking at him and their gazes clashed. Her pulse picked up and heat rose within her. What was he thinking, with that expression? Was he as desirous for her as she was for him at this moment? Or were her emotions tricking her, making her think, hope, that he somehow felt the same? He'd never really given her any hint that he had feelings like that for her, had he? She was probably just delirious.

Without speaking, she rose and they walked in tandem to the living room. Her heart pattered all the way, and then even more when the silence grew around them. *What was he thinking?*

He cleared his throat as though he was going to say something monumental, but when he spoke, he said, "Thank you so much for putting her to bed."

"Sure. No problem."

"I'm sorry it's so late. I really didn't mean to keep you."

"That's okay. But I should be going."

His throat worked. "Right. Okay. Well…" He raked back his hair. "I'll finish reading the proposal tonight, and we can go over any questions on that last section in the morning. Then we'll be, ah, good to go on phase two, I guess."

"Sounds good." But her mood slumped. Apparently he hadn't been thinking what she was thinking. It surprised her how disappointing that was, but she sucked in a deep breath and went to gather her things.

"Are you okay to drive?" he asked. "I can call a driver."

"I'm fine," she said on a laugh. It wasn't that late, and she didn't live that far away. "And thanks for buying dinner for Momma and the boys. That was very kind."

He waved her thanks away. "Least I could do, considering you've had me over two Sundays in a row. And, of course, because I stole you from them tonight."

"You didn't steal me. We needed this extra time. Besides, I enjoyed having a night off from the circus." They both chuckled, because they both knew the boys were a handful. "I also enjoyed dinner here, and extra time with Quinn. She's so sweet. And soooo much easier than the boys."

"Well, I'm glad to hear it."

"I...should go."

"Yeah," he said, but neither of them moved.

It was probably the tension, or the awkwardness, that forced her to finally turn for the door. It was hard leaving him, walking down the thickly carpeted hall to the elevator. But when she glanced back, he was watching her, lifting a hand in a wave.

And that made her smile all the way home.

Once the base proposal was finished, work really sped up, but honestly, that was all due to Celeste. Ben was stunned at how quickly and efficiently she worked. At this point in the project, she only came to him when she had a question or an update, which was great for the project, but not so great for his mood.

Days weren't quite as bright without seeing her. In fact, days were kind of a slog when she didn't pop in and warm him with that bright smile.

There had been a moment, that night she'd watched Quinn for him, when he'd thought something might have been brewing between them, but just when he'd been about to move in for a kiss—or say something equally disastrous—she'd left.

Then again, he hadn't made a move or anything. He hadn't told her how he was feeling. He hadn't had the courage. Things were so good between them, he hadn't wanted to take the chance.

He'd always been a little nervous around her, ever since high school. They'd only just found some kind of accord. And damn, he loved that they had. While his hopes that she might have changed her mind about him had blossomed recently, the last thing he wanted was to say or do the wrong thing and ruin everything.

The sad fact was, while he was really happy to be developing a friendship with her, he wanted more. Then again, he always had, ever since the first time she'd walked into his civics class way back when.

So, as always, he was cautious. He kept their conversations casual and on the job, unless she led the conversation into something more personal. Every once in a while, he would catch her looking at him, but he never had a clue what she was thinking, and he didn't have the nerve to ask.

Thank God his revived crush on her didn't get in the way of their work. They plowed through all the grant paperwork, assembled all the data—well, she did that—and finalized the application. Before they sent it off, it still needed to be reviewed by all members of the committee, as well as a few of the experts Char had contacted, but they were close.

And yeah. That made him a little sad too. When the grant was done, there would be no reason for her to see him. Not really.

He was stewing over this on a Wednesday afternoon—when he should have been working; he had an important meeting that evening—when Ellie knocked on his door.

"Sorry to interrupt, Mr. Sherrod," she said. "I need to talk to you."

His stomach tightened. *I need to talk to you* never ended well. "Sure. What's up."

"My mom is in the hospital. I'm going to need some time off."

Visions of his wife's car accident popped into his mind, along with the horrific memory of Quinn in that hospital bed. He came to his feet. "Oh my gosh. I'm so sorry. What happened?"

Ellie sighed. "They're saying it's probably appendicitis because she's having stomach pain and fever, but my brother is out of town and there's no one who can be with her right now."

"Ellie, no problem. You know family comes first. Don't worry about work. Just keep me posted on how things are going and when you think you'll be back. And if you need anything, let me know. Okay?"

"Thank you, Mr. Sherrod."

"It's Ben," he said for—what was it?—the *thousandth* time. No one called him Mr. Sherrod. Mr. Sherrod was his dad.

"Thank you, Mr. Sherrod." *Really?* "But who will watch Quinn?"

"Don't worry. We'll figure it out. Where is she now?"

She waved to the outer office. "With Char."

"Okay. Bring her in here, and go to your mom, okay? And again, don't worry about work at all."

"All right. And thanks for being so understanding."

Once Ben had explained everything to Char, she took over, as she usually did, sending her assistant to the kids' club to grab some art supplies, and set up a little table in Ben's office for Quinn. She was used to entertaining herself when he had to work at night, so, as they did then, they worked side by side. Every once in a while, she'd show him her drawing and he'd remark on what a fine piece of art it was, even when he didn't always know *what* it was. Almost all of them had that black Pepe scrawl on it somewhere.

When Celeste popped in with a few papers in her hand, she stopped short. "Well, hello, Quinn. Are you working with your dad now?" she asked.

Quinn jumped up and ran to her, of course, to show her the drawings and Celeste oohed and aahed appropriately. As she went back to her table, Quinn had a little swagger in her step.

"What's up?" he asked as Celeste came to his desk.

"Oh, I just finished this section, so I wanted to share it with you." She handed him the papers and he scanned the sheets. "Aren't you lucky to be able to have Quinn working with you," she said, more for Quinn's benefit than his.

He shot her a grin. "It's a perk of owning the business, I guess. Ellie's mom is in the hospital, so she had to leave."

"Oh no. Nothing serious, I hope?"

"They're thinking appendicitis."

"Oh, my. I hope she's okay."

"Me too. It's not the best timing, I have a meeting tonight that I can't miss and it's too late in the day to round up another sitter."

"What about the kids' club?"

He grimaced. "It's only staffed in the evenings on Friday and Saturday." He'd have to think about that for the future.

But, to his astonishment, she said, "Well, why don't I take her home with me?"

"What?" He stared at her.

"She can have dinner with us. You know she always loves to see John J., and he loves when she comes over.

And…" She snuck a glance in Quinn's direction and added, in a singsong voice, "We have a cat."

It was funny the way Quinn's head snapped up at that. "Please, Daddy," she signed, and then when he didn't respond quickly enough, she put on her sad little pouty face and signed again, "Please?"

"Well, I don't know…" he said, only to tease her a little. "I suppose it would be okay—" It was adorable the way she jumped up and ran over to give him a hug, and then she hugged Celeste for good measure.

"Happy," she signed. "Happy, happy, happy."

Celeste brought Quinn home with her that evening, but only because she had the boys' booster seats in her car. Otherwise, Ben would have had his driver bring her over.

John J. was especially excited to see Quinn. Pepe, however, ran for his life. He was a pretty chill cat, as far as cats went, but when Quinn came through the door and John J. hollered, "Woo-hoo," it had, apparently, wounded poor old Pepe's feline sensibilities and he ran for the hills.

"Look who's here," Celeste said to Momma. "Quinn's staying for dinner."

"Oh my goodness," Momma cooed. "Come here. Aren't you the prettiest girl today? Is that a ribbon in your hair?"

Quinn nodded and smiled and crawled up in Momma's lap. Probably because Momma had a plate of cookies.

"John J., can you set up a jigsaw puzzle for you and Quinn to work on while I make dinner?" Celeste asked. "What does everyone want to eat?"

"Spaghetti."

"Pizza."

"Lobster," Momma added to the boys' chorus in a wry tone.

Celeste chuckled. Amy would be home in a few days, and while Celeste would miss having the boys around, dinners sure would be easier. Momma would eat anything she made, even if they were leftovers. Even if it wasn't lobster. The boys, however, were pickier. "Okay. Spaghetti pizza, then," she said and all the kids howled with laughter. "Let me go see what I can find."

In the end, she made spaghetti, with a little mini pizza for Georgie, a salad and some frozen garlic bread. It was hardly a gourmet feast, but it was tasty and warm. They sat around the dinner table and chatted. The boys talked about their day—some video game they'd been playing and some terrible boring gardening they'd done at the sitter's. Celeste wondered if Amy knew Kim was having them do chores during the day, but it was probably better than letting them play video games all the time. At one point, John J. piped up with, "Quinn's birthday is coming up soon."

"Really?" Celeste glanced at her. "Your birthday?" And when Quinn nodded, "How old will you be?"

She very confidently held up six fingers.

"Wow. That's pretty old." She nearly laughed when Quinn nodded solemnly.

"She wants a kitten for her birthday," John J. said through a mouthful of spaghetti. Goodness, it was all over his face.

Celeste looked at him. "John J. How do you know that?"

He lifted a slender shoulder. "She told me, of course."

"Honey, Quinn doesn't speak," Momma said.

John J. put out a lip. "She talks to me."

Celeste stared at him for a moment. There was such certitude in his tone, and John J. wasn't one to make things up, so she asked, "Do you mean she uses words?"

He snorted and speared his spaghetti with his fork. "Of course. But she can only talk to me. And she can only whisper."

"Quinn," she said in a very measured tone, even though her heart was beating a mile a minute all of a sudden. "Do you talk to John J.?" Quinn stared at her, looking mutinous and maybe a little frightened. "It's okay," she said gently. "You can tell me."

Quinn's nod was nearly imperceptible.

Because it was clear the conversation made her uncomfortable, Celeste decided to veer away from the direct approach and said, in a cheerful tone, "Well, I think that's wonderful. It's so nice to have a friend to talk to sometimes, don't you think?"

To her relief, Quinn relaxed and she even smiled as she nodded. "Friend," she signed. "JJ friend."

"Yes. It's nice to have a good friend. Now, does anyone want dessert?"

Of course, the answer was yes.

After a little ice cream, Momma retired to her room—she liked to call it that when she snuck off to leave Celeste with the boys, *retiring*—but Celeste didn't mind at all. She put on a show the boys liked, and sat on the sofa next to Quinn, who was looking at a book. Quinn had hunted around for Pepe, but hadn't been able to find him, so she'd settled on a picture book of baby animals she found on the bookshelves Momma kept for the boys. "C'mere," Celeste said, patting the spot beside her. "I want to read the book too."

Quinn scooted over and they studied the pages for a bit, Celeste pointing out one animal or the other and chatting quietly as the boys' show wailed away in the background. Then she leaned closer and whispered, very softly into Quinn's ear, "You can talk to me too, you know," she said.

The little girl's eyes got wide and she shook her head, pressing her lips together.

"Why not?" Celeste asked. But of course, she wouldn't answer. "Can you tell John J.? Then maybe he can tell me."

Quinn thought about it for a minute, and then nodded, so Celeste called John J. over.

A flurry of whispering ensued and then John J. said, with a very serious expression, "She says she can't talk to other people because when she does, bad things happen."

Celeste blinked. Good glory. "She talks to you, though, and bad things don't happen."

John J. shrugged. "I'm her best friend," he said as though that explained everything. Goodness. Who could understand six-year-old logic? She couldn't.

But, man, she couldn't wait to share this news with Ben.

Chapter Nine

It was late by the time Ben finally pulled into the Tuttle driveway. He'd thought about calling Celeste and asking if Quinn could just stay over, but he'd decided against it. Mostly because he'd wanted to see Celeste.

When she opened the door with a strained look on her face it made his gut clench. "What is it?" he asked.

"Come in." She opened the screen and grabbed his hand. "I need to tell you what happened."

His heart lurched. "Is Quinn okay?"

"Yes. Yes. She's sleeping in Nat's old room. But, Ben, something happened. Tonight I found out that Quinn has been talking to John J." She went on to tell him about the conversation, and what John J. had told her. He was stunned. His heart was crushed to realize that Quinn believed that if she spoke bad things would happen. It killed him to know she had been carrying such a weight. But on the other hand, he was excited, for the first time in a long while, to have a glimmer of hope.

When Celeste finished, he stood there for a while, his mind spinning, then finally managed to say, "I had no idea she was talking to John J. I mean, actually *talking*."

"Me either. But, Ben, this is a huge breakthrough. I only hope I handled it all right."

He stared at her. *Handled it all right?* "Celeste," he said, "you did great. Just great." It seemed only natural to pull her into his arms and hug her. He loved that she hugged him back. "Thank you. Thank you."

She pulled away, just far enough to give him a smile. "Don't thank me yet. You need to have her assessed by a professional. Someone who has the skills I don't. Someone who knows how to convince her that it's safe to speak."

He loved the way she lifted him up, and the hope, the sparkle, in her eyes. "I'm ecstatic right now." Imagine, finally, a light at the end of the tunnel. And right in time for school to start.

"I know. Me too." Her grin was wide. Was she aware she was still hugging him? He was.

"I'll call Maisey first thing in the morning."

"Excellent. I can't wait to hear what she says."

He laughed. "Me too."

They both fell silent, and there was another one of those moments, where they stared into each other's eyes. The difference was, this time she was right there, in his arms, and she wasn't moving away. Heat rose between them, or at least it seemed so to him. Her eyes were wide and her lips were slightly parted and—it deserved another mention—she had not yet moved away.

It was only natural for him to lean closer, and when he did, her tongue peeped out. A slash of excitement speared him. A woman who didn't want a kiss would have pushed away by now, wouldn't she? She certainly wouldn't have dampened her lips.

But before he could seal the deal and kiss her, a door opened down the hall and Pearl called out, "Celeste?" She came around the corner as they leaped apart, but not before she caught a glimpse of the two of them in a clinch. Her eyes glinted and a smile teased her lips. Heat suffused him. He was certain it crawled all the way up to the tops of his ears. "Well, hello, Ben," she said.

"Hello, Pearl." He resisted the urge to straighten his suit jacket or rake back his hair like a teenager caught making out.

"Did you have a nice meeting?"

"Yes." A lie. It had been a pain in the butt. "Just here to pick up Quinn."

"Mmm-hmm." Her look was sly, but she didn't say anything that might mortify him, or Celeste. Thank God.

"In fact," he said, albeit reluctantly, "I'd better get going. It's late and I don't want to keep you up."

Celeste took him upstairs and gathered Quinn's things as Ben picked up his sleeping daughter, and then she walked him to the front door. There was an awkward moment there, but not for long, because she smiled at him and said, "See you tomorrow?"

"Yes. And thanks again. You know, for everything."

Her eyes warmed. "My pleasure," she said.

It wasn't until much later, when he was in bed and thinking about all that had happened today, and all that hadn't, that he realized her simple comment could have meant a myriad of things.

Ben was able to get an appointment for Quinn with Maisey the very next day. He was a little nervous, waiting for them to finish the session. The plan was that, after they were done, Maisey would send Quinn to the playground with the other children from the day care, and sit down with Ben and let him know what she'd been able to find out, if anything. There was still a chance that Quinn would continue to remain silent, and now that he knew what was driving her silence—or at least the reason behind it—he had a hard time blaming her. It was the first time he'd felt any hope since that terrible day when Quinn had woken up in that hospital bed after the crash that had killed her mother, and been heart-wrenchingly mute.

He was torn between heart-pounding excitement and preparing himself for another disappointment when Maisey finally called him into her office.

Her expression was unreadable. "Ben." It was concerning that she took him by the hand and led him to the chair across from the desk and said, "Please. Sit."

And once he did, and she didn't start talking soon enough, he said, "What? What happened? What did you learn?" Why wouldn't she just get to the point, already? "Is Quinn okay?"

"Quinn is fine. She's fine, Ben." Her smile relieved him a bit. "I just want to tell you what Quinn told me—"

"*Told* you?" His heart went into a hard tattoo.

Maisey shook her head. "Not with words, Ben. But she did tell me using sign language." And yeah, his stomach dropped. "Remember, Ben, this is early on, right? Let's take every small step at a time, okay?"

She seemed to need his agreement, so he nodded. "Okay. What did she tell you?"

"Well." She sighed. *Come on. Get on with it!* "Apparently when she was in the car with your wife," she began gently, "right before the accident, she was chattering and Vi told her to be quiet."

Ben nodded. There had been times when Vi hadn't had a lot of tolerance for Quinn's chatter. She'd been quite a chatterbox back then, even though a lot of her patter hadn't always made sense at three.

"But," Maisey continued, "Quinn wasn't quiet."

He nodded again. "Yeah. Sometimes when Vi told Quinn to be quiet, and Quinn hadn't wanted to, she'd just get louder." She'd been three. That was what three-year-olds did.

"Yes. But this time, when Quinn was rebellious, the accident happened. She told me, *If I talk, bad things will happen.* Ben, I think she blames herself for the accident."

He shook his head. "They were hit by a drunk driver." The highway patrol did a study of the tire marks and everything. But then a wave of emotion broke through his default logical response and shredded him. She was three at the time of the accident. Just a baby. Babies didn't operate on logic. Babies lived in a magical world and engaged in magical thinking. And in Quinn's mind, disobeying Vi, probably even talking louder, perhaps being angry at being shushed, had caused her whole world to come crashing down. Poor sweet Quinn. Poor sweet baby. To carry that weight. To feel that burden. His chest ached something fierce. "We need to tell her. We have to make sure she knows it wasn't her fault."

"Of course. And I explained that to her. But remember, Ben, these things take time. There's a complex psychological mechanism at work. This is a great breakthrough, it really is. But we need to let her unspool the intricacies in her own time. I'll keep working with her, now that I know what we're really dealing with—"

"And what can I do?"

She smiled then. "You be her daddy. Let her know she's safe and loved and we'll move on from there."

Okay. It wasn't perfect, but it was, at least, a start.

* * *

Later, that night, after he'd read Quinn a few books, he cuddled her in bed. "Baby," he said to her in a gentle voice as he stroked her hair. "You know it's okay to talk to me if you want. It's okay. You'll be safe." It was hard to believe he'd never thought to tell her that before.

She made a face.

"What? What is it? Tell me." He said it softly, but inside, he screamed. "You can whisper to me. The way you whisper to John J. Okay?"

She seemed dubious, but after a moment, she came up on her knees and leaned in. He felt her soft breath on his ear as she whispered, "Will *you* be okay?"

He wanted to melt. It was the first time he'd heard her voice in three years. And then he realized the enormity of what her question meant. She hadn't been keeping herself quiet for so long to protect herself. She'd been protecting the people she loved.

God. He wanted to howl. Instead, he pulled her into a fast, hard hug. "I'll be fine, baby. I promise. Is there something you want to say to me? Anything?"

She nodded.

His heart thudded like a bass drum.

He couldn't hold back the tears when she leaned in again and whispered, oh so softly, "I love you, Daddy."

And he held her close, and he wept.

Amy and Noah came back from their honeymoon on Thursday night and the house exploded with energy as the boys erupted in cheers and tears and hugs. After the boys excitedly recounted everything that had happened over the last two weeks, Amy and Noah regaled them all with all they'd seen in Alaska.

Technically, they still had a few days of their honeymoon left, but they'd decided to spend it with John J. and Georgie. Amy had missed her boys.

While Nat and Jax stayed a few more days in Victoria, BC, where their cruise ship had docked, Amy and Noah planned on taking the boys to an amusement park in Idaho. And yes, there were more cheers at this news.

But after they'd collected their boys and left, the house was oddly empty, almost eerily quiet. It was a good thing, because Celeste had a lot of work to do, but it was strange. She stayed home on Friday so she could focus on proofing the grant paperwork for review—she didn't need Ben's input at this point and there were too many distractions at the hotel—but she couldn't shake the haunting thought that something was…missing.

The last two weeks had been a crazy explosion of activity and deadlines, but now that the boys were gone and the grant work was wrapping up, it was almost a letdown.

The void that swelled into the space all that busyness had occupied was uncomfortable. It made Celeste take a hard look at her life, and she didn't like what she saw. Oh, she had her job and her committees and everything that had always sustained her soul—and of course, Momma needed her. But something was sorely lacking. The worst part was the realization that, while her life choices had fulfilled her in the past, they didn't anymore. At least, not as consistently.

Her mood got even darker at dinner that night, when Momma—who sat across from her at the near-empty table in the very quiet room—looked over at her and said, as casually as you like, "Now that the boys are gone, I think I'll go away for a few days."

Celeste gaped at her. "What?" Since her stroke, Momma had rarely left the house, much less *gone away*. But in truth, even before the stroke, she'd been something of a homebody, happy to putter in her garden. "Momma, what are you talking about?" She couldn't go away on a trip, could she? She couldn't even drive.

Momma shrugged. "Alexander has invited me to go with him to Greenwater."

Alexander? Celeste blinked, still stunned that Momma wanted to leave the house, much less go on a trip with Jax's dad. Granted, the two had developed a close friendship since Jax and Nat announced their engagement, and had been spending a lot of time together lately, but the thought of Momma going on a trip with a man other than Dad was…weird. Her brain was melting, so all she could ask was, "Wh-where's Greenwater?"

"Down the 410. From Enumclaw." She said it matter-of-factly, as though she expected everyone should know.

But even with that information, Celeste was in the dark. She'd google it later. For now, she asked, "Momma, why Greenwater?"

A sniff. "Well, because it's the best place to pick agates, of course."

And again, Celeste was speechless, other than a slightly squawked "Agates?"

"Yes, dear. Agates are very pretty, especially when you polish them up."

Well, she knew what agates were. And she was well aware of Alexander's rockhounding passions. Anyone who got close to him was. That was hardly the question, was it? "I… Momma…"

"Yes, dear?"

How could she say this without being offensive? Momma was a grown-up. She had the right to make her own decisions. But since her stroke, their roles had kind of reversed. Celeste had taken care of her every need for quite some time, to the point that occasionally, she felt like the parent, and now Momma was proposing a pretty wild idea. In the end she just said, "Momma, have you thought this through?"

Momma got a look on her face that resembled the one Georgie flashed when he was being rebellious. "What is there to think through? Alexander has invited me to go with him and I want to go."

"But who will help you get dressed?" She still struggled with buttons since her left hand didn't work.

She snorted. "He'll help me if I need help."

"Does he know which medications you need to take? And when?" A missed dosage could be a serious problem.

"You can make him a list."

"And what about—"

"Celeste." Momma waited until she had Celeste's full attention. "Life is short, honey. We have to take enjoyment where we can. I enjoy spending time with Alexander. And a treasure hunt sounds exciting. It's about time I took my life back."

Oh dear. On the one hand, the thought of Momma taking off on a trip without Celeste to take care of everything was horrifying. But on the other, Momma was right. Not only was it good for her to get out of the house, it was good for her to *want* to. After the stroke, Celeste had had the sinking suspicion that Momma was living her last days. She should be overjoyed that she was wrong...and she was. She just needed to shift her thinking, especially now that Momma had.

Oh, this would be so much easier if she had someone to talk to about it. But Nat was up in Canada and Amy was on her way to an amusement park in Idaho. She could probably reach them on their cell phones, but Celeste didn't want to ruin their trips by dumping this on them when there wasn't anything they could do. If Momma wouldn't be swayed by Celeste's logic, Natalie's charm and Amy's demands probably wouldn't register with her either.

So, in the end, Celeste simply smiled and said, "All right, Momma. I hope you have a wonderful time."

"Good," Momma said. "Because we're leaving tomorrow."

Tomorrow? Good glory. How long had they been planning this? Not that it mattered, not really. Tomorrow was simply another day, after all.

Besides, Momma was right. Life was short and it was silly, especially at her age, not to enjoy herself. She'd worked her entire life, raised her children—who were all grown—and she had survived a stroke. Why not take advantage of the good times when you had them?

So yes, she put on a happy face for Momma's benefit, but she couldn't deny that somewhere deep inside, panic raged.

She felt better about the trip the next day after she talked to Alexander when he came to collect Momma for their adventure. She explained all the things he needed to know about Momma's condition, her medications and any problems they might encounter—and he was able to soothe her nerves with his attention to her concerns and calm demeanor. He'd been to Greenwater many times, he told her. He knew the area, had a nice place to stay all lined up and even knew the best restaurants to visit. He seemed very confident about everything, but more importantly, he seemed just as excited as Momma for the trip.

"I usually have to go by myself," he said. "It's a lot more fun with someone else."

Well, she couldn't argue with that, but she did argue with Momma about her walker. Celeste insisted that they take it, just in case they needed it, because it had a seat for her if she got tired. Momma grumbled that it took up too much space in the trunk, but in the end, she agreed, but only because it made Celeste feel better.

How surreal was it then, to help them pack up Alexander's car and watch them drive away that Saturday morning? And how dismal was it to have the rest of the day all to herself? Most people would love that, wouldn't they? But for Celeste, it just exacerbated the feeling of emptiness she'd had when the boys left. All those thoughts came rolling back. The fact of the matter was, she'd built her life around her family, but now they were all moving on. At least, that was the way it felt. It was hard not to be maudlin as she made herself a sad little frozen dinner for one.

The only benefit to being alone in the house was that, as she worked, she could play whatever music she wanted, as loudly as she wanted. It was nice because she was in the mood for Beethoven, especially the more thunderous bits.

She had a frozen dinner on Sunday too, because she was too depressed to make anything or go out. Sundays had always been family days. Everyone came home on Sunday for supper or a barbecue or at least to check in.

There was always a huge meal spread out over hours, laughter, conversation, sometimes arguments...but still, it was wonderful. Celeste couldn't remember ever having dinner by herself in this house, much less on a Sunday. Yet here she was, in the big old house that had belonged to her grandparents...utterly alone.

Well, not all alone. Pepe was there too.

What a shame he wouldn't let her hold him.

To Ben's surprise, Celeste got the completed grant back to him on Monday morning—in record time. He was bummed that he'd missed her when she'd dropped it off— he wanted to tell her about what had happened with Quinn. But he set his disappointment aside and sent copies out to everyone who needed to review the proposal.

He delivered Sheida's copy to her, because they had a lunch date. They tried to meet up as often as their busy schedules would allow, and on this occasion, they chose Smokey's, which was a ratty little barbecue place off the main drag in town with the best ribs he'd ever tasted. It was also her favorite place, and it was usually very quiet because most customers just came there to grab takeout. The interior kind of lacked ambience, unless sticky tables appealed.

Sheida was already waiting for him at their usual spot in the back. She waved as he came in.

"Hey, Sheida," he said as he sat.

"Hi, Ben. I ordered your usual drink." She indicated the soda on his side of the table.

"Thanks." They'd been friends for so long, she knew what he liked. "I have a present for you," he said as he slid the file folder with her copy of the grant paperwork over.

Better to get that out of the way before the ribs showed up. This lunch was always a messy undertaking. He usually availed himself of the Big Pig Bib to protect his suit, and by the end of the meal there was always a pile of mangled napkins between them.

Her eyes widened. "Is this what I think it is?"

He grinned. "Yep."

"I can't believe it's done," she said as she riffled through the pages.

"Me either," he had to say.

"I can't wait to dig in." Her smile was wide as she tucked the file into her large purse that doubled as a brief-case. "So," she said after Baxter came by and took their orders. "How was working with Celeste?"

He assumed she was asking as an employer, rather than a friend, so he said, "She's great. Very professional and efficient. In fact, I wouldn't mind hiring her away from you."

"Don't you dare," she said with a laugh. And then, "So…no problems getting along?"

He shot her a look. She knew about his crush on Celeste way back when, because they'd been close friends in high school. But she was probably also well aware of Celeste's opinions about him and his company, or at least— he hoped—how Celeste *had* felt. It seemed her opinions had changed in the past few weeks. "No problems at all. In fact, we worked very well together. And get this, she helped me figure out what's really going on with Quinn."

Sheida leaned in. "Really?"

He told her the story of Celeste's discovery, and about Quinn's meeting with Maisey, and of course about that precious *I love you, Daddy*. By the end of his recounting, they both had tears in their eyes.

"Oh, Ben. That is so wonderful," she said.

"I'm hopeful. Maisey said it will take time, of course it will, to work through whatever is going on in her mind… but it was a huge breakthrough, and I owe it all to Celeste."

"I'm so happy for you."

"Thanks."

Sheida blew out a breath. "And I'm glad that you and Celeste are getting along. To be frank, I may have some other HHS projects I'd like to give her."

He shrugged. "I'm happy to work with her again. Anytime." It was true, but for more reasons than just her efficiency or how easy she was on the eyes. He'd enjoyed working with her so much. He was bummed that the bulk of the work was done. It would be hard not seeing her every day.

He'd have to figure out a way to make that change.

If Celeste had been lonely and bored all weekend, that all ended on Tuesday morning when both her sisters—and their husbands, and the boys—descended. The house went from being as quiet as a tomb to a carnival-like frenzy. Everyone had stories to tell over coffee and freshly baked cookies. Amy, Noah, Nat and Jax went on and on about the things they'd seen and done in Alaska and the boys were full of funny little anecdotes about their visit to the amusement park.

For her part, Celeste sat back, sipped her coffee and just enjoyed the company. It was nice having a few days off, which Sheida had insisted on, considering that the first draft of the application was done. This was a good time for her to make up for the nights and weekends she'd worked, as well as have a mental rest before the final review on the grant. Like a palate cleanser. But it was even nicer to have company again. She was so glad her sisters were home, or today would have been another dull and dreary day, like yesterday. She hadn't realized just how much she relied on her family to give her life meaning... until they hadn't been there.

"Where's Momma?" Amy asked after Jax and Noah finished tag-teaming their salmon fishing expedition story.

Celeste's stomach dropped. Um... "Well," she said in a nonchalant gust, "Momma and Alexander went away on a trip to Greenwater."

"Sweet," said Jax. "He must be looking for agates."

Celeste shrugged. "That's what they said."

"Wait," Amy cut in. "Momma went where? I figured she was off at a therapy session or something and that's why she wasn't here. She went...*away*?"

"Yep." Celeste nodded. "Road trip. They said for a few days. She left on Saturday, so she should be back anytime."

"Wait." Amy again. "You're saying Momma went away... with a man?"

"It's not just any man," Nat said. "It's Alexander."

Amy frowned. "I thought they were just friends."

Jax chuckled. "Friends can take a trip away together."

Yes, Momma said they were just friends, but Celeste had a sneaking suspicion it was becoming something more.

"Still," Nat said. "They are cute together."

Amy shook her head as though the idea was beyond her comprehension, but Celeste could hardly blame her. She'd been confused herself. Momma had always been Momma and the only man she'd ever been interested in was Dad. It seemed inconceivable that this might change.

But after a moment of thought, Amy blew out a breath and said, "Well, Daddy's been gone for years. She's probably been lonely. I suppose it makes sense."

"Besides," Nat said, "Alexander is wonderful."

"They've been spending a lot of time together. She's really enjoying it," Celeste said. She'd done a lot of thinking about it, and selfishness aside, she knew having a friend to do things with could really change a person's outlook on life. Celeste had seen it with many of the seniors she worked with.

"Well," Amy said. "I'm happy for her. Just surprised is all."

Celeste nodded. "I'm happy for her too, but dang, it's been quiet around here lately."

"We're back now," Noah said with a grin. "All your peace and quiet is gone out the window." And as though on cue, one of the boys stepped on the cat's tail, and Pepe yowled before scampering out of the room.

"Poor Pepe," Nat said, though she said it on a chuckle.

"Well," Amy said as she finished her coffee. "We'd better scoot. I have a ton of laundry to do. I'll come back when Momma gets home. Will you text me?" she asked Celeste.

"Of course."

Nat and Jax stayed, though, which was nice because Celeste wasn't quite ready to be all alone again.

"What have you been up to, Celeste?" Jax asked as he grabbed another cookie.

She blew out a breath. "Oh, my. It's been nuts. I've been working on a grant for that project I told you about—"

"The one you couldn't talk about?" Nat said with a glint in her eye.

"Yes. That one. A huge project, which isn't a problem,

but the deadline date changed, so I've been pretty much working on that nonstop."

"You gonna make the deadline?" Jax asked.

She had to smile. "It's nearly done now. Just polishing off the edges."

"Excellent," Nat said.

"See? Having a little peace and quiet wasn't so bad."

"It does feel pretty good to be so close to the end." She loved Jax's positive attitude, so she didn't mention how lonely she'd been, or any of the dark thoughts that had been haunting her. She didn't like being alone, she'd realized. And Momma wouldn't be with her forever. Thinking of the future was a little scary.

"And how's it been working with Ben?" Jax asked with a glimmer in his eye. Celeste felt heat crawling up her cheeks at the mention of Ben. He was never far from her mind, though.

Fortunately, she was spared from answering when Momma and Alexander pushed through the door and a whole new hullabaloo ensued as Jax and his dad caught up, and Momma—bustling with excitement because she'd found some agates—shared her adventures as well.

Funny how she looked at least ten years younger, beaming the way she was.

"Sounds like you had a good time," Jax said when they finally finished gushing about their little trip.

"It was just fine," Alexander said, shooting a grin at Momma.

She grinned back. "It was wonderful."

"So," Jax said with that glint in his eye. "Just before you came in, Celeste was telling us about the grant she's been writing with Ben."

"Ooh." Momma smiled. "I like Ben. He and Quinn have been coming over for supper while you were gone."

"Really?" Nat shot her a look. "And how was that?"

And even though the question was clearly for Celeste, Momma leaned in and said conspiratorially, "*Really* good. The other night I saw them *hugging*."

"Momma!" Good glory. Heat walked up her cheeks. "That wasn't a hug."

"It looked like a hug."

Celeste rushed to explain, because Jax and Nat were both gaping at her. "We'd just found out that Quinn has been talking to John J."

"Really?" Jax's brows rose. "You mean, really talking to him?"

"Yeah. She whispers to him, apparently. Anyway, I was just sharing that with Ben and he was excited."

Jax nodded. "I'll bet. That's pretty important news."

"He looked excited," Momma said, sotto voce, and Celeste sent her a reproachful glance at the poorly disguised double entendre.

"It was totally innocent." Why couldn't she just drop it? "Ben's not even interested in me that way. Not at all."

For some reason, Jax laughed. It was the spurty kind of laugh, when you just couldn't keep it in.

"What's so funny?" she demanded.

"Uh, nothing." He tried to look all innocent.

"Jax…" A warning.

"Well, come on, Celeste. You can't seriously think he's not interested in you at all, considering he was besotted with you in high school," he said.

Celeste gaped at him. Her heart thudded hard in her chest. "What?"

Jax gaped right back. "Wait. You didn't know he had a thing for you in high school? How did you not know that?"

"Of course I didn't know."

"I knew," Nat said. She turned to Jax. "Didn't everyone know?"

"Pretty much."

Celeste shook her head. "That's ridiculous." Surely it was. Wasn't it? She tried to think back, but high school was a little fuzzy.

"You wouldn't have noticed anyway," Nat said. "You were too busy hating him."

"I didn't hate him," she said…and they all gave her the side-eye. Well, she didn't hate him now. The conversation moved on, but Celeste didn't go with it. Her mind spun, whipping around and around trying to remember the past without her filters. Had he really had a crush on her? And how on earth had she been so oblivious?

Of course, she'd been a teenager then, but, honestly.

Oh goodness. Ben Sherrod had had a crush on her? Could that mean he still might be interested in her now? That she hadn't imagined his longing looks? Hadn't misread those awkward, staring silences they'd shared?

A rush of heat and excitement swamped her at the thought.

And then her stomach fell as she remembered. And yeah, it was something important. She frowned at Jax. "Wait a minute. Isn't Ben dating Sheida?"

His expression went flat and he stared at her. "What?" And then he laughed. *Laughed.* "Where on earth did you get *that* idea?"

"Everybody says so."

Jax laughed again. "Well, no one told Ben. Or Sheida. In fact, she's seeing a guy she met in Olympia."

Celeste felt her jaw drop. "What?"

Nat nodded. "Yeah. He's on that commission thingy she's on now. She's nuts about him. Did you really think she was dating Ben?"

"Everybody says so." This time with less conviction. And maybe a tiny trickle of…was that hope?

"Well," Jax said adamantly. "They're not dating and they never have. Their relationship is more of a brother-sister vibe. And I should know."

"Oh," Celeste said. "Okay." But her mind was in a whirl. And all of a sudden, she couldn't wait to see him again.

Chapter Ten

The week the grant was out for review, everything erupted for Ben. The Raskin project started to go south, so he'd had to go to the site and get everything sorted out—which took days. He hated being separated from Quinn, so he ended up making the drive back and forth to Olympia each day. By the time he got home, late every night, he was exhausted.

He thought a lot about Celeste and was tempted to call her, just so he could hear her voice. He was still itching to tell her about that breakthrough with Quinn, but every time he got the chance it was way too late to call. Besides, he wanted to tell her face-to-face. He wanted to see her expression.

By the time he'd straightened out the contractor in Olympia on Friday, the reviews of the grant application had come back from everyone—everyone except Angus. He wasn't surprised that Angus was dragging his feet until the last minute, as the deadline they'd set for comments was Friday at five.

Angus's review came in at exactly 5 p.m. on Friday afternoon. On the deadline. Ben had to laugh and shake his head at how obstreperous the old goat was; such passive-aggressive behavior was kind of funny as much as it was childlike.

Still, he was happy because this was the perfect excuse to give Celeste that call. He knew she'd want to know that all the comments had come back in.

Yeah. That was the reason.

Her phone rang for a while and he was just about to hang up when she answered, out of breath, "Hello?" She sounded unsure, and he realized that meant she didn't recognize his number. Dang. He'd put her number in his phone the moment he got it.

"Hi, Celeste. It's Ben."

She was quiet for a minute—trying to remember who he was?—and then she said, cheerfully, "Hey, Ben. Any news on the grant?"

It was silly for his stomach to drop when she dragged the topic straight over to work, but he forced a businesslike tone. "Yeah. I wanted to let you know I got all the comments back."

"Oh?" He liked the lilt of humor in her voice. "Even Angus's?"

Ben had to chuckle. "At five on the dot."

She laughed. "On the dot?"

"Yeah."

"That's hysterical."

"Hey, I know it's late, but, um, I'm available this evening if you want to do the review of all the comments tonight."

He expected her to say no right away—Friday night and all—so he was stunned when, without a beat, she said, "Oh, yes. Let's do that."

"Are you sure?"

"Yes." A definitive answer.

"Great. I'll get a sitter for Quinn and we'll make an

evening of it." Yeah. He cringed even as he said it. What a dorky way to put it.

But she said, "Awesome," in a chipper tone. "I'll get over there as soon as I can."

"Great. I'll be in the office until six, but after that I'll be up in the apartment." He cringed again when he realized how that sounded, but she didn't seem to bat an eye.

"Perfect. See you then."

"See you—" But she'd already hung up.

Dang.

He sucked in his breath and reminded himself that he was going to get to see her again. Finally. It had been far too long. Nearly a week. Had it really only been a week? It felt like longer. For a second, he thought about going up to his place and taking a shower, but decided that was a little too thirsty—this was a business meeting after all—and in the end he settled on just brushing his teeth in his office washroom.

Granted, that wasn't something he always did before a meeting, but hey, this meeting wasn't with just anyone. It was with Celeste.

She got there before six, so he was still in his office. It was something to look up from his paperwork and see her standing in the doorway. Had she been staring at him? But that thought had no traction because the next rolled right in. Dang, she was gorgeous. Her hair lay in a soft curtain around her face and her smile just made him feel warm inside. She was dressed in a bright summer dress and a pair of sandals.

"You're here," he said—brilliant opener.

"Sorry it took so long," she said in a gust. Was she out of breath again? Her cheeks certainly were pink.

"Naw. Not long at all. Do you want to start working upstairs?" He tried not to visibly flinch because, *Come on, Sherrod!*

Either she was oblivious to his unintended faux pas, or she was ignoring them, because her expression didn't change. "Sure," she said. "I have my laptop in my bag."

"Great." He grabbed the printouts of the comments and they headed for the door.

The ride up to the seventeenth floor was awkward, at least for him. She was fascinated by the view as they rode up the first ten floors, but after that, the elevator had an enclosed shaft and there was nothing to look at through the glass but a blank wall. She turned to him then—when there was nothing else to see—and smiled. "How is Quinn, by the way?" she asked.

"Oh, great. Awesome, really." Oh yeah, he'd been wanting to tell her this. "She actually spoke to me the other day. I mean, I got to hear her voice."

"Oh, Ben!" Her eyes shone. "That's fantastic."

He wanted to pull her into his arms, wanted to celebrate with her, but he held himself back. It was a business meeting, he reminded himself. Besides, he knew if he pulled her into his arms, he probably wouldn't stop with just a hug this time. He'd been thinking about kissing her for, well, the past two weeks at least. "I'm over the moon, Celeste. Maisey says these kinds of issues take a while to work through and to be patient with her, but at least we have a starting place. Thank you so much for working it out."

Celeste waved off his thanks. "I'm glad I could help, but it was really John J. that cracked the case." He knew she was being humble—and generous to share the credit—but it was really all on her. "Will I see her tonight?" she asked.

"I booked her in the kids' club. I figured we'd be able to work faster that way." *Liar. He'd wanted to be alone with her.*

"The boys love that kids' club," she said as the door opened on the seventeenth floor.

He gestured that she precede him out. "Quinn does too. They'll be bringing her up at eight." He checked his watch. "That'll give us an hour and a half to get a good start."

She made a face. "Have you reviewed the comments? Are they terrible?"

"Not too bad." He opened the door to his apartment and followed her in. "Mostly from Angus."

She grimaced, but with a smile. "This'll be fun. Well, where shall we set up?" she asked, scanning the space in the open great room. "Dining room table? Then we can spread out."

"Sure." They headed into the dining area by the kitchen. "Can I get you a drink?"

"Water's fine."

"And should I call down for dinner?"

She blinked. "Um, why don't I just make something? What do you have in the fridge?"

He winced. "Maybe I should just call down." She wasn't going to find much of anything in there to make a nice dinner.

But she did.

She found bread and cheese and butter and whipped up one of the best grilled cheese sandwiches he'd ever tasted. He thought it was funny that she dipped her sandwich into a blob of ketchup, but when he pointed it out to her, she insisted that was the way you were supposed to eat them, and she seemed pretty serious about it, so he didn't think she was kidding.

They ate as they reviewed the notes from the committee, with Celeste recording each issue—or nonissue in some cases—into her computer. It didn't take long to get through the list, but that was hardly a surprise. Celeste was so dang good at writing grants there weren't any gaping holes in her narrative. When he mentioned that to her, she just blushed a little and laughed and said, "Well, I have a lot of experience, I guess."

Most of the questions came from Angus—which was hardly a surprise—and Celeste didn't have a problem writing out an explanation for why they'd done what they'd done, so they moved along quickly. She also had the great idea of collating all the questions and answers into a single document for everyone, rather than responding individually; that way, everyone on the committee got a full view of all the questions and comments as well as a full accounting of all the communication that had ensued between members. Again, she was working from years of experience with committees, and he appreciated having the benefit of her knowledge.

Aside from the committee and the consultants, they'd had Sheida review the application as well, just to be sure they hadn't missed anything, and boy were they glad they did that, because she'd caught a couple of errors. While Celeste was right when she'd joked that the best way to kill a project was to send it to committee, sometimes, when the stars were aligned—or you were lucky enough to have two superstars like Celeste and Sheida on the team—it really worked out for the best.

Once they'd logged all the comments, made the changes to the original and did a final review of the paperwork... they were done.

Just like that.

Celeste gusted out a breath as she closed her laptop, and then sent him a smile. "We're finished."

"Wow. I can't believe it." While Ben was swamped with a rush of satisfaction, he was also slightly bummed. They'd still be working together on the project, but it would be limited to committee meetings and whatnot. Nothing as close or intimate as it had been. The thought made him feel a little cold. He pushed it away and focused on the bright warmth of a job well done. They didn't know if their application would be successful, and wouldn't know for weeks, but they'd pulled off a miracle getting it done in such a short amount of time. "Should I open a bottle of champagne?" he said, in light of the focus on celebration and all.

She sighed. "Oh, I'd love that, but I have to drive home. But I'll cheers you with this." She lifted her water bottle and he met hers with his.

"Good work, Ms. Tuttle."

"Good work, Mr. Sherrod," she said, and damn, he liked the look in her eyes.

It gave him courage, so he cleared his throat and said, "I've really enjoyed working on this with you, Celeste."

A beautiful flush rose on her cheeks, and she looked away, but back again quickly. "I've enjoyed this too."

"I'm glad we were able to, you know, get past the past." He hated when he stumbled over words, but he always seemed to, with her.

She didn't seem to notice. She said softly, "Me too.

I've…gotten to know you a lot better." Her blush deepened and she added, "And Quinn, of course."

He grinned. "She thinks the world of you."

"Aw. Likewise." She glanced at her watch. "Gosh, it's getting late. I should get home to Momma, I suppose."

Damn. He stood when she did. "Yeah. Sure." He headed for the door after her, his mood dragging on the ground. This was it, wasn't it? The last time he'd be alone with her…unless something changed.

To his surprise she stopped as she was passing through the living room—so abruptly he almost walked into her. Luckily he was able to stop in time. "Wow. Look at that moon," she said, pointing out the sliding glass door to the balcony.

"Yeah. It's pretty tonight." It was full and bright and beautiful, just like her. "Do you want to go out on the balcony?"

"Oh," she said, "I'd love that." He opened the door and followed her out and she gushed a sigh. "Goodness, Ben. It's gorgeous."

Was it? It was the view he'd always had. He tried to see it through her eyes, the undulating waves in the distance, the soft crash as they hit the shore, the reflection of the moon creating a silver ribbon down to the surf. Yeah. It was pretty, wasn't it? He hardly ever looked anymore. "Nice," he said because he couldn't manage much more. The breeze had kicked up and brought her scent to him, and it poleaxed him.

What stunned him even more was what she said after standing there for several minutes, just staring at the view. She turned to him with a tentative smile and said, "You know, Jax said the strangest thing to me the other night."

"What was that?"

For some reason her cheeks went bright pink and she looked away again. "He, uh, mentioned that you had, well, a crush on me in high school or something."

His belly did a big fat flop. Well, hell. *Thanks a lot, Jax.* Heat suffused his face. It flared when she peeped at him from beneath her lashes.

"Did you?"

So much for keeping his mortifying secret to himself. He couldn't lie and he certainly didn't want to, especially now when his feelings for her were changing so hard and so fast. But, she deserved a straight answer, so he sucked in a deep breath and said, "Yeah. I thought you were…cute."

"Cute?"

And then he added, because it needed to be said, "And you *hated* me." He said it in an overly melodramatic fashion to highlight the fact that he was no longer devastated by the rejection—though at one point, he had been.

"I didn't *hate* you," she said, but she looked away. "There was so much I didn't know about you. I just made assumptions, rather than bothering to get to know you. But now that I have, I realize that I was wrong. You're so…"

"So…what?" He wanted to know. He really did.

Finally, she met his gaze and held it. "You're…wonderful, Ben. You are a wonderful person and I'm, well, I'm ashamed that I didn't see that then." And yeah, he hated that, after that—that fantastic compliment—her gaze flicked away once more.

"Celeste." He waited until she looked back at him. "We were kids back then. It was a long time ago. We're both very different people now."

"Yes," she said. "We are. I still feel bad, though."

"Don't. I'm just glad that we're…friends now." Still, after everything, that word was hardly enough to describe what they were, or what he wanted them to be. But it would have to do.

"Me too," she said.

He opened his arms and she came in to him, and he hugged her. And he held her there, as they listened to the sea in silence.

Then, after a minute or so, she peeked up at him and smiled. It was a minxish offering that made something swirl in his belly. "At least you've recovered from that crush on me," she said in a teasing tone.

He was tempted to joke back, but something within him wouldn't allow it. Instead, he just stared at her. God, she was pretty. Her eyes shining, the wisps of her hair in the breeze. Her smile…

Suddenly, she stilled. Her smile faded. Her eyes widened. "You have," she said in something of a whisper. "Haven't you?"

In response he shrugged. What else could he do.

Because all he wanted in this moment, all he wanted with every breath and every hard thud of his heart, was to kiss her.

Celeste's mouth went dry.

He didn't deny it. At least not right away. In fact, his arms had closed around her just a tiny bit more. Goodness, he was warm and hard against her. She wanted to snuggle in, but couldn't drag her gaze from his. It was…hypnotic.

There was just something in his eyes. A hunger? A hope? She couldn't be sure, so she decided to ask. "What are you thinking?"

He blinked, slowly, those long dark lashes making a dramatic descent, as his mind madly calculated the options. He did that, she'd noticed, used silence as a shield sometimes, as he thought things through. She'd assumed it was arrogance or stubbornness back in the day, but now she knew better. He was simply taking his time, searching for the right words.

His lips parted, a fragrant breath huffed out, and then he chuckled. "Actually, I was thinking how much I want to kiss you right now."

Her heart gave a start. Her head spun. She gulped. "Oh." All she could think of, all she could manage. And then, with no thought at all, "Okay."

One word—that one word—changed everything.

Ben's body tightened against hers, his nostrils flared and he made a small sound in the back of his throat before lowering his head and tasting her. That was the only way she could describe it. Not a hard, hot kiss, not a tentative peck, but a feast. One slow and sensuous drag of his lips after another, he seduced her, and she couldn't help responding.

When she did, he tipped his head and deepened the kiss. Her heart pounded and her knees went weak and she wrapped her arms around his neck, just to keep herself steady. Her mind was in a welter, her body in a frenzy. Her pulse thrummed in places that hadn't thrummed in years, and goodness glory, it felt good. So good.

They would have continued, and who knew what might have transpired, but for some reason he pulled back. He didn't step away, so she took that as a good sign. But he did pull back, so she peered up at him through a haze of lust. "What?" she demanded.

He seemed a little befuddled too—and uncomfortable, if that rigid length in his trousers meant what she thought it did—but he managed, at least, to speak a full sentence. "There's someone at the door."

Well, crap. "Must be eight."

"Must be," he said. He gusted a heavy sigh. "I should probably get it."

"It's probably Quinn."

"Yeah," he said. "I know. I need a minute."

Oh.

She realized what he was saying and laughed. "Let me go get the door. You just take your time and cool down." She grinned and patted him on the chest.

"Hey, Celeste," he said as she turned away, so she looked back.

"Yeah?"

"We can…do this again sometime, can't we?" Gosh, it was so adorable the way he asked, as though he wasn't really sure she'd say yes.

When she waggled her eyebrows and said, "You betcha," he laughed. But what really got her was the relief that washed over his expression.

Maybe he really did like her.

What a wonderful thing to know.

Ben barely slept that night, lying awake thinking about that kiss. Damn, that had been something. Better than he'd imagined, better than he'd dreamed. She'd been so soft and sweet in his arms…he hadn't wanted it to end.

But then, neither had she.

That thought sent a thrill through him every time it popped up, and it popped up a lot. And left him smiling.

Yeah, she wasn't great for his sleep average. To make matters worse, Quinn woke up early that morning and decided to work off her extra energy by bouncing on his bed, and then, once he woke up, signed adamantly that she wanted to go out for doughnuts at Amy's bakery. Doughnuts at Amy's on Saturday had become a habit.

He was pleased to see Amy's smiling face when he stepped into the bakery. "Hey," he said. "You're back!"

She made a face, but said with a laugh, "Back to work."

"How was Alaska?"

"Oh, awesome. We loved it. We came straight back after we docked in Victoria, because we wanted to spend the last few days of vacation with the boys. We took them to Silverwood."

"Oh, wow. That must have been fun."

"It was." Quinn was getting antsy, so Amy smiled at her. "What are we having today, madame?" she asked.

Quinn smiled and pointed to the pink frosted doughnut. Huge surprise. She usually picked that one. Amy pulled it out and handed it to her, and Quinn went to sit at one of the parlor tables by the window where she devoted her attention to licking off the frosting. Ben sighed. God, he loved her. So much. He always loved her, but it hit him hard sometimes, when she did or said something that warmed his heart. Which reminded him... He shot Amy a grin.

"What is it?" she asked, and yeah, she knew him pretty well.

He leaned closer and said softly, because he didn't want to make a big deal around Quinn, "She spoke to me the other day." His grin must have been as bright as the sun. It almost hurt.

Amy's eyes went wide. "What? Ben, that's fantastic."

He nodded. "Apparently she's been talking to John J."

"Wait. What?"

He nodded. "Celeste figured it out."

"Celeste?" Amy blinked.

He shrugged. "Go figure. It was only one small part of the puzzle, but a great start. Maisey finally has something concrete to work with. Quinn's seeing her three times a week now."

"How did Celeste figure it out?"

He had to laugh at her befuddled expression. Yeah, when she'd left on her honeymoon, he and her sister had been barely speaking. "She was watching Quinn for me one evening. I guess it just came up in conversation."

"So…" Amy shot him a side-eye. "You and Celeste are getting along now?"

And how. "It's so much better. In fact, last night, we finished the grant application. Record time."

Amy's brows rose. "Last night?"

Well, hell, he didn't want to talk about last night. Not with Amy. So he shot her an innocent smile and said, "We've been working hard. It was a short clock."

"Well," she said. "I'm glad things are better between you."

"Me too."

"Oh," she said as she handed him his usual maple bar, "Coho Days kicks off tomorrow. Are you planning to come into town?"

He shrugged. "Maybe." The Cove, during Coho Days, was usually a zoo.

"Noah and I will be working the dinky doughnuts booth, but Celeste and Nat will be taking the boys around. Quinn might want to come."

"Really?" He'd been wondering how he might manage to spend time with Celeste again. "Yeah. I bet Quinn would like that," he said. And he grinned, because he might too.

Coho Days was the end of the summer festival the council and the chamber of commerce threw every year. It ran for a week, taking over most of the Old Town area, and included rides, a craft fair, puppet shows for the kids, live music in the park for the adults and, of course, a beer garden. It always kicked off the last Sunday in the summer. It was funny how, that Sunday, Ben was just as excited for Coho Days as he'd been as a kid. Of course, he had another reason to be excited, beyond the festival fun. He was going to see Celeste.

There was a jaunty kick in his step as he and Quinn made their way over to Amy's booth the next morning, where they'd all agreed to meet up. It was still early, so it wasn't very busy, but it still had that carnival atmosphere that stirred excitement in the soul. Amy was still setting up her booth when they arrived, so she sent him off to help Noah cart supplies over from the truck while she entertained Quinn with—yet another—pink doughnut, which Amy'd brought just for her.

He was busy unloading and stacking boxes when Celeste and the boys arrived, so he didn't even know they were there until he heard her voice as she called good morning to her sister. A shaft of pleasure slithered down his spine and he stood bolt upright and— Good God, she was pretty this morning. Her eyes had a sparkle and her lips tipped up in an alluring fashion. He loved that her smile brightened when she saw him.

"Oh, Ben," she said in a teasing voice. "I should have warned you not to show up too early today, or Amy would put you to work."

"Right?" he said, wiping his hands on his jeans. He didn't know why they were sweaty all of a sudden. "How are you doing, Celeste?" he asked, just because he wanted to say something, and that was the first thing that came to mind that he could say in front of Amy, Noah and the kids.

"I'm…good," she said in a soft tone. The shiver skittered through him again. "How are you?"

He couldn't help grinning broadly, because she was right here with him. "Very good." Their gazes locked and they stood there in a comfortable swirl of silence for a minute, until Amy shattered it.

"Well, those boxes aren't going to stack themselves, Sherrod," she said, but with a teasing lilt to her voice.

"Yes, ma'am," he said with a salute and then, very quickly, he finished the job he'd started. By the time he was done, Pearl, Alexander, Nat and Jax had joined them. Apparently they hadn't even tried to keep up with the boys as they'd bounded across the field. Who could blame them?

Once everyone was there—and all of the heavy lifting was done—Amy shooed them off by saying, "Oh, look. The merry-go-round is starting up. You should go and give it a whirl before it gets busy."

"Oh, my," Pearl said. "I haven't been on a merry-go-round for years."

"Well, let's go, then." Alexander took her arm, and all of the rest of them, except Amy and Noah, followed along.

But Celeste did stop to wave back and call, "Have fun." To which Amy rolled her eyes.

Everyone piled on the merry-go-round except Celeste—because she said it made her dizzy—so Ben decided to stay on terra firma with her. It would be nice to have a minute to talk without an audience, and since John J. was there to ride in the little princess carriage with Quinn, Dad was, apparently, chopped liver.

They stood side by side and watched, and waved, as the kids went by. He was busy trying to think of a clever opening, but before he could come up with something, she said, "Oh. I went ahead and submitted the application online."

"Great." Brilliant rejoinder. And then, equally brilliant, "Thanks."

She was silent for a moment, as though she was searching for something to say as well. Finally, she sighed and said, "Two days ahead of the deadline." Yep. They'd made it. "I can't believe it's done."

"Me either."

She shot him a sad look. "It's almost a letdown."

Was it ever. Except now, they were staring at each other again, so he dared a personal comment. "I'm going to miss working with you."

Man, the way her face lit up made him kick himself for not saying it earlier. "Thanks, Ben. I'm going to miss it too."

"Well," he said with a shrug. "We can still hang out." He nearly flinched. *Hang out?* That's not what he'd intended to say.

Fortunately, she smiled and nodded. "I'd like that."

"Great." He was about to say something about maybe having dinner sometime, but before he could form the words, the ride ended and the kids came raring at them, the boys chattering like mad and Quinn signing, "Fun, fun!"

"Aw," he said, lifting her up and spinning her around. "Did you like that, baby?"

She nodded and signed, "Pony."

"Pony ride?" he guessed, and all the kids nodded adamantly.

Even though there wasn't much of a chance for a private chat with Celeste again, he still enjoyed walking around the fairgrounds with her and watching the kids have fun. Pearl and Alexander tagged along with them for a while but then peeled off to find somewhere quieter to relax when the kids spotted the bouncy houses.

The event coordinators had thoughtfully set up some benches close to the inflatables, so he plopped down alongside Celeste, Nat and Jax to watch as the kids bounced themselves silly. It was such a pretty morning. There was laughter in the air, along with the tantalizing scent of delicious food, and Celeste was sitting by his side. Honestly, could a day get any better than that?

What a lovely day.

Celeste had a blast, just walking around the park with Ben. Granted they hadn't had much of a chance for a real conversation, with the kids close at hand, but he had said he wanted to spend more time together, so that was something.

After the kids got tired of bouncing, they made the rounds of all the vendors—especially the Art Gallery stall, where some of Nat's and Jax's work was on sale—and they ended up back at Amy's booth.

"Oh, thank God you're back," Amy said with a gust.

"I need a break." Indeed, her booth had been super busy every time Celeste had looked that way. "Nat, can you take over selling while I make a potty run? Noah knows how to run the fryer." Noah sent her a salute and Celeste tried not to laugh. But that was Amy. She put everyone to work if they got close enough. She wasn't afraid of making demands. In fact, she continued by saying, "Celeste, come with me," in a tone that brooked no denial.

So of course, Celeste followed Amy toward the porta potties, even though she had no intention of using one.

Neither, it seemed, did Amy. Instead, once they were out of earshot, she sidled closer to Celeste and said, "Is it me, or has something changed between you and Ben?"

Celeste's heart dropped. Not that she wanted to keep their fledgling relationship to herself for the moment… but she did. "We've been working on our *friendship*." And yes, she emphasized the word.

"Hah." Amy rolled her eyes. "You know I could always see through you. It's more than *friendship*. Don't get me wrong," she added quickly. "I think it's wonderful. I always thought you two had more in common than you would admit."

"More in common? What do you mean?"

"You both love this town. You love all that boring city council and committee nonsense—"

"It's not boring—"

"And you just…fit."

Celeste shot her sister a look. "We fit?"

"Mmm-hmm. Besides, I know he's always had a thing for you." *What?* Did everyone know except her? Seriously? "But I can tell something is different."

Celeste frowned at her. "Why do you say that?"

"Because it's true." Amy lifted a shoulder. "It's the way he looks at you."

"How does he look at me?"

"I don't know. Longingly?"

"Don't be ridiculous." He didn't look at her longingly. Did he?

"He's always looked at you like that, but now when he does it, he smiles."

"Maybe he has gas."

Her sister barked a laugh. "Why is it so hard for you to accept the fact that Ben Sherrod finds you attractive?"

It wasn't. She knew he did. He'd kissed her, for pity's sake. And my, it had been a really nice kiss. She really wanted another. What she didn't want was to talk about it with her sister. It was still too new. Too fragile. Too... indescribably sweet—

"Oh. My. God," Amy said in a series of three short staccato gusts.

Celeste glanced at Amy and immediately wished she hadn't, because Amy was staring at her, as though she'd just read Celeste's thoughts. How she hated when sisters did that. "What?"

"Something *has* happened, hasn't it?" Dang, she said it with such certitude. And double dang, she was right. Celeste couldn't hold back her smile, which, of course, confirmed Amy's suspicions. "Tell me," she hissed. "Tell me everything."

"I most certainly will not."

"Spoilsport." But she said it with a grin, and there was a little skip in her step. Probably because she'd finagled something almost close to a confession. "Oh, I'm happy. I mean, if something is...blossoming between you, I'm happy."

"Well, don't get your hopes up," she had to say. Because she'd been reminding herself to not do that for days now. But somehow, her silly heart wouldn't listen.

Chapter Eleven

Was it wrong that Ben kept watching for Celeste and Amy to return the whole time they were gone? Yeah, he was slightly obsessed and he knew it. Fortunately, Jax was there and he was keeping the kids entertained by doing magic tricks for them. When Ben finally saw Celeste heading back to the booth, he let out a breath he hadn't even been aware he was holding.

She rolled her eyes when she spotted him, but he didn't have a clue what that meant. Unfortunately, he didn't even have a chance to ask before Amy said, "Ben, can you help me grab something from the truck?"

He nearly glared at her. Really? But he forced a smile instead and said, "Sure." Amy had been a solid friend, a pillar of strength and a shoulder to cry on when Vi died. She'd helped him through countless dark nights of the soul, given him advice on raising a child by himself, and he thought the world of her. He would do anything for her. The trouble was, she knew it.

Still, it was always a pleasure to help her out when he could, return the favor as it were, if only in small ways. So he followed her to the truck even though he very badly wanted to stay and stare at Celeste.

But when they got to the truck, parked in the dirt lot at

the side of the fairgrounds, she whirled on him and smiled that huge cat-that-got-the-cream smile.

"What?" he said.

"I just had the most interesting chat with Celeste."

His stomach dropped, then soared. Then dropped again. What had she said? "Oh?"

"Please." Amy rolled her eyes. "Cut the nonchalant act and just tell me what's going on between you two."

He frowned at her because it wasn't something he wanted to talk about. Celeste was a very private person and he doubted she'd appreciate him gossiping to her sister. "That's a little personal."

For some reason, Amy grinned. How like her to be contrary. "Hah," she barked. "I knew it. I asked her if something had happened and of course she wouldn't say, but I could tell. I know her. And," she said, poking him in the chest with a hard finger, "I know you, Ben Sherrod."

"Really?" He crossed his arms over his chest, mostly to stop her from poking. "And what do you think you know?"

She sobered and leaned in. "I know that the both of you are shy—"

"I'm not shy." He was only shy with Celeste, and for good reason. She scared him to death. She always had.

"But it's obvious to me that something is going on between you—"

"Amy—" he tried to interrupt, but she wouldn't allow it.

"Don't bother with all your protestations."

Protestations? "I'm not—"

"All I want to say is this. If you should happen to want to ask her out, and if she says yes, which I'm pretty damn sure she will, I'd be happy to have Quinn sleep over."

Sleep over? What did Amy think he had in mind?

Oh. Right. Probably what he had in mind. Or what he wanted to have in mind, at any rate.

He couldn't stop the flush rising on his cheeks and he knew she saw it—it was like a neon light—but thankfully, she was gracious and didn't mention it. Instead, she said, "I can't believe it's taken you both this long to figure it out."

"Figure what out?" he asked, even though he knew. He'd been asking himself the same question.

She blew out a breath. "You two are so right for each other. And she's great with Quinn."

It was hard to hold back a smile. "Amy, are you trying to fix me up with your sister?"

"Who, me?" Her expression was all innocence. "I'm just saying… *If* you need a sitter, for an evening…or longer—" here she waggled her brows "—I'm here for you."

"Well, thank you."

She shot him a grin. "That's what friends are for."

Speaking of which… "What did you need me to carry?"

She blinked at him. "Oh. Uh…" She opened the truck and rummaged around and then came out with a couple of water bottles. "These."

"Really, Amy?" She was practically transparent. Not that he minded, though. He'd needed that kick in the pants, that incentive to finally ask Celeste out. He'd been wanting to for a while, but his fear that she might say no—born of his insecurities of the past—had always stopped him.

But things were different now.

Now he had a pretty good idea that she would say yes. Now he couldn't wait to ask.

While Ben and Amy were gone, the line at the dinky doughnut stand got really long, so Celeste hopped in and bagged up the treats as they came out of the fryer. It was kind of fun, and smelled delicious. But when Ben returned and said, "Anyone hungry for lunch?" ostensibly to the kids, she had to join the chorus of cheers.

"I'm starving," she said, taking off the pink apron Noah had handed her. She sent a mock glare at Amy. "These doughnuts smell too good. They're making me drool."

Amy laughed. "You go eat," she said. "But bring us back some burgers."

"Jax and I will stay and help," Nat said, as the line had built up again. "But can you bring us something too? Please."

Ben chuckled. "Of course. We'll be back soon."

As Celeste came up to him, and they followed the kids to the food court, their gazes clashed, and for some reason, his ears went pink at the tips. She knew what that meant, or thought she did, so it made her smile.

Because it was easier, wrangling the kids, they all ate their lunches at one of the picnic tables, with Ben and Celeste on one side and the kids on the other. It was chaotic but fun. She really enjoyed spending time with him—especially when there wasn't work or the pressure of a deadline looming over them.

When they were all done eating, Ben headed off to get four more orders of burgers and fries for Amy, Noah, Nat and Jax. He handed Celeste the bags—because it was hard for him to juggle the food and the tray of drinks—and they walked back to Amy's stall.

He let the kids get a ways ahead of them, and then, suddenly, stopped and turned to her with an intent shimmer in his gaze. It occurred to her how handsome he was in that moment, the way the summer sunlight made his eyes crinkle at the corners, the way it highlighted the curve of his chin, the lift of his lips.

"Celeste," he said, then he cleared his throat before he continued. "Would you…" His Adam's apple bobbed. The tips of his ears went pink. "Would you like to…have dinner with me?"

Her heart gave a hitch. Was he asking her out? On a date? How adorable would it be if he were asking her out, and was nervous. Suave, sophisticated Ben Sherrod?

But he wasn't really all those things. Was he? He put on a good show, but, now that she knew him better, she saw beneath the mask. She saw the boy who'd never been able to please his father, whose world had turned upside down more than once, and the man who had sacrificed much to save his family from bankruptcy. She felt like she saw *him* now.

As she stared at him in shock and delight—so intense she barely even noticed that his ears had gone even pinker—he added, "Amy said she'd be happy to take Quinn."

Oh, glory. Her stomach dropped. Had he talked about this with her sister? Egads. She wasn't sure how to feel about that. Even though she knew Amy had sussed out the fact that something was happening between her and Ben, she wasn't thrilled to have her know for sure. Not now. Not just yet. Celeste shuddered at the thought of the conversations she knew would be coming. Amy was like an FBI interrogator sometimes. She'd really missed her calling there.

"Um, are you okay?" Ben asked. Concern had flooded his face and she realized she hadn't answered his very nervous question about a dinner date.

"Yes. Yes." She put her hand on his arm to reassure

him. "I'd love to have dinner. And it would be fun for Quinn to have time with John J. as well."

"Great." He stood there and grinned at her, and she got the sense he hadn't thought any further than the invitation—along with the definite sense that he was delighted she'd said yes. Which made her feel warm. It was nice to have someone so sincerely want your company.

"Where should we go?" she asked.

He blinked, confirming her suspicion. "I, ah… Where would you like?"

She had to grin. *Good save.* "Well, I really like the Salmon Shack, and you like it too, don't you?" She'd seen him there before with Quinn.

"Yeah. I do. That's the place, then. Shall I pick you up at seven?"

It was her turn to blink. "Wait. Tonight?"

His smile was brilliant. "Why not tonight?"

"If it works for Amy, I'm all for it," she said, and she was. In fact, she was dizzyingly excited.

And that kiss…

That beautiful, unexpected, vibrant kiss. Oh, she'd felt so alive.

She realized then that she'd been staring at him through a moment of silence, and he, it seemed, had been staring at her. The corner of his lip kicked up, just ever so slightly, as though he'd been reading her thoughts and, indeed, joining in.

Ben slicked down his hair and checked himself out in the mirror. He was as nervous as he'd been on his first date in high school. More so, because this date was with *Celeste*.

He decided to book a driver for the evening, in case he had some wine. Okay, and also—maybe, a little—because it would look cool and he wanted to impress her. First, they swung by Amy's to drop off Quinn, who was beside herself with excitement because Amy had arranged a campout in the backyard with s'mores and everything. Of course, Amy had made him do the full circle fashion twirl in her living room so she could scope out his outfit. Thank God he passed muster.

He kissed Quinn good-night and then he was on his way to pick up Celeste.

Good lord. His heart was pounding. Why had he tied his tie so tight?

Heat suffused him as he made his way up the steps to her front door. He'd been there before, multiple times. Why was he sweating? He was a grown man, for pity's sake.

He paused before ringing the bell, to compose himself, just a little, but the second he pressed the buzzer, the door flew open and there she was. He stared.

God. She was gorgeous. Man. It knocked the breath out of him. "Celeste," he said in a wheeze. "You look wonderful."

"Gosh." The blush made her even prettier. "Thank you. You don't look so bad yourself." Her gaze strafed him up and down and she smiled. "Hubba-hubba." When he didn't respond, because his wits had apparently left him, she glanced at the flowers in his arms and said, "Are these for me?"

"Oh." He thrust them at her. He hadn't known if he should get her pink roses or red, so he'd settled for a mix.

"These are beautiful." She didn't seem to notice his

robotic awkwardness, which was a mercy. "Come on in while I put them in a vase."

He followed her into the living room, but paused to say hello to Pearl and Alexander, who were playing cribbage on the sofa, while Celeste ducked into the kitchen to tend to the flowers. He'd always admired Alexander, ever since Ben had been a kid and Jax's dad had recognized that he'd needed some kind of father figure, and filled that role for him.

"Well, hello there, Ben." Pearl lowered her glasses on her nose. "Don't you look handsome. Hubba-hubba." He had to grin. Well, at least now he knew where Celeste had gotten that from.

He tugged down his suit jacket. "Thank you."

"It's fun to dress up once in a while, isn't it?" she said. "And where are you two going tonight?"

"The Salmon Shack," Celeste said, coming out of the kitchen. "Look, Momma. Ben brought roses."

"Oh," Pearl said. "Those are pretty. Well, you two better get going." Then she turned to Ben and said, in a stern voice, "Don't keep her out too late, young man."

"Momma!" Celeste squawked.

Alexander chuckled. "Don't worry about the time," he said. "I'll stay with Pearl until you get back." He paused to wink at Ben. "No matter how late."

But yeah. Ben's rampant fantasies of taking Celeste home and making love to her until dawn were kind of dashed, right then and there. Family did that sometimes.

When they arrived at the Salmon Shack, they were guided to a table on the deck overlooking the water. The view was gorgeous, bathed as it was in the hints of a coming sunset. As they sat and stared out at the rippling water, a beautiful sailboat glided by and she sighed.

"Pretty, isn't it?" he said.

"I've always found sailboats to be terribly romantic."

His smile widened. "Funny," he said. "I always thought fishing boats were romantic."

He loved her laugh. He loved that he was able to make her laugh.

Dinner, when it came, was fantastic. They enjoyed some fabulous wine, great food and entertaining and easy conversation. They talked about his adventures and hers, growing up and in recent years.

It wasn't until dessert, however—a rich chocolate mousse, which they shared—that things got really interesting.

"So, what kind of music do you like?" she asked after they'd shared a litany of their favorite foods.

He flushed. "Um… I'm kind of boring. I like classical music."

She stared at him. "That's not boring at all. I love classical."

"Really?"

"Really."

Imagine that. "Who's your favorite composer?"

She pursed her lips. "Hard to choose. Vivaldi, probably."

He lifted his wineglass. "Vivaldi's great."

"Who's yours?" she asked.

"Beethoven." Obviously.

"Mmm. Love the *Moonlight Sonata*."

"And the symphonies," he had to mention.

"Oh, yes. Of course. Okay." She leaned in. "What's your favorite instrument?"

He nearly winced. *Uh-oh.* "Ah, I'm kind of weird." Might as well let her know now.

She grinned. "Try me."

"Okay. It's a tie. I love the cello..."

"Same." She nodded. Her eyes were bright, her attention rapt. Locked on to him. It was intoxicating. Too bad he was about to ruin it all by making her laugh. But he had to tell her the truth. If they were, indeed, on their way to a deeper connection, she needed to know.

"And the...oboe."

She sat back. Her jaw gaped, just a bit, and she swallowed hard. "No."

He shrugged and huffed a laugh. "I'm afraid so. I'm... kind of obsessed with it."

"Me too." She shook her head. "Oh my God. I've never met anyone else who answered oboe."

He lifted a brow. "You ask that question a lot?"

Her cheeks pinkened and she meticulously refolded her napkin. "Only as a screening question."

"A screening question?" He nearly laughed, but then he realized, a person's favorite instrument said a lot about them. The oboe was quiet but resonant. Maybe a little sad and plaintive at times, occasionally playful and sprightly, but always woody and reedy and rich.

Okay. Yeah. He was an oboe nerd.

But then, so was she. It pleased him immensely.

"Oh, I'm a firm believer in screening questions," she said. And then, with a wry smile, "Which explains why I'm single, I suppose."

"Hey, nothing wrong with screening applicants for a job, right?"

She laughed as she set her hand on his. "Spoken like a true businessman."

He barely heard her words because—and it bore repeating—she'd set her hand on his. Through numb lips, he said, purely on autopilot, "So, what kinds of answers have you gotten to that question in the past?" Even through his stupor, some part of his reptilian brain was still functioning, whispering, *Yeah, check out the competition.*

"Oh," she said, going back to folding the napkin. He wished he hadn't asked, because it had deprived him of her attention. And her hand. "Most of the guys I've dated never got past question one."

He blinked. What had question one been? He couldn't remember.

Fortunately, she continued on, giving him a clue. "Most of them were into rock and roll, some country. A couple New Age. Not that I don't love all kinds of music," she said hastily. "I do. But classical, well, that's a passion of mine."

He nodded, but as she had listed out all those kinds of music, a new question had formed in his mind. "Uh… How many guys have you dated?" Well, crap. He hadn't meant it to come out like that. "I mean, have you dated a lot?"

She chuckled at his chagrin. "Not a lot," she said. "But I did do a little speed dating once upon a time. Screening questions are very efficient when speed dating."

"Oh? Any luck?"

She held up her hands. "Still single here."

"So…no one?" The conversation dropped down a note, suddenly very serious.

She took a moment. Sipped her wine. "Ah, I did live with a guy for a while."

"How was that?"

He hated that she flinched. He totally recognized the emotion in her face. "Not good."

"You don't have to tell me about it if you don't want to."

She took another sip of wine, maybe for courage. "No. I don't mind." She flicked a look at him. "If you want to know."

"I do."

Celeste drew in a deep breath. "Okay. Well, his name was Randall. I met him when I was in nursing school in Portland. He lived next door. He was a musician." She paused to flutter her lashes. "He was older than I was, and charming. Man, was he charming." She sighed. "Oh, I thought he was so sexy." Yeah, something bitter curled in Ben's belly. "I think he could tell I was besotted, because he flirted with me constantly. Then, one day, he asked me out and we started dating. And oh my, he lavished so much attention on me, I felt like a princess. When he suggested that we move in together, I thought I'd died and gone to heaven. Everything was wonderful. We were in love...or so I thought." She gave a self-deprecating laugh. "*I* was in love. I thought he was too. But things started to change. When he lost his job at the symphony and had to rely on gigs, he couldn't always pay the rent, so I took care of it. I'd finished nursing school by then and had a wonderful job in a pediatric ward at a local hospital. That's when I started getting interested in working with kids."

"So you liked it?"

"Loved it. Even though it was sometimes sad, it felt good to be able to make a difference every day. But the shifts were long and varied. When I was on nights and weekends, sometimes Randall and I didn't see each other for days."

Ben nodded. "That can really be tough on a relationship."

"It was more than that, though. I didn't realize, but I'd only seen the positive side of him up until then. I thought he walked on water, so when things started to go sour, I didn't want to see it."

"What happened?"

She blew out a breath. "He started to say mean things to me in private." She looked away. "I mean really nasty, horrible things. Then in public, with our friends. One of my friends tried to warn me. She recognized the signs because she'd been in an emotionally abusive relationship before, but of course, I wouldn't listen. I let him convince me that the problems in our relationship were my fault—because I was working too much, or I complained about his drinking, his unwillingness to look for a job that could help pay the bills…all that. In the end, I would have done anything to make him happy, to try to save what I thought we had. It was something I'd never experienced before—what do they call it? Gaslighting?"

Ben nodded. He was familiar. "So what happened to end it?"

She blew out a breath. "Luck. I got sick at work one day."

Ben lifted a brow. "That was luck?"

A wry smile crossed her face. "Yep. Just a touch of the flu, but since I was running a fever, they sent me home—hours early. He hadn't been expecting me. Obviously."

"I take it he wasn't alone?"

"He was not." She looked away again, as though the past were too painful to face. "I walked in on him with another woman. They were having wild sex on the kitchen table."

"Wow."

She leaned in and hissed, "On the *kitchen table*. *My* table. Where I *ate*. Ugh."

"That must have been painful."

"It was, but I'm glad it happened. Sometimes I wonder how long I would have stayed in that horrible relationship if I hadn't walked in on them. But I was so furious. I started packing my things right away. He tried to stop me. Tried telling me it was my fault because I hadn't been giving him what he needed, but my delusion had evaporated. I could see right through him. He hadn't been my dream man. He'd been the dream *of* my dream man. He'd been a reflection of what I really wanted—a cultured, generous, loving man who loved all the things I loved and had the same values. A man who wanted a future…with me. But it had all been a lie, or maybe a game. I'd been convenient. I found out later that there had been others."

Ben winced. With all his problems with Vi, infidelity had not been one of them. "I'm sorry."

She surprised him by laughing. "I'm not. Even though it was traumatic—the whole relationship there at the end—I learned a lot about what I wanted. And what I didn't."

"Good for you." He toyed with the rim of his wineglass. "Anyone since you moved here?"

She sighed. "I went out on a few dates, but I… There hasn't been anyone I've been seriously interested in." She looked down. "Until now." When she peeped up at Ben, a shard of electricity shot through him. But the intensity of the moment probably spooked her because she said, in a rush, "How about you? Anyone since Vi?"

He refused to release her gaze. "Same." No one he'd been interested in. Not remotely. Except her.

She needed to know. Now, after all this time, he was free to express it. It was scary, but damn if it didn't feel fantastic when she held his gaze. So he said—and God knew where he got the courage—"Only you, Celeste."

She looked stunned as she took this in, but after a moment of reflection, she said, in even more of a rush, "Are you ready to get out of here?"

"Yes."

"Is Quinn at Amy's?"

A nod. "Nightcap? My place?"

"Get the check."

And yeah. He did. Damn fast.

As they slid into the butter-soft seats of his town car, Ben said to the driver, "Back to the hotel, please, Greg," in a voice that hardly cracked at all.

Heat rose on Celeste's cheeks—that the driver knew where they were going, and probably why—but she had to ignore her embarrassment. She'd been thinking of a night like this, longing for it, since the moment Ben's lips had touched hers. Her body pounded with tension, excitement and maybe a little fear. She ignored that too.

This was one of those times Momma talked about, where you had to take happiness when it came your way. Celeste resolved to enjoy this moment, this time they had together, with every one of her senses, live only in the here and now, rather than the past or the future. Philosophers said the past and the future were illusions and *now* was the only time that really existed. And she wanted to live in this *now*, forever. Especially when Ben shyly reached over and took her hand in his.

She glanced at him and their gazes locked.

He stroked her slowly with his thumb and her heart nearly shot out of her chest. *Good heavens.* When she reciprocated, just as gently, just as shyly, his nostrils flared.

Exhilaration jangled her nerves. The last time his nostrils had flared like that he'd—

Oh yes. He pulled her toward him, wrapped his arms around her and kissed her. She'd never been kissed in the back seat of a town car before…but then, she'd never been kissed quite like this before either. It was a rampage.

Oh, it started off soft and sweet, if not a little hungrily, but before long, with his forays and her ripostes, they were both fully engaged in a purely carnal conversation. And it was delicious.

She was on fire. Alight. Couldn't get enough.

Slowly, gently, he pulled away and she opened her eyes. Goodness, he was handsome, ringed in that golden umbra…

Oh dear. All of a sudden she realized that the aura around him was the lights from the hotel behind him. "We're here," he said softly.

"Oh," she said with a small huff. "That was a fast drive." She stepped out of the car on wobbly legs, but Ben must have guessed as much because he was there to steady her. The lobby was quiet as they crossed to the elevators—thank God. Celeste had been to Ben's apartment more than once. She'd never thought twice about what it might have looked like, but tonight, for some reason, she felt conspicuous.

All right, she knew the reason. It was because this time, she had naughty intentions.

Fortunately, so did he. The minute the elevator door closed, he pulled her back into his arms. They kissed without coming up for air until the elevator dinged, warning them that if they didn't get out, they were going back to the lobby, and neither of them wanted that.

She hurried down the hall to his apartment door and he fumbled for his key card—dropped it—and then finally got them inside. She was worried that once they were inside, alone, the old awkwardness would consume them again, but Ben didn't give it a chance. He pulled her to him and pressed her up against the wall, as the door closed itself, and picked up right where they'd left off in the elevator. And oh, it was glorious, being here, alone with him in his big, beautiful, empty apartment.

They were alone. In each other's arms. *Finally.*

When he caressed her neck as he nipped at her mouth, there was no one there to see. When he stroked her arm, cupped her breast, dragged a thick thumb over her nipple—and, God, that was glorious—there were no interruptions. She couldn't help herself from making a guttural sound in her throat.

"Do you like that?" he whispered, growled.

"Oh, yes. Yes."

"Good." He did it again. "I like it too."

"Ben," she said.

He stilled instantly, ceased tormenting her, and she realized her tone might have been threaded with something akin to a plea. Then again, it had been. "Celeste?" He peered at her through the shadows. "Are you okay?"

"Yes." She could barely speak. Her voice was a rasp. "But I think we need the bedroom now."

He stared at her in silence for a second. A vein thrummed in his temple. His tongue came out and dabbed at his lips. And then, without warning, he whipped her up into his arms, and muttering something that sounded like, "Right now," he marched with her, there in his arms, into the bedroom and dropped her on the bed.

She laughed when she bounced, and he shot her a wicked grin and followed her down. But, to her chagrin, he reversed himself almost immediately with a muttered "Damn" and went to riffle around in the bedside table. And then, again, another "Damn" as he headed into the bathroom.

She realized all of a sudden what he was searching for so madly, and she threw her head back and laughed. While she hated to wait, what a lovely anticipation this was. It thrummed through her with every pulse.

And when, from the bowels of his bathroom, she heard his triumphant "Aha!" she laughed again, this time with joy. Because she knew what was coming.

But oh. She didn't. Not really.

Celeste had made love with a man before. She'd undressed a man, and had him undress her as well. But it had never *felt* like this. It had never *been* like this. Her excitement was at a fever pitch, and his was as well. Still, she was curious about him, and wanted to stroke every inch she uncovered, explore every glorious expanse of his skin.

He was curious as well, and attentive, making it a point to bring her to the point of bliss again and again as he made his discoveries. And torment—oh, the man was a master.

A stroke here, a nibble there, a few long, deep exploratory ventures into areas tender beyond words, and he had her thrashing and moaning and begging for more.

But his patience with her, his generosity, did not come without a cost. When she opened her eyes after she'd recovered from a very unexpected orgasm, he was there, above her, watching her. There was hunger and need on every line on his face.

How unfair of her.

She opened her arms to him and welcomed him in, and he came to her, entered her, filled her.

Oh.

Oh, oh.

It was… It was bliss. They fit perfectly.

He made a sound, like a sigh, then eased out. The emptiness ached, so she urged him, implored him, to come back in, and he did. And then he began to move. Slowly at first, but then with an increased speed. With each thrust he ratcheted her up to a higher and higher loft until she was there on the edge of it all for a timeless moment before tumbling again into the glorious abyss.

But he wasn't done. He wasn't finished with her yet. He was moving still, and moving her still, lifting her up again and yet again and dashing her around like the waves in a turbulent sea. His lunges got faster and even faster yet, until they were both out of breath and covered in sweat and striving madly, desperately, together, for something neither of them could quite reach by themselves.

And this time, when she reached the heavens, when the world exploded in a flash of colors before her…he was right there with her, staring into her eyes, at one with her. It was a look she'd never seen in a man's eyes before.

Simply put, adoration.

As he had filled her in body, this filled her soul, fed her and left her sated and complete.

When the tumult diminished, leaving her satiated and sleepy, he eased down beside her and took her into his arms. She nestled in, rubbing her cheek against his chest. Had she ever felt so fulfilled?

Never.

Never even close.

"Are you…okay?" he asked, caressing the hair from her cheek.

She chuckled. She didn't mean to; it just came out. "I'm awesome. How are you?"

She liked that he grinned at her. Loved that he kissed her nose. "Never been better," he said. "That was…fantastic."

"Stupendous." She waited a beat before she said, with a cheeky grin, "Wanna do it again?"

He kissed her, this time on the lips, even through his laugh. "I'd love to, but I'm gonna need a minute. I did promise you a drink in my ploy to get you up here. Do you want one?"

She pulled him closer and cuddled against his heat. "I'd rather just do this."

"Mmm." He nestled his face in the crook of her neck, which made her sated nerves jump back to life. He teased and explored and she did the same, reveling in this, a softer kind of lovemaking, not so frenetic or hungry, but rousing nonetheless.

And it turned out he didn't need that much time to recharge after all.

They made love three times that night. Three. Ben had counted them. Each had been better than the last—though each one had been so different, it was really hard to judge them. And why would he? Every time with her was a new discovery, a revelation. Her passionate side, her sensual side, her comical side...

After they made love for the third time—in the bathtub because she kept splashing him with the bubbles—they did finally get around to that drink. He poured her a neat whiskey, because she'd never tried that particular blend, and they sat in his living room, wrapped in fluffy hotel robes, and sipped on the warm golden spirit as they listened to one of his favorite albums filled with Vivaldi's oboe concertos.

She sat with her eyes closed and listened, and he watched her, slowly sipping his whiskey. He could stare at her forever while she listened to Vivaldi, he decided. She was luminous. When the album ended, she sighed and wiped something from her eyes. "That was beautiful," she said.

"Mmm." *She* was beautiful.

She looked at him and gusted, "I should probably go. I can't be too late."

Damn. He'd forgotten that Alexander was waiting. "Celeste, I want to do this again," he said.

He loved that she grinned. "My. You do have stamina," she teased.

"I'm serious. When can I see you again?"

She laughed.

"What? Too thirsty?"

She stood and smiled at him over her shoulder as she headed for the bedroom—unfortunately, only for her clothes. She looked like the *Mona Lisa* with that smile.

He padded after her and dressed alongside her. There was no way he wasn't seeing her home. "I'm serious," he repeated after he'd tied his shoes and then stood to zip her up. "When can we see each other again?"

She turned into his arms and smiled at him and he was tempted to unzip her again, right then and there. "As soon as we want, I think," she said.

"Good."

Yeah. It was good.

Life was good.

He didn't think he'd ever been happier.

Chapter Twelve

Celeste was floating on air when she walked into the house after Ben dropped her off at her door, probably because he'd kissed her there. Ironically, Momma and Alexander were still on the couch, playing cribbage as though nothing magical and life-changing had happened at all.

"How was dinner?" Momma asked.

"So nice." Celeste had to turn away, to pretend to smell the roses on the table, because she was sure she was blushing. It had been better than nice. So much better. And it hadn't been just the sex, although that had been astounding. Her body was still humming. It was the way that—now that they'd managed to shave off all the rough edges between them—they fit. "Did you know he likes the oboe too?" she had to ask.

Momma's eyes widened. "A man of rare good taste," she said.

Yes. He was.

She thought about it as she got Momma ready for bed, after Alexander said good-night, and as she lay in bed herself waiting for sleep to come. Throughout her dating life, with Randall and the other men she'd considered, she'd been looking for something that she just hadn't been able to name, but now she knew what it was. Because she'd found it with Ben. Yes, part of it was the things they had in common—from music to books to their philosophy of life—and the comfort that came with that, but it was more than just that. It was also the things they didn't have in common too. Now, rather than causing conflict between them, their differences spurred spirited debate, which made their conversations interesting and stimulating and crackling with contrast. Now that they'd found a space to accept each other as they were—though if she was being honest, she was the one who'd shifted the most— the tendency for conflict they'd experienced in the past had melted away into the background. The result was surprisingly scintillating.

Every moment with him made her feel…alive.

Life had suddenly become exciting again.

All because of him.

The next few weeks, Ben and Celeste saw each other as often as they could. It was a challenge at times, balancing their responsibilities with Quinn and Momma—and his job and hers—but since they were both determined to spend time together, they made it work.

Once school started for Quinn, they often convened in his apartment for a private lunch…and a little afternoon nookie. More than once, they made leisurely love to Beethoven's *Appassionata* because it was absolutely transporting.

Most of their dates were casual, a lunch here or a dinner there—time together when they could grab it—but they had some fancy dates too. Ben took her to Benaroya Hall in Seattle to see Yo-Yo Ma play his cello—*fantastic*—and another time they took a brunch cruise on Elliott Bay with views of the breathtaking Seattle skyline. And then, when Momma and Alexander took another trip, they lounged at her house for a few days as Amy watched Quinn.

Occasionally, they went on double dates with her sisters and their husbands because, by now, of course, everyone had realized that they were dating and there was no keeping it a secret. And Celeste didn't care. She was enjoying herself too much to worry about what other people thought, or what might happen if it didn't work out.

And how astounding was that? When the summer began, she would have laughed in someone's face if they'd told her that she and Ben would be a couple by September. Back then, it would have been unthinkable. She'd considered him an enemy then, or an adversary at best. Now it was different.

She *knew* him now. She could see past the mask he sometimes wore to hide his vulnerability. Or maybe he let her in more.

Then again, she had let him in as well.

It had been scary, telling him all her deepest secrets, trusting him to respect them and be gentle with her. But he'd honored her sensibilities on every count. Aside from that, Amy had been right. They did have a lot in common. They were both logical and measured in their reactions, both appreciated the merits of a well-made spreadsheet and both felt more comfortable in a quiet, uncluttered environment. Oh, and their senses of humor matched. That was a huge one.

Sometimes they included Quinn in their outings too, and Celeste really enjoyed having her along because she was such a bright soul. Quinn still wasn't talking like other kids did, but she was pretty good at using sign language to get her point across.

Aside from all that, Ben and Quinn were now coming regularly to Sunday suppers at home and the two of them had eased seamlessly into the Tuttle family unit. It had felt the same with Jax and Noah, when they'd started dating Nat and Amy, so that gave Celeste tremendous hope for the future of their relationship.

Hope could be a scary thing, though. She had to remind herself, many times, when her expectations got too lofty, that it was still early on. They knew each other better, and it seemed that things were moving along nicely, but it had felt that way with Randall too at first, and look how that turned out. So she vacillated between that hope and worry that something, somewhere, would go wrong.

It usually did, didn't it?

For Ben, the weeks following the breakthrough in his relationship with Celeste were the best he could remember in a long time. Granted, having a relationship like this with her was something he'd dreamed about—and lamented not having—as long as he could remember.

But the reality was far better than he could ever have imagined—and it just got better and better as they fell into a routine of spending time together, learning more about each other and exploring the possibilities. He couldn't have been happier. Things were going so well, he'd even been toying with the idea of bringing up the possibility of something more permanent. Trouble was, he didn't want to rush it.

He knew she'd been burned in a relationship before

and the last thing he wanted to do was rush her, but the thought was certainly on his mind. A lot.

And okay, he might have been a little nervous about bringing it up too. It was a huge step, and while he'd been besotted with her since high school, she'd only just started really getting to know him.

Ben was just finishing up work for the day on a Friday in late September—thinking about the dinner plans he had with Celeste—when his phone rang. He made a face. He hated complications on a Friday afternoon, which, ironically, was usually when they cropped up. With a heavy sigh, he steeled his spine and picked up the line. "Yes, Char?"

"Hey, Ben," she said. "You have a call from a Maxwell Carver. Do you want me to take a message?"

Since he'd been so deep in thought about Celeste, and his anticipation of seeing her tonight, it took him a second to connect the name. They'd been expecting word about the grant funding, so he knew he had to take the call, but his feelings were mixed. If the grant funding was approved, that would be great, but if it wasn't, it would put quite a damper on the evening. Still, he needed to know. "Sure, Char. Put him through."

"Maxwell," he said as the call transferred. "Please tell me this is good news."

He relaxed a little when Maxwell chuckled. "Yes. Good evening, Mr. Sherrod."

"Ben. Please."

"Ben, then. Yes. I have good news. I just heard back from the review committee and the grant for the medical equipment has been fully funded. I'll be sending you the paperwork and the official notification, but I wanted to let you know right away."

"Oh, Maxwell. That's excellent news. Thank you so much for letting me know."

"No problem. Say, is Celeste there? I'd love to say hello."

Ben paused for a moment, but only to grind his teeth a little. "Ah, no, unfortunately. She's not in the office."

"Oh." Such a small word to carry so much disappointment.

"I'll be sure to pass on your regards when I see her, though."

"Oh. Okay. Well, thank you, Mr. Sherrod, uh, Ben."

"Thank *you*."

Was it wrong that he smiled to himself, maybe whistled a little, as he made his way down the hall to get ready for his date? Because he was having dinner with Celeste.

And Maxwell Carver wasn't.

After work on Friday, Celeste went straight home and checked in with Momma, who was getting ready to have dinner with Alexander, then she changed for her date with Ben. They'd planned to meet at Bootleggers at six. The trendy bar and grill was just down the street from Amy's bakery, so she figured she would head out now, spend a couple hours browsing the shops, chatting with Amy at the bakery and visiting her friend Lynne, who had a bookshop nearby, before meeting up with Ben. During the whirlwind of the past weeks, she'd been so wrapped up with Ben she'd neglected her other relationships. It would be good to catch up. Since it was a nice day, and she had time to spare, she walked. It was lovely.

When she pushed through the bakery door, she was

happy to see Nat had popped by as well. Celeste greeted both her sisters with a hug. "Well," she said as they all sat down at a parlor table by the window with a coffee and lemon tart. "How are you guys liking married life?" she asked. It had been a little more than a month since the wedding, but every time she'd seen her sisters, their husbands had been present. This was a great chance for some girl talk.

"I'm loving it," Nat said.

Amy grinned. "Me too. It's so nice having a man around the house."

"And the boys?"

"We're adjusting. But Noah is so great with them."

"What are you adjusting to?" Nat asked.

Amy rolled her eyes. "Noah's not as strict as I am. Sometimes it feels like I have three boys instead of two."

Celeste chuckled, mostly because Amy was very particular about everything, especially the boys' behavior. Granted, they had all been raised in a fairly strict household too, so it made sense. "That must be fun."

"Right." Amy took a bite of her tart. "It doesn't help that Georgie is developing a little bit of a resistance to authority."

Yes. Celeste had noticed that while she was watching the boys. "He's growing up," she said.

"Now that he's in the second grade he thinks he should be the boss of everything."

"He'll learn," Celeste said gently.

Amy blew out a breath. "I know. But enough about me. How are *you* doing?" She fixed her attention firmly on Celeste.

"I'm great." It was true.

"And how is everything with Ben?" Nat asked.

"We have a date tonight."

"Nice," Nat said.

Amy, as usual, wasn't so easy to fob off. "That's not an answer," she said. "How are things *going*?"

Celeste toyed with her fork. "Things are good." She shivered, even though it wasn't cold. "Really good. Should I be nervous?"

Nat patted her hand. "Ben's a solid guy. He's not gonna pull a Jekyll and Hyde on you like Randall did," she said. "Besides, you've known Ben for years."

"And I didn't *like* him for years."

"Only because you made assumptions about him," Amy said.

Yeah. She had. Celeste was glad that she'd had the opportunity to really get to know him. It was appalling to think that she could have missed all this…joy if she hadn't been willing to overlook her prejudices. And what ridiculous prejudices they had been. "Well," she said, "I know him now." The real Ben Sherrod.

"And?" Honestly, Amy was relentless.

Celeste blew out a breath. "And he's…wonderful." He was.

But still, a cloud of intangible doom seemed to hover, just there on the horizon, casting a pall on her happiness. She couldn't, of course, mention that to her sisters. That was something she had to keep to herself.

After getting dressed and dropping Quinn with the sitters at the kids' club, Ben headed for town. He was excited to see Celeste sipping a glass of wine at the bar when he stepped through the door of Bootleggers, and not just because he had great news to share with her. He always looked forward to his time with her. He sidled up to the bar beside her and shot her a grin. "Hey, you," he said.

Her expression brightened when she saw him. "Hey." Her smile was sweet and a little shy. Color rose on her cheeks.

"Sorry I'm late."

"You're not late. I just got here." She picked up her glass and, in tandem, they headed to the dining area. Bootleggers was a seat-yourself kind of place—at least until it got busy. "I had a nice afternoon. I stopped by the bakery and chatted with Nat and Amy—"

"How are they?"

"Good." She sighed. "They seem to be really happy. It was nice to have a chance to talk, you know, just the three of us."

"I can imagine." He held her seat for her.

"And then," she said, after she got herself settled and he sat across from her, "I popped in to see Lynne at the bookstore."

"Oh. And how's Lynne?" He loved this—just small talk. Just staring at her across the table. Just being together.

"She's fine. It was good to catch up. I've been so busy, and of course, she's been busy, so we really haven't spent much time together lately."

He nodded. He hadn't been spending much time with his friends either, because he'd been focusing on her. He made a mental note to reach out to Jax. It had been a while since they'd gotten together—just the two of them. "Well, I had an interesting day," he said.

"Really?" He loved the way she looked at him. Loved her smile.

"I got a call from Maxwell Carver this afternoon," he said. Man, it was fun to see her face light up like that. But then her smile dimmed; it felt like the sun had gone behind a cloud.

"Tell me it's good news."

All he wanted was to see that smile again, so he nodded. "Great news." And yeah, she smiled and all was right with the world again. "The medical equipment has been fully funded." He took her hand across the table. "Congratulations, Celeste. You did it."

"*We* did it." He loved that she laced their fingers together. That she didn't pull away. At least, not until Vic came by to hand them their menus. They didn't really need them, though, as they'd both eaten here many times before. They ordered the famous coconut shrimp, as a starter, and she ordered the Chinese chicken salad. He, however, had a hankering for the tri-tip.

While they waited for their food, they chatted about the clinic project, and some other things that had happened during her day or his, and of course, they talked about Quinn.

"Is she excited for her birthday next week?" Celeste asked.

He nodded. "Man, I can't believe she'll be six."

"Time flies. The boys are growing like weeds too."

"I still need to buy her a present. I want to get her something special." He shot Celeste a look. "Any suggestions?" As a female, and someone who knew Quinn well, she might be able to help him out.

Celeste chuckled. "She wants a cat."

He grinned wryly. "I've noticed. But don't you think she's too young for a pet?"

"She's very gentle with Pepe…when she can catch him."
She grinned, but then she shrugged. "We never had pets because we moved so much, so I don't know. I'd ask Maisey.
She'll probably have a good assessment if Quinn is ready
for that kind of responsibility."

"That's a great idea. I will."

"Are you planning a party or anything?"

His cheeks went red. "Well, other than John J., she
doesn't have a lot of friends."

"Well, we can do something small. Just family." Oh,
how he liked that she put it that way. "We can have a party
for her at our place, if you like. Or Amy's. You know how
much she loves throwing kids' parties."

"Thanks, Celeste. I think she'd like that. And I'll talk to
Maisey about the idea of getting Quinn a cat." He hated to
think that his daughter might be lonely. Granted, her unwillingness to speak probably played a factor in her lack of
friends, but it wasn't the only thing. He blew out a breath.

Her attention was fixed to his face, so she noticed.
"What is it?" she asked.

He shook his head. "Nothing, really. I've… Well, I've
been wondering if we should move out of the hotel," he
said.

"Really?" Celeste lifted a brow.

Ben nodded. "If we lived in a neighborhood she'd have
more kids to play with, wouldn't she?" And then maybe
she'd have more of an incentive to overcome her fears and
communicate with them. She talked to John J., after all.

"Probably. But it depends on the neighborhood, I guess."
She toyed with the stem of her wineglass, then peeped up
at him. "I do think living in a hotel might be…lonely for
a child."

His chest ached at the suggestion, but only because it was something he'd been wondering about already. He nodded. "I'll have to think about that. Now that she's in school, it's probably time to move." Yeah, now that Quinn was in school, everything was changing. But it wasn't just that, was it? Celeste's advent into his life had caused a lot of changes too, mostly in his thinking. She'd shaken up his complacency. Made him want more.

Once Celeste got in touch with Amy, and with the two of them on the case, they had Quinn's birthday party set up in no time, which was a relief for Ben because stuff like that wasn't his forte. It would be a simple event, a barbecue with rented bouncy houses and a small petting zoo in Amy's sprawling backyard. The invite list included the Tuttle family and a few school friends that John J. recommended. It turned out Quinn did have some friends after all.

When he and Quinn arrived at Amy's that next Saturday, Celeste greeted them at the door. "Happy birthday, Quinn!" she said, pulling his daughter into a hug. "Are you ready for your party?"

Quinn, grinning from ear to ear, nodded. "Fun," she signed.

"Yes," Celeste said. "It's going to be fun." She shot a smile at him and he couldn't help but grin back. He gave her a kiss and said, "Thanks for doing this."

"Thank Amy," she said on a chuckle. "She did most of the work. I told you, she loves this kind of stuff."

"Quinn!" John J. bellowed from the top of the stairs. He came raring down in a tumult that had Ben's heart in his throat, but he didn't fall, thank God. He took Quinn's hand and led her out to the backyard, chattering like crazy about everything they were going to do and all the fun they were going to have; Ben and Celeste followed at a more leisurely pace. When they stepped outside, his eyes widened. Celeste had given him a heads-up about what they'd planned, but it looked a lot better than he had imagined. In addition to the bouncy houses and the petting zoo—which Quinn made a beeline for—Amy had decorated the patio cover in pink and purple streamers and there were balloons everywhere. The patio was set up with a long table and chairs, as well as some lawn furniture scattered around, as a seating space for the adults to hang out. Of course, there was a gorgeous cake—an enormous pink doughnut that made Ben laugh when he saw it.

Amy came up to him and he gave her a hug. "Aw," he said, "this is fantastic."

"I'm glad you like it." She handed him a beer.

"I take it you made the cake?"

She winked. "I thought it was apropos."

Definitely, since pink doughnuts were Quinn's favorite. "Everything looks great."

"Come on over and say hi to Momma."

He made his way to Pearl, who was sitting in the shade with Alexander. Jax and Noah, who were over by the grill, trying to tame the flames, sketched him a wave and he waved back. It was so nice, being here with his friends like this. So nice having friends like this.

Yeah. Maybe it was time to move into a house. He hadn't realized how much he'd been missing by living up on the seventeenth floor. A yard, for one thing.

Pearl stood as he neared, and she opened her arms to him. As he hugged her, he couldn't help thinking of his mom and how much he missed her, how much he wished she could be here too. But maybe she was, in spirit. "Hello, Pearl. How are you?"

"I'm fine."

"You're looking beautiful today."

Indeed, she had a sparkle in her eyes. "I can't tell you how much I've been missing girly parties. I mean, grand-sons are wonderful, don't get me wrong, but I'm tired of dinosaur parties."

Ben chuckled, then reached out to shake Alexander's hand. "And how are you doing, Alexander?" he asked.

Alexander lifted his beer. "Can't complain."

Celeste went to help Amy set out the food, and when he offered to help, she waved him off. "No. You just relax and have a nice time." So he did. He sat and chatted with Pearl and Alexander for a bit, then made his way over to the grill to talk with Jax and Noah, who'd started grill-ing burgers and franks. He kind of felt like a third wheel because he didn't know the first thing about cooking on a grill. It was still fun, though, standing there, nursing his beer and chatting with his buddies. Kids had started showing up and Ben was gratified that Quinn seemed to fit right in. He'd been worried about that. He shouldn't have been.

Once the first batch of burgers was done, Noah loaded them onto a tray and took them over to Amy, while Jax put the next batch on. He glanced at Ben with a serious look. "How've you been, buddy?" he asked. "It's been a while since we've had a chance to catch up."

"Yeah. I'm sorry about that. I've been good."

A grin split his face. "No need to apologize. I understand. Seems like things are going well with you and Celeste."

Ben blew out a breath. "Yeah. Really good."

"I'm glad. She deserves a guy like you. And I know how much you like her."

"Love her." He flinched as the word came out. He'd been thinking it, but had never given it this kind of power before. Funny, it tasted good. He liked it.

Jax studied him for a moment, but then nodded, as though this fact was something he accepted, or had always known. "You're a good match, I think."

"I do too."

"How does Quinn feel about it?"

"Quinn loves her. They get along great."

"That's a plus. So, what are your plans?"

Ben had to chuckle. "Are you the big brother now, asking my intentions?"

He lifted a brow. "Kinda."

Gulp. "Ah, well, since you asked… I'm pretty serious about her. I'm, um, thinking about proposing." Yikes. It was the first time he'd voiced that out loud too.

Jax's eyes went wide. "Really?"

"Yeah. I'm just not sure if she's ready for, you know, the next step. It wasn't that long ago that she hated my guts."

"I don't think she *hated* your guts. She just didn't like them very much."

"You know what I mean. I don't want to move too fast and scare her off."

Jax chuckled. "Yeah. I had the same concerns about Nat. But the fact is, you never know how she's feeling unless you ask. Right?"

"Right." Of course he was right. All Ben had to do was dig up the courage to take that chance.

Celeste had a blast at Quinn's birthday party. She always enjoyed Amy's parties, but this one was special. It was for Quinn.

Gosh, she adored her so much. She wanted everything to go off without a hitch, and it did. Quinn's little friends were adorable, the food was delicious—if a little charred for her taste—and everyone she loved was here, and Ben was by her side.

They ate together and he stood beside her as Quinn blew out the candles on her cake, his arm cradled casually around her waist. The best part was watching Quinn open her presents, because witnessing her sheer joy was a delight. After opening each of her gifts, she got up from her chair to hug the person who'd given it to her. She loved the Disney princess dress Amy had bought her, and jumped up and down when she opened the tiara and scepter Celeste had gotten her. She had to put the sparkly crown on right away.

"Oh my goodness," Ben said, his eyes wide. "You look like a princess." And Quinn practically glowed. But there was one gift left. The best one of all.

"Open the present from your daddy, Quinn," Celeste said, handing over the small box. Yes, it was the smallest gift, but everyone knew that small boxes often held the best presents. Ben had talked to Maisey about getting Quinn a cat and she'd thought it was a great idea. He and Celeste had gone to the county shelter during the week to learn more about the adoption process and scope out the available cats. They'd both been overwhelmed at how many there were to choose from, and in the end, Ben had decided that it might be better to let Quinn choose.

Quinn's smile was bright as she ripped into the present and it didn't even dim when she revealed the stuffed cat inside. She picked it up and hugged it and signed, "Thank you, Daddy."

Ben went down on his knees beside her. "Well, honey, that's not the whole present."

Her beautiful baby blue eyes went wide.

"You see, now that you're six, I think it's time for a real kitty. After the party, we're going to go pick one out and bring it home. Would you like that?"

Quinn's jaw dropped. "A kitty?" she signed. "A kitty for me?"

"Yes, baby," he said. "Would that make you happy?"

In response she threw herself into his arms and bellowed, out loud, "Woo-hoo!"

Ben held her tight and when he glanced up at Celeste, there were tears in his eyes, and her heart melted.

Celeste went with them to the shelter to pick out Quinn's kitty, which was a good thing because Ben had someone to talk to while his daughter made her selection. Quinn sat on the floor in the room they had set up for meet and greets, surrounded by adoptable cats of all ages, colors and sizes, petting and playing with each one in turn. He was starting to wonder if maybe he should have just picked one out himself the first time he'd come by, when Quinn finally made her choice.

In the end, after thoroughly considering all the available cats, she picked up an orange-and-white kitten with a confused look in its eyes, a slender nose and pronounced whiskers—one that looked a lot like the cat on the cover of *The Tale of Tom Kitten*, in fact. Cradling her precious bundle, she brought it to him.

"Is this the one?" he asked, and she nodded.

"Oh," said Celeste. "Yes. I think you picked the best one." Which made Quinn glow.

Knowing they'd be coming home with a cat today, Ben had already gotten everything he'd need, including a litter box and food, as well as a carrier. So, once they'd paid the fee—and convinced Quinn that they had to put the cat in the carrier so it would be safe—they bundled Quinn and her new pet into the back seat of the car and headed home.

It was such a great feeling, having Celeste there with him. "Thanks so much for coming," he said, and she laughed.

"Oh, I wouldn't have missed it for the world." And, judging from her smile, he knew it was true. He hated dropping her off at her house that evening, because he wanted her to come home with him—and maybe stay, forever—but she insisted. "You guys have a busy night ahead of you, making your new cat feel at home. Besides, you're coming over tomorrow, right? For Sunday dinner?"

"Right." Oh, good. They wouldn't be apart for too long.

"Do you like your present, Quinn?" he asked his daughter as he tucked her into bed that night. She'd wanted to sleep with the kitten—who she'd decided to name Tom, even though it was a girl—but the internet had suggested making up a cozy bed in the carrier, and closing it in the bathroom during the night, with the litter box close at hand…at least until the animal became accustomed to its new home.

Quinn nodded and signed, "Happy."

He hugged her and kissed her head. "I'm glad you're happy, sweetie. You got some pretty awesome presents, didn't you? And the party was fun too, wasn't it?"

Her grin was brilliant as she made a nodding sign with her fist. "Yes."

"Good. I'm so glad you got everything you wanted."

It plucked at his heartstrings when she pulled back and frowned at him. "No," she signed.

"No? Not everything? Was there something else you wanted? You can tell me, you know."

He meant figuratively, but when she went up on her knees and cupped her hand around his ear, as she had the last time she'd spoken to him, his heart started to patter. Then it stilled when she whispered, "Daddy, why can't I have a mommy?"

He stared at her, speechless. On the one hand, he was thrilled that she'd felt confident enough to speak to him again. On the other, his heart ached. He'd had no idea that she'd been wanting a mother—and the fact that it hadn't occurred to him until now made him feel a little small. Was he a terrible father? Why hadn't he ever asked?

When he didn't answer her, at least not quickly enough, she signed, "JJ, mommy."

"Yes, honey. John J. has a mommy."

And then, to his utter shock, she put out a lip and said, out loud, and in a fabulous, miraculous, demanding tone— no whisper at all—"I want a mommy too."

Oh. God. Tears pricked in his eyes. "Do you?" he rasped, because his throat had closed up with joy, or something.

"Yes, Daddy." Again, out-freaking-loud.

"Well," he said, wrapping her into his arms and hug-

ging her—only partly so she wouldn't see the tears stream-
ing down his face. "We'll just have to see what we can
do about that."

Celeste couldn't wait to see Ben and Quinn on Sunday afternoon. Yesterday had been such a beautiful day,
and watching Quinn with her new kitten had been heart-
melting. She really was a beautiful child and so sweet.
But then, so was her father.

Yeah, she got all squishy inside when she thought about
him.

When the bell rang—and she knew it was him, because the rest of the family never rang the bell—her heart
jumped and she leaped to her feet and ran to greet him.
She was glad he was early, because she missed him.

Celeste yanked open the door and her smile must have
grown five times when they locked eyes. "Hey, you," he
said.

"Hey." She turned to smile at Quinn, but her smile
dimmed when she saw Quinn's frown. She had her arms
crossed over her chest too. *Uh-oh.* "Quinn, honey, what's
wrong?"

"She's mad," Ben said.

"Oh?"

"She wanted to bring her kitten today and I told her no."

"Oh dear." Celeste bent down to Quinn's level. "I'm
afraid your dad is right, honey. Sometimes cats don't like
to have other cats visit and we wouldn't want Pepe and
your kitten to get into a fight." And, when this explanation didn't mollify, she added, "Why don't you come in
and see if we can find Pepe?"

With a little luck—and a handful of cat treats—they

were able to coax Pepe out, and before long, Quinn had him on her lap and was petting him happily as Momma and Alexander chatted nearby.

After a moment or so, Ben took her hand. "Can we talk?" he asked.

Her heart jerked at the solemnity in his expression. "Ah, sure."

"Outside?"

Um... "Okay." She led him out to the backyard. It had once been a charming re-creation of an English garden—Momma's passion—until John J. and Georgie had come to stay. Now there were holes and mounds and what looked like racetracks pitting the grass and snaking through the rosebushes. The arbor had a pretty bench, so she headed there. "What's up?" she said as she sat.

He didn't answer right away, and his ears were pink at the tips, so she knew it was something important. It took some effort, but she waited for him to put the words together.

"Quinn spoke to me again last night," he said after a minute. "Out loud."

"Out loud?" Her heart lifted. "Ben, that's amazing."

"I know. I'm so thrilled."

"What did she say?"

For some reason, his throat worked for a moment and his ears went even pinker. He looked away. "I, ah... She said, very adamantly, that she, uh, wants a...mommy." He flicked a glance up at her as he said that last word, as though judging her reaction.

Of course, her stomach did a somersault and her heart kicked into gear. But she restrained herself and offered a small smile, though she allowed it to reflect her delight. "Did she?" she said softly.

"She did." His Adam's apple worked. "You know…" Could his ears get any pinker? "That's something we've never talked about. How do you, ah, feel about kids?"

Oh. Oh, my. Her pulse thrummed. "Me? Well, I love kids. And I love Quinn, Ben. She's… She's wonderful. But…" It was her turn to struggle with words. In the end, she said simply, "But, Ben, what are you saying?" A little clarity would help.

"Just… I can't think of anyone better for the job than you." He flinched as soon as he realized what he'd said. "Damn. I didn't mean it to come out like that."

Celeste tried to be somber—it was a somber moment after all—but she couldn't help smiling. Was he saying what she thought he was saying? What she hoped he was saying? Her heart soared at the prospect. "How did you mean it to come out?" she asked in a teasing tone.

"Look, you're great with Quinn. She adores you and it's clear you adore her too."

"I do."

"But that's not why I want to marry you." Her heart trilled at that! "Oh, it's part of it, but it's so much more than that. I want to be with you, Celeste. I want you to be my wife. I want to listen to oboes and cellos with you until we're old and gray." He looked at her, straight in the eye. "You're the one, Celeste. I…love you. I think I always have."

Oh, God. He said it. He said the words! "Ben." She set her hand on his cheek. "I love you too. I never imagined… I never thought—" But she didn't get any further, because he kissed her. He kissed her for a long while, and it was truly sweet. When he finally lifted his head, and she had recovered her senses, she said, because she'd been thinking about it too, "And other children?" She peeped up at him. "Are you interested in having more children?"

He stared at her for a moment, then grinned widely. "I wouldn't mind a little boy. Or two?"

She smiled. "Good. I always thought I'd have at least three kids. But what about Quinn? Do you think she'd be okay with me as her mommy?"

His eyes twinkled. "We should talk to her about it, but I'm pretty sure she'd like the idea. So…what do you say? Will you marry me, Celeste?"

"Oh, Ben. Yes. Of course I will." She pulled back when he went in to kiss her again. "But only if Quinn approves."

His eyes went wide. "I'll go get her now."

He was back in a flash with Quinn, whom he sat between them. "Quinn, do you remember what we talked about yesterday?" he asked. "About you wanting a mommy?"

Her eyes went large. She nodded solemnly.

"Do you think you'd like Celeste to be your mommy?"

Quinn looked at her. Her eyes shone. She nodded.

Celeste's heart, of course, melted. "I'd love to be your mommy, Quinn," she said, reaching out her arms. When Quinn came into them and hugged her as tight as she could—and Ben cradled them both in his embrace—she nearly burst into tears. Oh, how precious was this? All of it? Everything she'd ever wanted. Everything she'd ever dreamed of. All hers, and forever. Suddenly all her fears and worries—that dark scuttling cloud that had been stalking her—vanished and the sun broke through. Ben wasn't Randall. Things weren't going to fall apart. Everything was going to be okay. Everything was going to be great. It *was* great.

But the best was yet to come, because when Amy and her boys arrived, and John J. burst out into the backyard, Quinn wriggled from their embrace and ran to him. "Guess what," she said to him in a loud, proud six-year-old voice. "Celeste is going to be my mommy!"

"Woo-hoo!" said John J.

"Woo-hoo," said Quinn.

And they danced and danced.

Epilogue

Excitement filled Ben's chest as he pulled into Pearl Tuttle's driveway. It always did that when he was about to see Celeste when they'd been apart—even if it had only been a few hours. Though it was over a year since they'd started dating, that hum of anticipation was still there. He suspected it always would be.

But today was extra special, so there was extra excitement. The summer sun was warm in the sky and there was a soft breeze coming in from the sea; it was a perfect day for an outdoor wedding.

He parked the car, then went to grab the case of champagne and sparkling grape juice from the trunk. As he pushed his way through the door, the scent of lilacs assailed his nasal cavity, and he nearly sneezed. "Wow," he said as he caught sight of the living room. It was lavishly decorated and positively awash with flowers.

Nat, who was setting the table for the brunch that would follow the wedding ceremony, poked her head around the arch leading into the living room and grinned. "Ben. You're here." She eyed the box he carried. "Is that what I think it is?"

"If you think it's bubbly, then yes."

"Excellent. Let's put it in the kitchen." She led the way and held the door as Ben stepped through.

Jax, who was basting a roast—which smelled much better than the lilacs—shot him a grin. "Hey. You made it on time."

"I didn't dare be late."

"Not with the champagne," Nat said with a laugh.

Ben set the box on the counter and then transferred a couple bottles to the fridge to keep them cool. "Where is everyone?" Though the house was decorated and the meal preparations were underway, it was quiet. Pearl's house, on a Sunday, was rarely quiet.

"The babies are napping and Momma is resting," Nat said. "Big day, you know. And the kids were getting rowdy, so Amy and Noah took them along to pick up Sheida and Alexander."

"And Celeste?" Nat should have known that was what he was really asking. Even though he'd only been gone for a while—checking in at the office and then picking up the wine—he'd missed her.

Nat smiled. "She's out in the backyard."

Ben's chest tightened. He furrowed his brows. "She's not putting up decorations out there, is she?"

Nat patted his shoulder. "No, Ben. Noah and Jax did those earlier."

Jax chuckled. "Don't worry. We've been keeping an eye on her, buddy. Not letting her lift a finger."

"Good." She had the tendency to want to be busy and the doctor had told her specifically to keep off her feet. "I'd better go check on her."

"You'd better," Jax said with a grin. "You might not get another quiet moment the rest of the day."

How true. Once the kids returned and the guests started showing up, the place would be a zoo. It usually was on a Sunday, but today promised to be even more chaotic. Even more reason to keep Celeste from the heart of the fray. As Ben headed to the back door, he smiled to himself. It was amazing how life had fallen into place since he'd found her. She'd smoothed out all the jagged edges of his world, soothed his soul. He'd never been happier. And neither had Quinn. His daughter had truly blossomed, thanks to Celeste's influence.

When he stepped out onto the back patio and scanned the garden—which today sported a large white lattice arch and a phalanx of chairs for the ceremony, all swathed in lilacs—his gaze found her without hesitation. As he stared at her, his heart swelled. She sat on the arbor bench in the shade with her eyes closed and her hands crossed over her belly. God, she was gorgeous.

She must have sensed his presence because her eyes fluttered open and she smiled. Of course, he made a beeline to her. He couldn't not. She lifted her hand to him and he took it as he sat beside her. The diamond he'd given her flashed in the sunlight; the sight of it on her slender finger made him happy all over again. "You're back," she said in a sleepy voice.

"Mission accomplished." He studied her face. Was she pale? "How are you feeling?"

She chuckled. "I'm fine."

"You weren't doing any heavy lifting, were you?"

At this her brow rumpled. "I told you I wouldn't."

"Okay. Because the doctor said—"

"I'm fine." She set her hand on her belly. "We're both fine."

He had to join his hand with hers, there, over the child they'd created together. The little baby bump fluttered and he couldn't hold back his grin. *Soon. Soon you'll be here, little one.* "I know you're fine," he said. "I know you're strong. But all this excitement…"

"All this excitement is wonderful." She glanced over to the archway and sighed. "It reminds me of our wedding."

"Our wedding was awesome." He didn't remember much of the actual event, because he'd been so nervous, but the pictures hanging on the walls of their new house over on the Point were pretty.

"It was awesome, wasn't it?" She gusted another sigh, but it was one of deep contentment. "I'm so happy for Momma and Alexander."

"Me too."

She met his eyes; everything about her glowed. "If they even know half the joy we have, Ben, how could I not be delighted?"

He felt something warm rise up in him, filling his chest. "Have I told you lately that I love you?"

She smiled. "Mmm-hmm."

"Let me say it again anyway. I love you, Celeste."

She smiled then, with a twinkle in her eye, and said, "I know."

Yeah. That was it. They knew. They both knew. That was a huge part of the peace, the perfection of what they had. No matter what…they *knew*. He kissed her then, something gentle and tender, though it lingered.

It would have lingered longer, there in the sweet summer breeze, but a cacophony exploded into the yard as the kids spilled onto the lawn.

"We're back," Quinn announced once she spotted them.

Then she made a face and said to John J., who, as always, was right by her side, "They're kissing again."

John J., sagely, shook his head. "Grown-ups do that a lot, I've noticed."

For his part, Georgie just made a face.

It wasn't long before everyone else followed the kids out onto the lawn and began taking their seats for the ceremony, so Ben helped Celeste up—it was a challenge for her these days—escorted her over and got her settled in the front row.

For all the work everyone had done on the decorations, the ceremony itself was very simple. Pearl hadn't wanted anything fancy, and neither had Alexander, so they'd settled for this backyard ceremony with family and a handful of friends. But still, it was powerful.

Whenever two people made the decision to join their lives, to be faithful companions together, it was a beautiful thing. Maybe this ceremony hit him so hard because his happiness was so complete, he wanted it for everyone, but as he watched Pearl and Alexander facing each other, holding hands and listening to the preacher, his heart swelled. He looked around at the company, his dear friends and family, and thought how perfect it all was.

His buddies Jax and Noah sat with their wives—his *sisters*—cuddling their new babies in their arms. *Family.*

His nephews, Georgie and John J., trying to keep still as the ceremony droned on, boring to young ears. *Family.*

His precious daughter, the light of his life, too bubbly and energetic and *talkative* to keep from whispering to John J. as the ceremony proceeded. *Family.*

And Celeste. The love of his life. The keeper of his heart. The woman who had made him whole. She was even more than family somehow. She was part of him. And any day now, she'd be giving him another precious, long-awaited gift. Another child to expand their joy.

This was it. This was life at its best. He was so thankful they'd finally found each other, that they'd had the chance to come to know each other anew, that they'd been able to put the past in the past and head into the future…together.

How lucky was he to have this second chance? To have her in his life?

How blessed was he?

Indeed, he'd never been happier.

As the pastor finished the ceremony and happily introduced the new couple at the altar, Celeste squeezed his hand and he looked at her with a smile. His gut clenched at her chagrined expression. "Sweetheart?" he asked softly. "What is it?"

She grimaced and eased closer and muttered, in something of a groan, "Ben, I think my water just broke."

Oh, God. It was time!

His heart raced, his mouth went dry, his mind spun. And all he could think was, *Thank* God *there's a medical clinic just over the hill.*

The clinic they'd made happen.

Together.

* * * * *